Eliza Robbins

Elements of Mythology

Classical Fables of the Greeks and Romans

Eliza Robbins

Elements of Mythology
Classical Fables of the Greeks and Romans

ISBN/EAN: 9783337161309

Printed in Europe, USA, Canada, Australia, Japan

Cover: Foto ©Andreas Hilbeck / pixelio.de

More available books at **www.hansebooks.com**

ELEMENTS OF MYTHOLOGY;

OR,

CLASSICAL FABLES

OF

THE GREEKS AND ROMANS:

TO WHICH ARE ADDED,

SOME NOTICES OF SYRIAN, HINDU, AND SCANDINAVIAN
SUPERSTITIONS, TOGETHER WITH THOSE
OF THE AMERICAN NATIONS:

THE WHOLE COMPARING

POLYTHEISM WITH TRUE RELIGION.

For the use of Schools.

BY THE AUTHOR OF

"AMERICAN POPULAR LESSONS."

"Thou shalt have no other gods before me."

TWENTY-FIRST EDITION, IMPROVED.

PHILADELPHIA:
MOSS, BROTHER & CO., 430 MARKET ST.
1860.

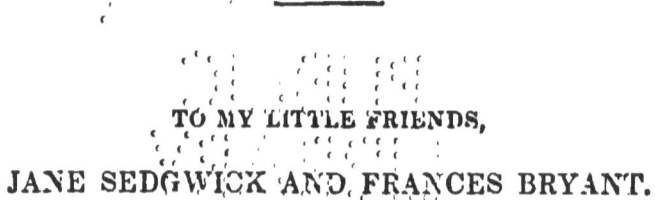

TO MY LITTLE FRIENDS,

JANE SEDGWICK AND FRANCES BRYANT.

IN the hope that it may be useful, this book of MYTHOLOGY is affectionately offered to you, by your friend,

THE AUTHOR.

PREFACE.

This book of Education is one of a series of simple and easy works for the use of schools. It may appear to have less of the character of *utility* than its predecessors; but the object of them all, humble and merely elementary as they are, is to raise the mind above mere utility, not only to employ the faculties of the young upon what is necessary to be known, but to elevate them to the love and enjoyment of the beautiful, in nature, in art, and in literature—to inspire a taste for the luxuries and refinements of intellect—to make them understand prose, and take delight in poetry—to discipline the reason, and excite the imagination.

I know that the stories of heathen gods and goddesses are somewhat out of date—that recent poetry derives its greatest power from sentiment, from delineations of the human heart, from external nature, and from genuine history. But we must preserve our old poetry, and its connexion with the fine arts, and with the fictions and superstitions of other ages and countries. We cannot comprehend our New Testament, nor multiplied allusions to classic authors. who, by their association with our

3

own literature, have become necessary to be somewhat known by all readers; nor can we understand sculpture and painting, unless we know how all these are illustrated by fictions of pagan antiquity. Too many of these fictions are unfit to meet the eye of innocence, but so far as any of them convey a moral, so far as they throw light upon the history of mankind, so far as they have been incorporated in our literature, either with the design of instruction or of ornament, they require to make a part of useful education.

Not to make a compend of this character too minute to be interesting, and too meager to entertain, is the most I have attempted in these Elements of Mythology, except that I have constantly endeavoured to suggest a comparison between true and false religions, and to make children feel and be grateful that "the glorious gospel of the blessed God" is a dispensation of infinite wisdom and infinite mercy —that it is a marvellous light and a fountain of knowledge, as well as a guide to all virtue —that it dispels all phantoms from our life, and all darkness from our death—that it makes our worship a pure and simple service, our faith a clear conviction, and our devotion an undivided homage.

I trust it is not a forced application to make a book of mythology one of a religious tendency. It is my own view of the subject, and I cannot but believe that the holiness and happiness of the Christian world will be rendered more evident by comparison with the times of that ignorance which God suffered long to exist—now happily succeeded and effaced by the certainty of revealed truth. By bringing fictions into contact with the facts of religion, I hope I shall in no case impair the sentiment of reverence, and that Christian piety will lose nothing by the assumption that natural religion was an elementary principle of human feelings and opinions, amidst the self-deceptions and gross abuses which grow up, like stifling weeds with it, in the divers faith and ordinances of paganism.

To cherish the love of truth, to contribute to the formation of a just taste in literature, to employ the understanding *principally* in the acquirement of knowledge, to make reason the instructor of memory, and not memory the caterer of reason, is the purpose of all the little books I have written. To those who are employed in the education of the young, who think conscientiously and with interest upon the philosophy of instruction, and whose theory is the rule of their practice, I commend this book.

Philadelphia, October 22, 1830.

CONTENTS.

8 CONTENTS

ELEMENTS OF MYTHOLOGY

THOSE young persons who live in the present age of the world, and who are educated as Christians, often hear of other gods besides that true and only God who is represented to them as the father of all intelligent beings, and the maker of every existing thing. They learn from this, that men have not all, and always, worshipped that pure and holy Spirit, who has been represented to them as the only proper object of trust and praise: and in reading the Scriptures they perceive, that God has forbidden the worship of images. They must naturally ask, what nations have worshipped idols, and why they have worshipped them.

This question is answered by the fact, that when men first spread themselves over the habitable earth, they forgot and altered the revelation which God had made to Adam, Noah, and other patriarchs, and invented new and false gods, whom they adored. It pleased God to select one nation, to whom, in order to preserve the knowledge of himself in the world, he revealed himself in a particular manner.

The fables connected with the false religions of antiquity are still carefully preserved. They constituted the religious faith of civilized nations; are often mentioned in ancient and modern history and poetry, and are often very amusing. Mythology,

9

or the history of fable, is necessary to be known, because it explains many books, statues, and pictures, and enables us to comprehend the value of our own simple and true faith—the doctrines taught by Moses, the prophets, and the Lord Jesus Christ.

The fables of Greece and Rome are the most interesting and the best known, therefore they must take the first place in the following compend of mythology, which is designed to bring into one view, for the use of young persons, some of the most remarkable fables, and best known usages, of ancient and modern paganism.

MYTHOLOGY is the history of the gods and god desses who have been worshipped by heathen nations in different countries and ages of the world.

Heathens, or pagans, are people who are not acquainted with the true and only God, and who worship false divinities. Heathens sometimes worship images of the deities whom they reverence. The worshippers of images are Idolaters, the images are Idols, and the worship is Idolatry.

Men were first taught by God himself, that there is a God. Instruction directly from God is Revelation. We learn from the Bible that God *manifested*, or made himself known to some good men, and instructed them concerning the worship and conduct which he requires of human beings.

The most remarkable individuals whom God appointed to instruct mankind concerning himself, were the Patriarchs, the Prophets, and lastly our Lord Jesus Christ. The *patriarchs* to whom God more especially revealed himself were Adam, Noah and Abraham. *Patriarch* signifies a father.

As soon as Adam was created, God imparted to him the knowledge of himself and of the uses to which his gifts were to be applied. The first and second chapters of Genesis contain this fact. Adam was formed nearly six thousand years ago. Sixteen hundred years after Adam, God taught Noah his own character and will. Four hundred years after Noah, Abraham was also instructed how to serve God acceptably; and four hundred years after Abraham, and fifteen centuries before the birth of Christ, Moses, more fully than any of his predecessors, was instructed in the nature of a holy worship.

After Moses, *prophets*, at different times taught mankind their duty to God. The prophets were persons instructed by God concerning himself, and concerning events which were to happen after they were foretold. Moses was a prophet when he foretold, " The Lord thy God will raise up unto thee a prophet from the midst of thy brethren like unto me." This prophet was our Saviour Jesus Christ, who came into the world as Moses had predicted.

Moses was succeeded by other prophets. Elisha, Isaiah, Jeremiah, &c. were prophets. The patriarchs, the prophets, and Christ taught that God is one—a spirit infinitely wise, powerful, holy, just, and merciful; and that he requires all human creatures to serve him in truth, that is, to confess or worship him before men; to love him with the whole heart: and to keep the commandments.

Those persons to whom God revealed himself thus were all of one nation; they were the Hebrews, and dwelt on the eastern border of the Mediterranean, in Palestine, anciently Judea. The Hebrews are styled the *chosen people*, that means, they were chosen by God to be instructed in a true religion, and to teach it to the rest of mankind.

The other nations of the world were partially taught the character of the Supreme Being by the Hebrews. All other nations believed in a *plurality*

of gods, or many gods.   This is Polytheism.   The
history of the fabulous divinities is Mythology

The good men who knew and loved the true God,
endeavoured to make their *contemporaries*, persons
living at the same time with themselves, love and
serve him also ; and many believed them, and *walked with God*, as the scripture says, which signifies,
that they believed in God, and worshipped him only.

Who are heathens ?
How did men first learn that there is a God ?
Who are the most remarkable persons to whom God has
revealed himself ?
At what different times were these revelations made ?
After the patriarchs, who at different times instructed man-
kind in true religion ?
Did the patriarchs and prophets teach one doctrine ?
To what nation did God particularly communicate himself ?
What was the religion of the rest of mankind ?
Were those that believed in the true God numerous ?

As Noah, Abraham, and Moses, did not live at
the same time, but several centuries passed away
from the death of one till the lifetime of another of
those holy men, there was time for men to forget
the instructions of one, before they should hear the
same truth from another, of those *inspired* persons

At the present time, whatever truth is discovered,
is immediately printed in books : in civilized countries people are generally taught to read, and therefore a known fact is not likely to be lost or altered.
When Noah and Abraham lived there were no letters or writings, and all knowledge was preserved
by *tradition*.

Tradition is an account of past events related by
the old to the young, and again related by the person who first heard it to others still younger than
himself   When a father tells his son, *My father*

told *me* that he planted *yonder* tree, I tell *you* that he did *so*; when you shall have a son, tell *him* that your grandfather planted that tree, and let *your son* tell *his son* this fact. The history of the tree be:omes a *tradition* in that family.

By tradition the knowledge of God was preserved n the world till the time of Moses; then the comnandments were engraved on tables of stone, and God's law could be read to the people. Long before this time, all that God had taught the patriarchs concerning himself had been altered or *corrupted*, as it was told from one person to another.

Wicked men particularly described God, 'or *the gods.* as they called the Supreme Being,) to be as wicked as men had become themselves. They invented a god of *wine* for the drunkards, of *gold* for the covetous, and of *dishonesty* for the thieves, &c.

Those who were not taught the true nature of God, worshipped the works of God, and also adored good men as divine beings. The sun, moon, and stars, the sea, the rivers, and the elements were worshipped, instead of him who made them all.

How came men to forget the exact instructions of the patriarchs?
How is truth certainly preserved at the present time?
What is tradition?
When was God's will first recorded in writing?
How did wicked men represent God?
What besides the Supreme Deity became objects of wor ship?

The mythology of the Greeks and Romans is that which is now most important to be known. This mythology is introduced into all *classical poetry. Classical poetry* is that which is left of the poetry of the Greeks and Romans, and which is still read. English poets, and almost all modern poets of other countries, often allude to the ancient mythology.

Painters have drawn beautiful pictures of the gods and goddesses, and sculptors have represented them in admirable forms. It is impossible to understand ancient and modern poetry, or to comprehend the beauty and propriety of the finest works of art, without some acquaintance with the history of ancient fables.

The Greeks were first civilized by colonies of Phœnicians and Egyptians, and it is probable that the religion of the Greeks was a mixture of Phœnician and Egyptian faith and worship.

The pagan deities of Greece were divided into classes : the Celestial, the Terrestrial, the Marine, and the Infernal Gods. The gods of heaven, of earth, of the sea, and of hell. The principal of the *celestial* gods was Jupiter—the supreme divinity of paganism, the father of gods and men.

Besides Jupiter, five gods and six goddesses were of the higher order of deities, namely, Neptune, Apollo, Mercury, Mars, and Vulcan. The six goddesses were Juno, Minerva, Ceres, Venus, Dian , and Vesta.

Besides the gods there were demi-gods. These were originally men who had performed great actions, and whom, after their death, men worshipped.

Personifications of certain ideas were deified by the ancients ; as Courage and Pain, Prudence and Honour. Courage is a quality of the mind, it is the absence of fear, and a virtue. A picture of courage would be a figure of a bold man ; this picture would make a *person* of a *virtue ;* it would be a *personification.* The Greeks and Romans worshipped these personifications.

What mythology is most important to be known ?
What is classical poetry ?

SATURN.

CYBELE.

Who besides poets have celebrated pagan deities ?
Whence did the Greeks derive their religion ?
How are the heathen gods classed ?
Who are the chief gods and goddesses ?
Who are demi-gods ?
What is a personification ?

SATURN.

THE most ancient divinities of the Greeks were
Heaven and Earth ; the former was a god called
Cœlus, and the latter a goddess named Terra.
Cœlus and Terra were the parents of Titan and
Saturn. Titan, the elder son, gave up to his brother
Saturn, his right to reign over the dominions of his
parents, that is over heaven and earth.

Saturn, the same as Chronos, signifies Time.
Saturn, when he took the kingdom of the world,
agreed always to devour his male children ; as the
Hours and Days, portions of time, cease to be as
soon as they exist. But according to the fiction,
Rhea or Cybele, the wife of Saturn, concealed one
of her sons, and had him secretly educated. This
son was Jupiter. Neptune and Pluto, two other
of Saturn's sons, were saved.

When Titan discovered that one of his brother's
sons, contrary to a promise which Saturn had made
him, was permitted to live, he made war upon
Saturn ; conquered both him and Cybele, and confined them. They were released by their son Jupiter, who deposed Saturn, and afterwards ruled the
universe instead of his father.

Saturn, upon the usurpation of Jupiter, took refuge in Italy. He was kindly received by Janus,
the king of the country. Saturn, in gratitude for
the hospitality of Janus, endowed that prince with
extraordinary prudence, with a knowledge of future
events, and a perpetual remembrance of the past.

2*

That part of Italy where Saturn took refuge, was called Latium, and lies along the Mediterranean. One of its ancient kings was Latinus. The language spoken in this region, and afterwards in Rome itself, was the Latin.

Saturn was highly honoured in Latium, and became king of the country. The hill, afterwards called the Capitoline, was named Saturninus from Saturn, and from him all Italy has been sometimes styled Saturnia. Saturn taught his subjects agriculture, and other useful arts, and made them so happy, that the time of his reign was called the Golden Age. Saturn is represented as an old man, with a scythe in his hand.

At Rome, a festival was annually celebrated in honour of Saturn. At first, this festival, called the Saturnalia, lasted but one day; its duration was afterwards extended to three, four, and five days in succession. During the Saturnalia, business was suspended at Rome, schools were shut up, and unbounded hilarity prevailed. The slaves were released from toil, and permitted to say and do what they pleased, even, it is said, to ridicule their masters.

Who were the parents of Saturn?
Who was Saturn's brother?
What does Saturn signify?
Who were Saturn's sons?
Who deposed Saturn?
Where did Saturn take refuge?
Where is Latium?
How was Saturn regarded in Latium?
How is Saturn represented?
What was the Saturnalia?

CYBELE.

See plate, page 16.

RHEA, or CYBELE, the wife of Saturn, is sometimes called Ops, and sometimes Berecynthia. Cybele was regarded as the mother of the gods, and
was thence called *Magna Mater*—the Great Mother. Cybele was the first who fortified the walls
of cities with towers, and she is therefore represented with a crown of towers upon her head, and
seated in a car drawn by lions.

The priests of Cybele were sometimes called
Corybantes, they are usually represented dancing
and striking themselves.

Who was Cybele, and how is she represented ?
Who were the priests of Cybele ?

VESTA.

VESTA was the daughter of Saturn and the goddess of fire. Numa Pompilius, the second king of
Rome, raised an altar to her, and instituted those
celebrated priestesses who bore the names of Vestals, or Vestal Virgins.

At first, the vestals were only four in number,
but were, afterwards, increased to seven.

Roman virgins, from the first families at Rome,
and destined for the service of Vesta, were chosen
between the age of six and ten years. The time
of their consecration to the goddess lasted thirty
years, and it was not till after this term that they
were free from their priesthood, and at liberty to
marry. During the first ten years they were instructed in the duties of their profession, they practised them during the second ten, and in the last ten
years, they instructed the novices.

The chief employment of the vestals consisted

in constantly maintaining the sacred fire, which burned in honour of Vesta.

This fire was renewed by the rays of the sun yearly, during the calends of March, or latter part of February.

The preservation of this fire was considered as being so important, that when it happened to expire, all public spectacles were forbidden till the crime was punished.

This event was the subject of general mourning, and considered as a most direful presage. If either of the vestal virgins had neglected her duty, or violated her vows, nothing could save her from the dreadful death of being buried alive.

The temple of Vesta was said to contain, besides the consecrated fire, the Palladium, or sacred image of Minerva, and the images of Lares and Penates, or household gods, which Æneas saved from the destruction of Troy, and brought to Italy.

The vestal's vow was, never to suffer the sacred fire to become extinct, and never to associate with any man.

Who was Vesta?
Who were the vestals, and what was their discipline?
Was the fire of Vesta's temple sacred?
To what punishment were the vestals exposed?

JANUS.

JANUS was a king of Italy, who received Saturn when he was expelled from heaven by Jupiter. The true history of Saturn must be, that he was a wise man, who was driven from some little kingdom by a successful usurper, who was perhaps his son; and, as a fugitive prince, escaping from injustice, was hospitably received by Janus.

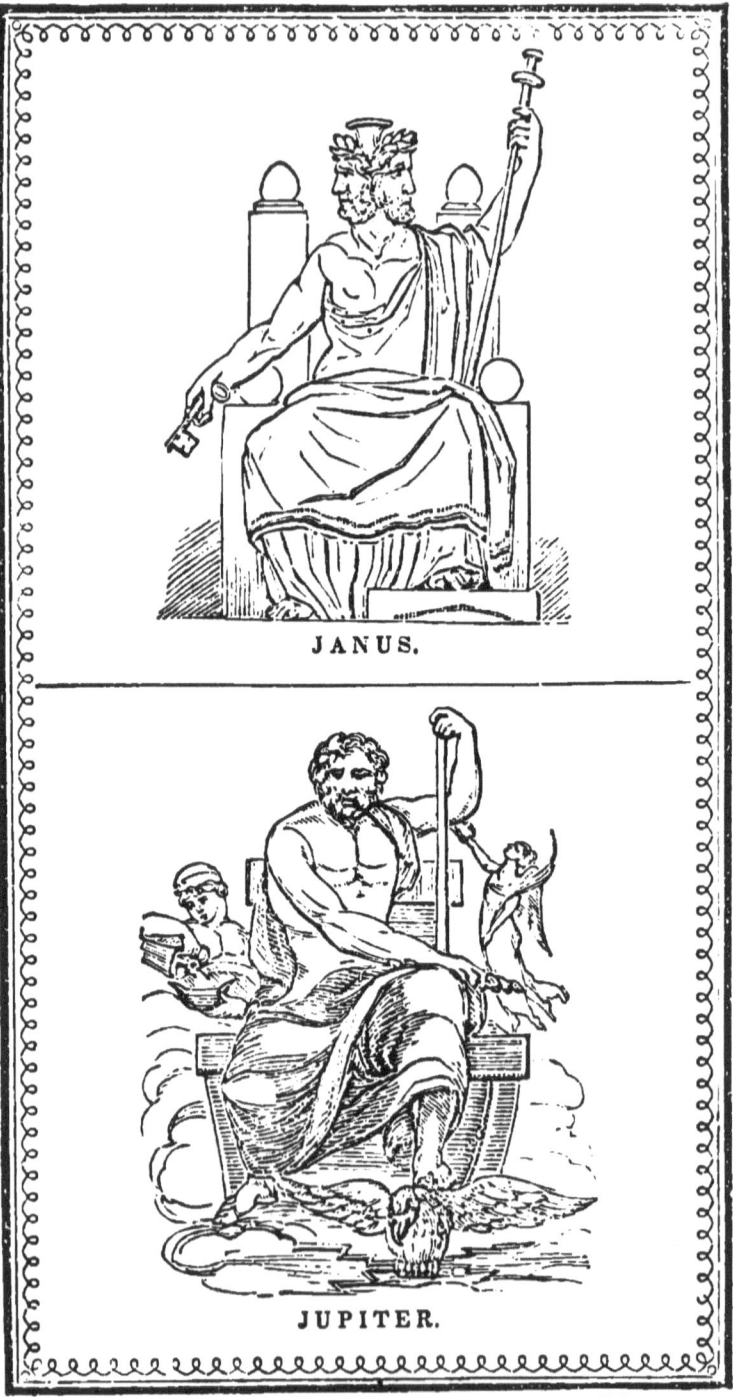

JANUS.

JUPITER.

The people of Italy were probably, at that remote period, less instructed in the useful arts and the comforts of life, than the inhabitants of Crete, over which the usurper Jupiter acquired dominion. Janus was a patriotic king, one who wished to make his subjects wiser and better, and who devoted himself to improving them; therefore, he gladly admitted Saturn to a share of the government, and acquired useful knowledge from him.

Janus, from his wisdom, was regarded as a prophet, and was supposed to be as well acquainted with the *future* as the *past.* This double gift of *looking before and after,* was nothing more than the *experience* and *foresight* of a wise man; nevertheless, ignorant people supposed that he was a *supernatural* being, and therefore, after his death he was *deified.*

It is probable, that Janus regulated the divisions of time among his subjects, as the first month of the year was called in honour of him, January. In some of his temples, the statue of Janus was surrounded by twelve altars, which denoted the twelve months of the year.

Janus was worshipped at Rome as the god of the year, as the patron of new undertakings, and the arbiter of peace and war. He was represented with two faces. These two faces indicated the *double reign* of Saturn and Janus; the double knowledge of the *past* and *future;* the *double attribute* of *peace-maker* and *war-maker.* He was supposed to open and shut the gates of heaven.

The images of Janus had in one hand a key, to denote his power in heaven, and in the other hand a sceptre to express his authority upon earth. The Roman king Numa instituted a festival in honour of Janus, which was celebrated at Rome on the first day of the year.

On the first day of the year, the Consuls entered upon their office, and the people were entertained with *spectacles*. New enterprises were dated from this day, but they commenced after it : for on the day itself, business was suspended, quarrels were forgotten, mutual presents were made, and the time was spent in mirth and friendly intercourse. This agreeable mode of spending the *New-year's* day has been much followed by Christian nations even to the present time.

The temples of Janus were shut at Rome during the time of peace ; but these occasions were rare. First, in the long reign of Numa ; secondly, at the conclusion of the second Punic war, B. C. 232 ; and three times by the emperor Augustus. During the last time our Saviour was born in Judea, then a Roman province.

The circumstances of our Lord's birth, himself the subject of an earthly empire, and the founder of a moral kingdom which shall extend to the end of the world—his coming into the world, the prince of peace, while mankind enjoyed a memorable peace, has often been noticed as a remarkable occurrence.

Who was Janus, and what is the meaning of the fable of Saturn ?

Why did Janus admit Saturn to be the partner of his throne?

How was Janus regarded by his subjects?

Why were the images of Janus sometimes surrounded by twelve altars ?

How was Janus worshipped at Rome ?

How were the attributes of Janus expressed by images of him, and who instituted a festival in honour of him ?

How did the Romans celebrate New-year's day !

When was the temple of Janus shut ?

What has been particularly noticed concerning the birth of Christ ?

JUPITER.

See plate, page 21.

JUPITER was the supreme god of the heathens, the governor of heaven and earth, the father of gods and men, the lord of the elements, and the dispenser of every blessing to mankind. His names were Optimus Maximus, or the Best and Greatest; Jove, king of gods and men; the Thunderer, as master of thunder and lightning.

When Jupiter deposed his father Saturn, he divided the empire of the universe among himself, as king of heaven and earth, Neptune, the lord of the ocean, and Pluto, the ruler of the infernal regions. He is said to have been educated in the island of Crete.

Very solemn worship was paid to Jupiter. The animals offered to him in sacrifice, were sheep, goats, and bulls with gilded horns. Flour, salt, and incense were used in these sacrifices. The oak and the olive were sacred to Jove.

Jupiter is represented under the figure of a majestic man, with a venerable beard, seated on a throne. In his right hand he held a thunderbolt, and in his left, a sceptre of cypress wood. The Titans are beneath his feet, and an eagle by his side. The sceptre is the symbol of his majesty.

The ancients represented this god as having a face of great dignity and beauty. His head was surrounded with rays and clouds. Beside him were placed two urns, one of *good*, the other of *evil*. From these he distributed benefits or afflictions to mankind.

Terror is one of Jove's principal attributes. Homer describes him thus:

He whose all-conscious eyes the world behold,
The eternal Thunderer, sits enthroned in gold.
High heaven the footstool of his feet he makes,
And, wide beneath him, all *Olympus* shakes.

3

He speaks, and awful bends his sable brows,
Shakes his ambrosial curls and gives the *nod*—
The *stamp of fate*, and sanction of a god ;
High heaven, with trembling, the dread signal takes,
And all Olympus to the centre shakes.
> *Iliad, Pope's translation.*

Jove's peculiar habitation, and that of the other celestial gods, was supposed to be Olympus, a mountain of Greece ; though Dr. Clarke, a very learned man, supposes Olympus to be a name com mon to high mountains in the ancient world. *Fate* signifies a fixed purpose of the gods,—a determination of the divine mind which could not be altered. When Jove *nodded*, or inclined his head, that motion expressed his unalterable will.

Jupiter, in Homer, answers a petitioner thus :

Depart in peace, secure thy prayer is sped,
Witness the sacred honours of our head ;
The nod that ratifies the will divine ;
The faithful, fixed, irrevocable, sign ;
This seals thy suit, and this fulfils thy vows.
—He spoke, and awful bends his sable brows,
Shakes his ambrosial curls, and gives the *nod*,—
The stamp of fate, and sanction of the God :
High heaven, with trembling, the dread signal took,
And all Olympus to the centre shook.   *Iliad*, Book I.

Virgil, the Roman poet, represents Jove's power over nature, with great effect, thus :

Great Jove himself, whom dreadful darkness shrouds,
Pavilioned in the thickness of the clouds,
With lightning armed, his red right hand puts forth,
And shakes with burning bolts, the solid earth ;
The nations shrink appalled ; the beasts are fled ;
All human hearts are sunk and pierced with dread ;
He strikes *vast Rhodope's* exalted crown,
And hurls *huge Athos* and *Cerannia* down.
Thick fall the rains ; the wind redoubled roars :
The god now smites the woods and now the sounding
  shores.   *Æneid, Pitt's translation.*

Rhodope was a mountain of Thrace, Athos of Upper Greece, and the Acroceraunian ridge may be seen in modern Turkey, north of Macedonia.

Just, wise, and powerful as Jove was represented by the heathens, he had not the infinite purity of the true God, for his worshippers, in their blindness, admitted many vices in his character, and related concerning him many scandalous adventures.

Jupiter's enemies were the Titans and the giants : the former were the sons of his uncle Titan, who imprisoned Saturn ; and the latter were sons of Terra or Earth, who attempted to dethrone Jupiter. The giants, in their invasion, that they might scale the heavens, are said to have piled mount Pelion upon Ossa. Jupiter defeated them all.

Jupiter had several oracles ; that of Dodona, in Epirus, and that of Jupiter-Ammon in Lybia were the chief.

What are Jupiter's attributes ?
How did Jupiter divide the universe ?
What worship was paid to Jupiter ?
How is Jupiter represented ?
How does Homer describe the terrors of Jupiter ?
Where was Jove's peculiar habitation supposed to be ?
How does Virgil describe Jove ?
Was the character of Jupiter perfectly holy ?
Who were Jupiter's enemies ?

The ancients supposed that Jupiter often loved mortal ladies ; however, he did not appear to them in his own awful character, but assumed the shape of some man, or animal. One of these ladies, Semele, the daughter of Cadmus king of Thebes, entreated the god to appear to her as he did to Juno. Jupiter had sworn by the Styx to grant her whatever she should ask, so he was forced to keep his word, and he entered her apartment in the terrible majesty of the thunderer, surrounded by clouds and lightning. The celestial fire caused the instant death of Semele.

To Leda, he appeared as a swan. This lady was the wife of Tyndarus, king of Sparta ; she was the mother of four children celebrated in poetic history. Helen and Clytemnestra, Castor and Pollux. Helen was the beautiful wife of Menelaus, king of Sparta, and Clytemnestra was married to Agamemnon, king of Mycenæ, who was brother to Menelaus.

One of the most remarkable adventures of Jupiter was the rape of Europa. *Rape* means bearing off in haste. Europa was a beautiful virgin, the daughter of Agenor, king of Phenicia. Jupiter saw her in the meadows, surrounded with her maids, diverting herself with gathering flowers. To gain the attention of Europa, Jupiter assumed the form of a white bull, and mingled with the herds of Agenor.

Europa admired the beauty of the animal, approached and began to play with him as with a great but gentle dog ; when he lay down at her feet she sprang upon his back. This was what the wily god desired, and he immediately withdrew himself slowly to the shore of the Mediterranean, plunged into the sea and swam off with his lovely burden to Crete. Crete is a European island, or nearer to Europe than to Asia or Africa. Europa afterwards married the king of Crete, and her name was given to one quarter of the world.

The following is a fine description in verse of the flight of Europa. The poet supposes that Cupid and sea-gods, admiring her beauty, accompany her as she is borne over the waves.

> Now lows a milk-white bull on Asia's strand
> And crops with dancing head the daisied land.
> With rosy wreaths, Europa's hand adorns
> His fringed forehead and his pearly horns ,

Light on his back the sportive damsel bounds,
And pleased he moves along the flowery grounds;
Bears with slow steps his beauteous prize aloof,
Dips in the lucid flood his ivory hoof;
Then wets his velvet knees, and wading laves
His silky sides amid the dimpling waves.
Beneath her robe she draws her snowy feet,
And half-reclining on her ermine seat,
Around his raised neck her radiant arms she throws,
And rests her fair cheek on his curled brows;
Her yellow tresses wave on wanton gales,
And bent in air her azure mantle sails.
While her fair train with beckoning hands deplore,
Strain their blue eyes, and shriek along the shore;
Onward he moves; applauding Cupids guide,
And skim on shooting wing the shining tide;
Emerging Tritons leave their coral caves,
Sound their loud conchs, and smooth the circling waves,
Now Europe's shadowy shores, with loud acclaim,
Hail the fair fugitive and *shout her name.*

Darwin's Botanic Garden, Canto II.

Capitoline Jupiter.—A statue which adorned the temple of Jupiter at Rome. The finest Jupiter in existence is one in the Vesospi palace at Rome. On a medal struck in the time of the emperor Vitellius, is an impression like the famous statue of the capitol.

Did the ancients suppose that Jupiter loved human females, and what is related of his appearance to Semele?

How did Jupiter appear to Leda?

How did Jupiter deceive Europa?

Was Europa easily allured to trust herself to the god in his assumed form?

Who has given a fine description of the flight of Europa and what is it?

What is the most famous statue of Jupiter at present in existence?

APOLLO.

APOLLO was the son of Jupiter and Latona. He has been called "the god of life, and light, and arts." He was the cause of disease, and the restorer of health. He is often called Phœbus the god of day ; and was supposed to be the patron of poetry, music, and the fine arts. Apollo was perfectly beautiful. He taught the arts of divination and *archery*, or the management of the bow and arrow. In hymns addressed to Apollo as the god of health, he is called Pæan.

Apollo is sometimes represented with rays around his head, to show that he was the dispenser of light, and is often mentioned as the sun himself. We sometimes hear of Sol. Sol appears to have been a name for the sun, distinct from Apollo. Apollo frequently appears with a lyre in his hand. He is sometimes drawn in a car, commonly called the chariot of the sun. Apollo's chariot was drawn by horses which no hand but his own could control.

Many absurd and immoral actions are imputed to Apollo, as well as to other of the heathen deities.

Apollo had a son named Esculapius. Esculapius was the best physician of antiquity ; he prolonged the lives of so many mortals, that Pluto complained to Jupiter that Esculapius prevented his dominions from being peopled, therefore Jupiter struck Esculapius with lightning and killed him.

Apollo, enraged at the death of Esculapius, destroyed the Cyclops, huge one-eyed giants who had forged the thunderbolts of Jupiter. The Cyclops were servants and favourites of Jupiter, so he was angry at Apollo for destroying them, and expelled him from heaven as a punishment.

When Apollo dwelt upon earth, he employed himself in tending the flocks of Admetus, king of

APOLLO.

MERCURY.

Thessaly. Admetus treated Apollo so kindly that
the god promised, whenever the former should be
summoned from the world by death, that his life
should be spared, provided he could find another
person who would die in his place. A mortal disease afterwards seized Admetus, and his wife, Al-
ceste, offered herself to die instead of her husband.
This act of generous devotion has often been com
mended.

It is asserted by the poets that Apollo raised the
walls of Troy by the music of his harp ; and that
a stone upon which he laid his lyre became so melodious, that whenever it was struck, it sounded like
that instrument. Having unfortunately killed a
very beautiful boy, called Hyacinthus, by the blow
of a quoit, Apollo caused to spring up from his
blood, the flower called after his name.

Among the stories which relate to Apollo, is that
of Phaeton. Phaeton was the son of Apollo and the
nymph Clymene. Epaphus, a son of Jupiter, one
day told Phaeton that Apollo was not his father.
The youth, distressed at this, repaired to the god,
and complained of Epaphus. Apollo consoled him,
and to comfort him, promised that he would bestow
upon him any gift he should ask. Phaeton petition-
ed to be allowed to drive the chariot of the sun for
one day. Apollo in vain assured him that he could
not govern the horses ; but Phaeton, notwithstanding,
persevered in demanding of his father to grant his
request.

To keep his word, Apollo'intrusted his chariot to
Phaeton ; but the latter, unskilled in the management
of the celestial coursers, suffered them to run wild,
and they would have set the world on fire, had not
Jupiter struck Phaeton into the Po, where he was
drowned. His sisters, the Heliades, mourned for
him and were metamorphosed into poplars by

Jupiter. This story is told by Ovid, the Roman poet.

Apollo's most famous achievement was the de· struction of the serpent Python. This serpent was probably only a pestilential disease which he cured. The Greeks, at their festivals, used to exhibit the destruction of the Python. A priestess of Apollo was called the Pytha in honour of the god's achieve· ment.

The laurel was sacred to Apollo. 'It was bestowed upon poets as a reward for their excellence.

The most famous *oracle* of the Greeks was that of Apollo at Delphi, in Phocis. An oracle signifies a truth from God. The Greeks supposed that Apollo instructed the Pythia in what he wished mortals to do; and all who could, repaired to the temple of Apollo to inquire at the oracle whether it was best or not to commence any undertaking.

The Pythia was a poor old woman who was in· toxicated or disturbed in mind by the respiration of vapours from the ground, and her cries were pre· tended to express the will of the god. The priests made the Pythia sit in the temple of Apollo upon a *tripcd*, or three-legged stool, and then they explained her frantic words to those who consulted the oracle.

There scarcely exists in any country a museum or gallery of the fine arts, which does not contain one or more statues of Apollo. Of these, that which is universally preferred is the Apollo which adorns the Vatican palace at Rome. Casts of this statue may be seen in almost every considerable town in the United States. It is commonly called the *Apollo of Belvidere*. Belvidere is the name of a court of the palace, which commands a very fine prospect.

Who was Apollo?
How is Apollo represented?

Are immoral actions imputed to Apollo ?
Why did Jupiter expel Apollo from heaven ?
With whom did Apollo dwell while he was on earth !
Did Apollo love Hyacinthus ?
What rash promise did Apollo make to Phaeton ?
What happened to Phaeton ?
What were Apollo's achievements ?
Where was the most famous oracle of Apollo ?
Who was the Pythia ?
What is the most admired statue of Apollo ?

MERCURY.

See plate, page 31.

–The God who mounts the winged winds,
Fast to his feet the golden pinions binds,
That high through fields of air his flight sustain,
O'er the wide earth, and o'er the boundless main.
He grasps the wand that causes sleep to fly,
Or in soft slumbers seals the wakeful eye ;
Then shoots from heaven to high Pieria's steep,
And stoops incumbent on the rolling deep.
Homer's Odyssey.—Pope.

The Greek Mercury was the son of Jupiter and Maia. He was the god of eloquence, of arts and sciences, and the messenger of Jupiter. He was the inventor of weights and measures, and conducted departed souls to the world of spirits.

Mercury is represented as a young man ; wings were fastened to his sandals and to his cap, and in his hand he held the *caduceus.* This was a wand entwined with two serpents. The caduceus had a power to induce wakefulness, or to cause sleep. Mercury, besides his higher offices, was the god of thieves, of merchants, and of highways. Statues of Mercury were often placed in roads to point out the way to travellers.

The mythologists say that Mercury was born at Mount Cyllene in Arcadia, and that in his infancy he was intrusted to the care of the Seasons. His cunning and dexterity in stealing were remarkable. He stole the quiver and arrow of Apollo, and robbed Neptune of his trident, Venus of her girdle, Mars of his sword, and Vulcan of his anvil.

The cunning and add ess of Mercury recommended him to those gods, and Jupiter chose him for his special messenger. The king of heaven presented to him his winged cap called the *petasus*, and with wings for his feet called *talaria.* He had also a small sword which could render him invisible, which he lent to Perseus.

Mercury is supposed to have been the Hermes of the Egyptians. The ancient Egyptians are considered as the original inventors of the arts, science, and religion of Greece ; though the arts and sciences flourishing at a later period in Greece, and deriving improvement from successive races of men, seem to have been brought to much higher utility and beauty by them than by any other people.

The Hermes of Egypt was probably some philosopher, who was distinguished by various knowledge and inventive talent. The Egyptians impute to Hermes the invention of commerce, of geometry, of astronomy, and of hieroglyphic characters.

Who was the Greek Mercury ?
How was Mercury represented ?
Where was Mercury born ?
What were his gifts ?
Who was the Hermes of Egypt ?
What inventions do the Egyptians impute to Hermes ?

MARS.

MARS was the god of war. He was commonly depicted by his worshippers as a warrior completely armed, and attended by Bellona, his sister, a goddess, fierce as himself. They were represented in

MARS.

VULCAN.

a chariot drawn by two wild horses, whose names were Flight and Terror.

Discord, Clamour, Anger, and Fear attended the chariot of Mars. The *dog*, for his eagerness in pursuit of prey; the *wolf*, for his fierceness; the *raven*, which feeds upon the slain; the *cock*, for his wakefulness, were all consecrated to a god, who was himself without pity, forbearance, or fear.

Men worshipped Mars, to engage his assistance against their enemies, or through fear of his power They could not feel love and trust in a being who was neither just nor benevolent. Mars was dreaded upon earth, and detested in heaven. In the Iliad, Jupiter addresses him thus:

> Of all the gods that tread the spangled skies,
> Thou most unjust, most hateful in our eyes!

The Romans were a more warlike people than the Greeks; they held Mars in higher reverence than the former people. The priests of Mars at Rome were called Salii,—they had the care of Ancilia, or sacred shields. These shields were sacred to Mars, and were held in superstitious reverence by the Romans.

In the early ages of Rome, a shield was found, of a shape which was not known among the Romans. An oracle was consulted by the person who found the shield, in order to learn its origin. The oracle declared that the shield had fallen from heaven, and that Mars would favour the people who should preserve it, and that they should overcome their enemies and conquer the world; that is, all the civilized world, which then included the countries round the Mediterranean, and which the Romans several centuries after completely subdued.

Numa Pompilius, second king of Rome, in order to secure the shield from being lost, caused several to be made, so exactly like it, that it was almost impossible to distinguish the original. Their form was oval. Their number was twelve; as was that of the priests, or Salii, at first, though afterwards they were increased to twenty-four.

Bellona had a temple at Rome. She usually harnessed the terrible horses of Mars, and with dishevelled hair, and frantic gestures, drove them through the field of battle. Victory was also an attendant of Mars. She had several temples in Greece and Rome. Games were instituted in honour of Victory.

A figure of Victory was often placed upon the car of a Roman conqueror when he appeared in triumph. Victory was then represented as flying, holding a crown, a branch of palm, and a globe

Who was Mars?
Who attended Mars, and what animals were sacred to him!
How was he regarded in heaven and on earth?
What nation chiefly honoured Mars?
What reverence was attached to the Ancilia?
What king instituted the Salii?
Who was Bellona?
How was Victory represented?

———

VULCAN.

See plate, page 37.

VULCAN was the god of fire, of smiths, and of metals, and the armorer of the gods. The working of metals is a most important circumstance in the civilization of man. By very little thought we instantly perceive that without the use of iron we could not cultivate the earth, prepare our food by the help of fire, possess any fine cutting instruments, or carry on any manufacture. For want of such accommodations we should be in the lowest state of savage life.

The ancient Greeks sometimes imputed the art of

forging metals to Prometheus. Perhaps Prometheus first discovered that metals were capable of fusion, and taught the art of manufacturing them to mankind; but Vulcan, according to the mythology was skilled in this mechanic operation, and was, in fact, a labourer at the anvil.

> "Obscure in smoke his flaming forges sound,
> While bathed in sweat, from fire to fire he flew;
> And puffing loud the roaring bellows blew."

In the book of Genesis it is said that Tubal-cain, one of the first men, was " an instructer of every artificer in brass and iron." This Tubal-cain might have been the same man whom the Greeks described either as Prometheus, or as Vulcan, but the fable says, Vulcan was the son of Jupiter and Juno. Vulcan is sometimes called Mulciber, and Lemnius.

It is said that Jupiter, taking offence at Vulcan, kicked him out of heaven, and that he fell into the island of Lemnos, and was lamed by his fall. At Lemnos he set up his forges, but afterwards moved to the volcanic islands of Lipari, near Sicily, where he forged Jupiter's thunderbolts.

> Nor was his name unheard or unadorned
> In ancient Greece : and in Ausonian land
> Men called him Mulciber; and how he fell
> From heaven they fabled, thrown by angry Jove.
> From morn
> To noon he fell, from noon to dewy eve,
> A summer's day ; and with the setting sun,
> Drops from the zenith, like a falling star,
> On Lemnos, the Ægean isle.
>
> *Paradise Lost*, Book L

Venus was the beautiful wife of Vulcan.

> ————when of old, as mystic bards presume,
> Huge Cyclops dwelt in Ætna's rocky womb,
> On thundering anvils rung their loud alarms,
> And leagued with Vulcan, forged immortal arms;

Descending Venus sought the dark abode,
And soothed the labours of the grisly god.
With radiant eye she viewed the boiling ore,
Heard undismayed the breathing bellows roar,
Admired their sinewy arms and shoulders bare,
And ponderous hammers lifted high in air ;
With smiles celestial blessed their dazzled sight,
And beauty blazed amid infernal night.

Botanic Garden, Canto I.

Vulcan wrought a helmet for Pluto, which rendered him invisible ; a trident for Neptune, which
shook both land and sea ; and a dog of brass for
Jupiter. He also constructed invincible armour for
Achilles and Eneas. The former a Greek, and the
latter a Trojan hero, who were engaged in the siege
of Troy. Vulcan also fabricated palaces of pure
gold for the celestial deities.

At Athens and Rome, festivals were kept to his
honour. Upon Mount Etna a temple was dedicated
to him, which was guarded by dogs, whose sense
of smelling was said to be so exquisite, as to enable
them to discern whether persons who came there
were virtuous or vicious, and who fawned upon, or
drove them away accordingly.

The Romans, in their most solemn treaties, invoked Vulcan ; and the assemblies in which they
discussed the most important affairs, were held in
the temple of Vulcan. At Memphis, in Egypt, also,
was a most magnificent edifice raised in honour of
this god, before which stood a colossal statue seventy
feet high.

The fiction of the *thunderbolts* proceeded from
the notion of ignorant people concerning the phe-
nomenon of *thunder*. The sound of thunder re-
sembles that of a heavy blow from some powerful
instrument, as a cannon-ball, which breaks into a
thousand fragments whatever it strikes. Thunder
is known to be the explosion of the electric fluid,

and its dispersion into the atmosphere, accompanied by the evolution of fire.

Before natural philosophy made this discovery, ignorant people fancied that thunder was an expression of the divine anger, and that it was produced by the *bolts* of Jupiter. These bolts were supposed to be sharp and barbed points, driven with a terrible force from the mighty arm of Jupiter, and which carried destruction before them. The ancients sometimes marked the spot where they supposed a thunderbolt had fallen, enclosed the place, and held it in reverence.

Who was Vulcan, and of what use is the manufacture of metals ?

Whom did the ancients suppose were the first workers of metals ?

Whom say the Hebrew scriptures was the first metallurgist ?

What is the history of Vulcan ?

In what verses is Venus described as visiting Vulcan ?

What did Vulcan manufacture !

What was the worship of Vulcan ?

How was Vulcan honoured at Rome ?

THE CYCLOPS.

The Cyclops were the workmen of Vulcan; they were probably very strong men, employed in the most laborious services of society. In Peloponnesus some of the first edifices were constructed of vast stones, which still remain. The arrangement of these stones, before the machines existed which have since been invented to assist labour, must have required immensely strong men. This is therefore called, from the Cyclops, the Cyclopean architecture.*

Vulcan had many Cyclops; the chief were Brontes, Steropes, and Pyracmon. The Cyclops

* Dr. Clarke.

were of prodigious stature, and had each but one eye, placed in the middle of their foreheads ; lived on such fruits and herbs as the earth spontaneously affords, and had no laws. All this only describes rude men, living by hard labour in a state of poverty.

The fiction of the Cyclops being one-eyed arose from the fact, that when they were exposed to the most violent action of the fire with which they wrought, they were forced to shield their faces with a piece of stiff leather, that had in the middle of a single perforation through which they looked.

Virgil thus describes the Cyclops at their work

Amid the Hesperian and Sicilian flood,
All black with smoke, a rocky island stood,
The dark Vulcanian land, the region of the god.
Here the grim Cyclops ply, in vaults profound,
The huge Æolian forge that thunders round.
The eternal anvils ring the dungeon o'er ;
From side to side the fiery caverns roar.
Loud groans the mass beneath their ponderous blows,
Fierce burns the flame, and the full furnace glows.

* * * * * * *

The alternate blows the brawny brethren deal ;
Thick burst the sparkles from the tortured steel.
Huge strokes, rough Steropes and Brontes gave,
And strong Pyracmon shook the gloomy cave.
Before their sovereign came, the Cyclops strove
With eager speed, to forge a bolt for Jove,
Such as by heaven's almighty lord are hurled,
All charged with vengeance on a guilty world.
Beneath their hands, tremendous to survey !
Half rough, half formed, the dreadful engine lay ;
Three points of rain, three forks of hail conspire,
Three armed with wind ; and three were barbed with fire
The mass they tempered thick with livid rays,
Fear, Wrath, and Terror, and the lightning's blaze.

Pitt's Translation

Who were the Cylops ?
What mode of life did the Cyclops follow ?
What is meant by the Cyclops being one-eyed ?
What is Virgil's description of the Cyclops ?

PANDORA

THE name of Pandora signifies *all gifts.* Pandora was originally a beautiful female image, formed by the skill of Vulcan, and carried to heaven. There Jupiter endowed her with life ; Venus gave her beauty; Pallas, wisdom, and Juno, riches ; Mercury taught her eloquence, and Apollo, music.

With these accomplishments Pandora was a perfect woman, and she was sent by Jupiter in a box to Prometheus. Jupiter, it is said, was angry at Prometheus for the manifold blessings which the latter had bestowed upon mankind, because Jupiter himself chose to be regarded as the supreme benefactor of the human race.

To revenge himself upon Prometheus, Jupiter sent him the gifted Pandora for a bride. She was enclosed in a box with diseases, war, pestilence, famine, discord, envy, calumny, and all the evils which Prometheus had endeavoured to banish from the earth. Prometheus, dreading some concealed evil, refused the present of Jupiter; but Epimetheus, the brother of Prometheus, felt greater curiosity, and opened the box. The beautiful Pandora instantly appeared, and with her came forth all the train of calamities which were concealed in the box, but Hope remained behind.

The meaning of this allegory appears to be, that the most beautiful and estimable things in this world, are sometimes connected with the most grievous misfortunes, but that, in every affliction, man is com forted with the hope of relief and of better days.

PROMETHEUS.

Thy godlike crime was to be kind,
 To render with thy precepts less
 The sum of human wretchedness,
 And strengthen man with his own mind.—*Byron.*

PROMETHEUS was, doubtless, one of the first civil-
izers of mankind. He first yoked the ox, and dis-
ciplined the horse : he taught the use of fire, and
the fusion of metals, and he also is said to have been
the inventor of letters ; he instructed men to cultivate and refine their manners, and to examine the
laws of nature, that the treasures hidden in the earth
might be brought forth and made serviceable.

Because Prometheus employed fire more curiously
and successfully than other men, he is said to have
stolen it from heaven. He was accused of having
taken this fire from the chariot of the sun ; he probably obtained it by concentrating the sun's rays, as
may be done by a burning-glass ; and this, ignorant
persons considered stealing from heaven. It was
asserted that he formed statues, into whom he trans-
fused fire from heaven, which gave them life.

Jupiter, not having succeeded in making the benevolent Prometheus unhappy, sent Mercury and
Vulcan to seize and chain him to mount Caucasus.
There a vulture was commanded to prey upon his
liver, which was reproduced so soon as it was devoured, so that he was doomed to eternal sufferings.
Hercules killed the vulture, and liberated Prometheus.

The hatred and vengeance of Jupiter against Prometheus gives a very unworthy notion of the god's
character. We reverence God because he is infinitely great and powerful ; and we love him because
he is as good as he is powerful ; and we know that
whatever good we do to our fellow-creatures is acceptable to him, and is, indeed, commanded by him

To punish a benefactor of mankind for his benevolence, is not suitable to the character of a benevolent
being.

Æschylus, the Greek dramatic poet, in his drama
of Prometheus, describes Prometheus as being bound
to the rock by Force and Strength, instead of Vulcan
and Mercury. *Force* and *Strength* may signify the
power and cruelty of bad men who were enemies of
Prometheus, and who might have confined him in
some solitary place, on account of his generous
services to his fellow-men.

In modern history many distinguished benefactors
of mankind have suffered greatly from the *force* and
strength of powerful tyrants. The discoverer of
America was sent to Spain in chains, after having
given a new hemisphere to Europe: and Galileo,
the Italian astronomer, was put in prison because he
demonstrated the motions of the heavenly bodies.
The malignity of his enemies is a more rational
cause for the sufferings of Prometheus than the
vengeful and jealous treatment of a god.

What signifies the name of Pandora?
How did Jupiter dispose of Pandora?
Did Prometheus receive Pandora?
What is the meaning of this allegory?
Who was Prometheus?
Of what was Prometheus accused?
How did Jupiter persecute Prometheus, and who was his
deliverer?
Is it natural to suppose that a god would persecute a good man?
How does Æschylus represent the sufferings of Prometheus?
Does modern history furnish similar examples?

JUNO.

See plate, page 49.

JUNO, the queen of heaven, was the sister and
wife of Jupiter. Though a celestial goddess, the

mythologists say she was born upon earth. It is disputed whether Juno's birth-place was the island of Samos or the city of Argos. At the latter place she was accounted a *tutelary* or guardian goddess.

At Rome, Juno was worshipped in the earliest age of the city. Tatius, the colleague of Romulus, instituted rites in her honour. At Rome she was called Juno Matrona, the *matron* or mother, and was regarded with the highest veneration.

Juno was haughty, vindictive, and jealous. She often quarrelled with her husband, and was implacable in her anger. The ancients, however, represented her under different characters. The Romans had a mild Juno, who had a benevolent and gracious countenance.

In general, Juno appears as a queen, seated upon a throne, holding in one hand a spindle, and in the other a sceptre, Her deportment was majestic, and her countenance severe, and a radiant crown was on her head. Near her was commonly placed her favourite bird, the peacock.

Juno bestowed empire and riches. When she appeared before Paris on Mount Ida, she offered him a city. The poppy and the lily were sacred to her, and she is sometimes exhibited with these flowers in her car, when she appears as the queen of the air, and is borne through the heavens by peacocks, and attended by Iris, the goddess of the rainbow.

IRIS

In the Hebrew Scriptures the rainbow is the symbol of peace, God's peace with the guilty world, which was punished and pardoned. When the first bow was set in the cloud this gracious promise was uttered, " henceforth, summer and winter, day and

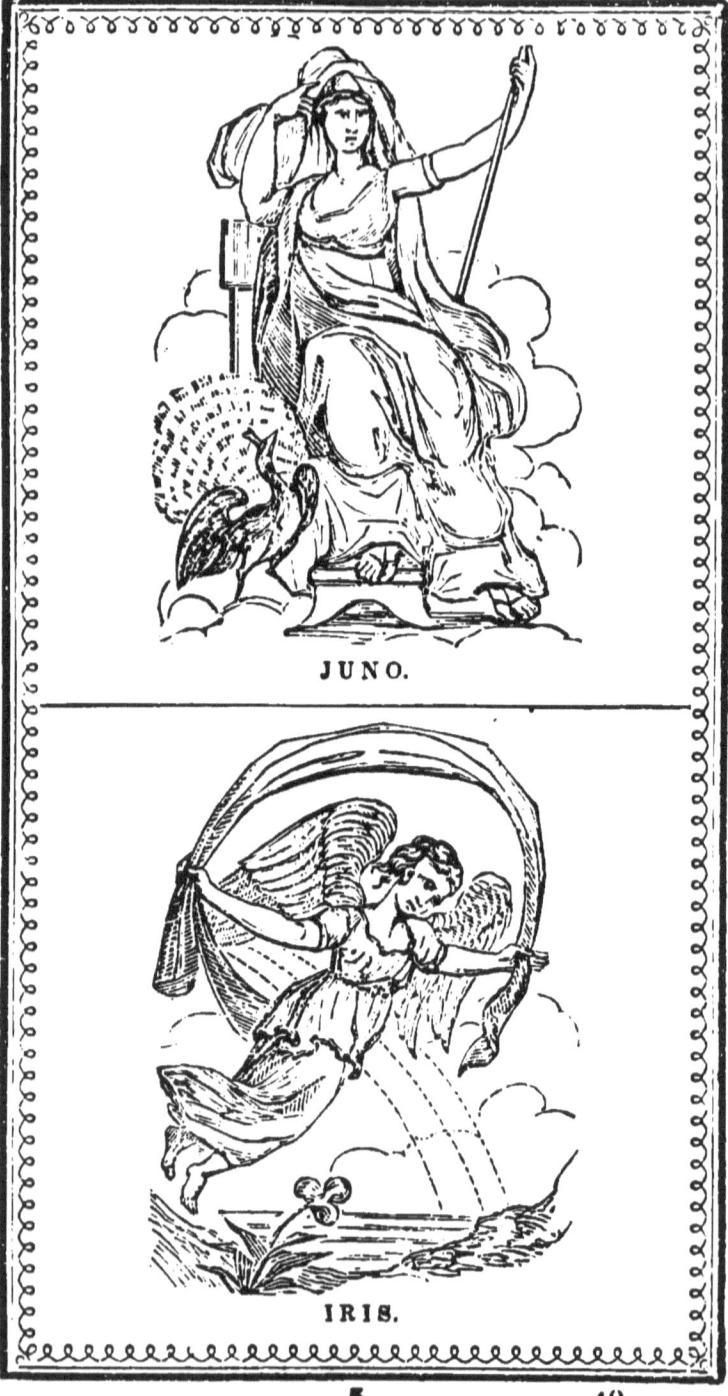

JUNO.

IRIS.

night, seed-time and harvest shall never fail." *Gen.* ch. ix. ver. 12.

The heathens seem to have known that the rainbow intimated God's goodness, for they personified this meteor under the figure of Iris, who was the messenger of peace to the dying. Iris was a beautiful female, the constant attendant of Juno, and more particularly the messenger of that goddess.

Iris was frequently employed by Juno to stir up strife among men. She is commonly represented with wings, and with her head encircled by a rainbow. The most benevolent office of Iris was to disengage the soul from the body, and she descended from heaven on this errand. Iris attended only dying persons of the female sex.

Who was Juno ?
Was Juno worshipped at Rome ?
What was the character of Juno ?
How is Juno represented ?
What was Juno's prerogative ?
What was the promise of God on the first appearance of the rainbow ?
Why was Iris represented as a divine messenger ?
Had Iris any other office than those of favour to mankind ?

HEBE AND GANYMEDE.

HEBE was the daughter of Jupiter and Juno. She was the goddess of youth, and had the power of imparting to others her own perpetual healthfulness and vigour. Hebe is, in fact, the personification of youthful beauty. She is represented as happy and innocent.

Hebe is always represented as a beautiful virgin, crowned with flowers, and attired in a variegated garment.

Jupiter, on account of her beauty, chose Hebe for his cup-bearer.

The gods of the heathen were not represented as *pure intelligences*, that is, as *spirits* without animal wants. They ate, drank, slept, and went journeys.

When the Israelites adopted the idolatries of Syria. the prophet Elijah reproves the worshippers of Baal by this derision, " Cry aloud, for he is a god ; either he is talking, or he is pursuing, or he is in a journey, or peradventure he sleepeth and must be awaked." 1 *Kings*, ch. xviii.

Homer, in the first book of the Iliad, describes the gods as having left the high Olympus, and being absent in Ethiopia.

> The sire of gods, and all the ethereal train,
> On the warm limits of the farthest main,
> Now mix with mortals, nor disdain to grace
> The feasts of Ethiopia's blameless race.
> Twelve days the powers indulge the genial rite,
> Returning with the twelfth revolving light.
>
> *Iliad*, Book I.

The heathen deities, like mortals, had their day and night.

> The radiant sun, to mortal sight,
> Descending swift, rolled down the rapid light,
> Then to their starry domes the gods depart,
> The shining monuments* of Vulcan's art.
> Jove on his couch reclined his awful head,
> And Juno slumbered on the golden bed.
>
> *Iliad*, Book I.

Jupiter, however, is supposed never to have slept.

> The immortals slumbered on their thrones above,
> All but the ever-wakeful eyes of Jove.
>
> *Iliad*, Book II.

The food of the gods was not supposed to be formed of the gross aliments of earth.

> For not the bread of man their life sustains,
> Nor wine's inflaming juice supplies their veins.

---

* These domes were separate habitations of the celestial gods, constructed by Vulcan.

Their sustenance was nectar and ambrosia. The former their drink, and the latter their food. These imaginary aliments were more delicious than any known to mankind. Hebe presented nectar to Jupiter in a golden cup.

Once, when Hebe was offering nectar to Jupiter, she fell. This carelessness offended his majesty, and she was deprived of the honour of serving him.

When Hebe was dismissed, Ganymede was chosen to succeed her.

Ganymede was a prince of Troy. His occupation was the care of flocks on Mount Ida. He was exquisitely beautiful, and an eagle carried him from earth to heaven, where he poured out nectar for Jupiter.

Who was Hebe ?
Were the heathen gods supposed to be spirits ?
How did the prophet Elijah deride this false notion of God ?
Does Homer represent the gods as *omnipresent*, that is, filling every part of the universe at once ?
Did the heathen deities sleep ?
What was the food of the gods ?
Why was Hebe dismissed by Jupiter ?
Who was Ganymede ?

MINERVA.

See plate, page 55.

MINERVA was the goddess of Wisdom. Wisdom is the knowledge of what is right and true, and of what is best to be done, when intelligent beings are called upon to act. Wisdom also includes the will to do what is right, and the love of goodness and truth. The God whom we worship is infinitely *wise*.

The heathens personified Wisdom under the character of Minerva. Solomon, the wise Hebrew king, also personified wisdom in the book of Proverbs, and represented her as the counsellor of God in the creation of the world. "The Lord possessed me in the beginning of his way, before his works of old. I was set up from everlasting, from the beginning, or ever the earth was.

"When there were no depths I was brought forth; when there were no fountains abounding with water. Before the mountains were settled; before the hills was I brought forth: while as yet he had not made the earth nor the fields, nor the highest part of the dust of the world.

"When he prepared the heavens, I was there: when he set a compass upon the face of the depth: when he established the clouds above: when he strengthened the fountains of the deep. When he gave to the sea his decree, that the waters should not pass his commandment: when he appointed the foundations of the earth: Then I was by him, and I was daily his delight, rejoicing always before him."

Minerva was the daughter of Jupiter. The poetic fiction concerning her is, that Jupiter being tormented with an excessive pain in his head, applied to Vulcan to open it with a keen axe; and upon his doing so, Minerva instantly sprang forth, a goddess armed.

Minerva was the tutelary, or guardian goddess of Athens. That city was called by one of her names, Athenæ; its original name was Cecropia, from the founder, Cecrops. Minerva was also called Pallas, from a Greek word, signifying bearing a javelin. She is often called in Homer, the "*blue-eyed maid*," for she never married.

The fable relates, that Neptune and Minerva disputed for the honour of giving a name to the capital of Attica. The gods decided that whichsoever should bestow the most useful gift upon the citizens, should give a name to the city. Neptune gave them a *horse*, and Minerva an *olive tree*. The latter gift

MINERVA.

CERES.

was the most valued by the inhabitants of Cecropia and from that time they called their city Athenæ.

Minerva was represented as a beautiful woman, of a countenance somewhat severe. On her head was a golden helmet, and her breastplate was also of gold. In her right hand Minerva bore a beaming lance, and in her left a buckler, called the Egis.

The Egis of Minerva had embossed upon it the head of Medusa. Medusa was one of the Gorgons, a sea nymph—she offended Minerva, and the goddess transformed her beautiful hair to frightful serpents. Thus disfigured, Medusa became an object of aversion and horror. Perseus, a prince of Argos, was employed to cut off this terrific head.

Perseus, in this expedition, was assisted by the gods. Mercury gave him a cimeter, and the wings from his heels; Minerva lent him a shield, polished like a mirror: and Pluto bestowed upon him a helmet which rendered him invisible. Thus equipped, Perseus flew to Spain, where he found Medusa, and unseen himself, presented the mirror to the Gorgon; —while she was gazing at herself, he cut off her head.

Perseus afterwards presented the head to Minerva, who placed it upon her shield; and so frightful was it, that those who beheld it were turned to stone.

With the bright wreath of serpent tresses crowned,
Severe in beauty, young Medusa frowned:
Erewhile subdued, round *Wisdom's* Egis rolled,
Hiss the dread snakes, and flamed in burnished gold;
Flashed on her brandished arm the immortal shield,
And terror lighted on the dazzled field.—*Botanic Garden.*

The Egis was not often thus employed,—it was only used to affright the bad. The meaning of this fable is, that if men in the midst of crimes are overtaken by the terrors of the wise and just God, they are suddenly stopped in the midst of their wicked purposes, and terrified at their own guilt, by a power who is of purer eyes than to behold iniquity with complacency.

The Palladium was an image of Pallas, which was supposed to have fallen from heaven.

The Palladium was preserved with great vigilance in the citadel of Troy, because an Oracle had declared, that, as long as it remained there, the city would be invincible against all the attacks of its enemies. Diomed and Ulysses, two of the Grecian heroes, contrived to convey the Palladium away, and Troy was taken.

Eneas, the son of Venus, and the great ancestor of the Romans, is said, by some of their writers, to have recovered and brought it with him into Italy. They assert that this celebrated image was deposited in the temple of Vesta, as a pledge of the stability of the empire and dominion of Rome. Hence, the word Palladium is sometimes used figuratively, to signify the preservation or safeguard of any valuable object. As, for example, the palladium of American liberty, or its security, is the virtue of our citizens.

The Parthenon, called from one of Minerva's names Parthenos, was the most splendid and beautiful temple of antiquity, and was erected in honour of this goddess at Athens. On a conspicuous part of this temple was sculptured the different worshippers of Minerva—young and old, bond and free ; and by means of these figures, which have been preserved, we are enabled to know the style of dress common to the Athenians.

Who was the heathen goddess of Wisdom—and what is signified by Wisdom ?

Who personified Wisdom, and how ?

What is the description of heavenly Wisdom in the book of Proverbs ?

What is the poetic origin of Minerva ?

How is Minerva represented ?

Of what city was Minerva the guardian ?
Why was the name of Minerva given to Athens ?
How was Minerva's Egis distinguished ?
Who assisted Perseus in this enterprise ?
What use did Perseus make of Medusa's head ?
What does the fable of the shield signify ?

The Panathenæa was a festival, celebrated in honour of Minerva. It occurred in our month of June. The principal inhabitants of all the towns in Attica, resorted to Athens on this occasion, bringing with them numerous victims for the sacrifices. Horse races, wrestling matches, and musical performances were exhibited for the public entertainment at this festival.

The songs sung at the Panathenæa were commonly the eulogium of some citizen, who had performed a distinguished service to the state. Thus the achievements of heroes were kept in the memory of the Athenian people, and served as lessons to others who might wish to serve their country. An olive wreath was bestowed, as a mark of the public approbation upon those that excelled in any of these competitions.

At this festival a very interesting procession was formed. It was composed of different classes of the citizens, and those who appeared in it were selected for their fine appearance. First advanced old men, still vigorous, who were of a majestic and venerable form—these bore in their hands branches of the olive tree. The old men were followed by those of middle age, clothed in polished armour, and after them proceeded youths under twenty years of age.

The young persons were of both sexes—the boys clad in plain garments, and the girls dressed with simplicity, and carrying baskets of cakes and flowers.

as offerings to the goddess. These were of honourable families, and were attended by the daughters of foreigners settled at Athens. The latter carried a folding seat for the young girls to rest upon, and an umbrella to screen them from the sun ; they also carried water and honey for the *libations*. Foreigners, or sojourners as they were called, who resided at Athens, held a rank inferior to natives of the city

Musicians, some playing on the flute, and others upon the lyre, *rhapsodists*, who sang passages from Homer's poems, and dancers of singular grace accompanied the procession, and passed through the streets, amidst a crowd of spectators. When the whole reached the temple of Minerva, a magnificent sacrifice ended the solemnity, and the assembly dispersed to different places, where they concluded the day in feasting and mirth.

The most celebrated statue of Minerva in ancient times, was that of the Parthenon, thirty-nine feet in height, formed of ivory and gold. It was the work of Phidias, produced by the request of Pericles. The Athenians were offended at Phidias, because it was discovered that among certain figures, engraved upon the shield of Minerva, he had placed likenesses of himself and of Pericles. In consequence, this capricious people banished Phidias, and he withdrew from Athens to Elis, where he was beloved and cherished, and where he made a statue of Jupiter, that was reckoned among the seven wonders of the world

What was the Palladium ?
Who carried the Palladium to Italy ?
What was the Parthenon ?
What was the Panathenæa ?
What were the songs sung at the Panathenæa ?
What procession appeared at Athens at this festival ?
How did young persons appear at the Panathenæa ?
How was the Panathenæa concluded ?
What was the most celebrated statue of Minerva ?

CERES.

See plate, page 55.

CERES, the daughter of Saturn and Ops, was the goddess of agriculture. She first instructed men to plough the soil, to sow seeds, to reap the harvest, to thresh the grain, to make flour and bread, to enclose fields, and to mark out the limits of each individual's property.

In the first ages of society, men fed upon wild fruits, and the flesh of wild animals taken in hunting —they are then in a *barbarous* state. When they discover the use of vegetable substances, and acquire the art of procuring them from the fields, *they have advanced one step in civilization*—they are in the agricultural state. Ceres, possibly, might have done much to advance her contemporaries from a savage condition, to one of greater industry and comfort.

Ceres might have made some improvements in the art of cultivating the earth. The Egyptians worshipped a goddess, called by them Isis; who, like the Ceres of the Greeks, conferred the gifts of corn, bread, and separated property. The mythologists say, that Isis and Ceres are the same goddess, worshipped under those different names, in different countries in the pagan world.

The image of Ceres was that of a tall female, having her head adorned with ears of wheat. Her right hand was filled with poppies and corn, and her left carried a lighted torch. Ceres had splendid temples, and she was worshipped by husbandmen in the fields, before they began to reap. Sacrifices to her were also offered in the spring, and *oblations* of wine, honey, and milk.

Virgil mentions this rural observance :

To Ceres bland, her annual rites be paid,
On the green turf, beneath the fragrant shade :

When winter ends and spring serenely shines,
Then fat the lambs, then mellow are the wines:
Then sweet are slumbers on the flowery ground ;
Then with thick shades are lofty mountains crowned.
Let all the hinds bend low at Ceres' shrine ;
Mix honey sweet, for her, with milk and mellow wine.
Thrice lead the victim the new fruits around,
And Ceres call, and choral hymns resound.
Presume not, swains, the ripened grain to reap,
Till crowned with oak in antic dance you leap,
Invoking Ceres ; and in solemn lays,
Exalt your rural queen's immortal praise.—*Pitt's Virgil.*

The worship of Ceres was universal among those who received the religion of Greece. The most solemn ceremonial of that religion was the festival of Ceres, celebrated at Eleusis, a town in Attica, and particularly honoured by the Athenians. These solemnities were called the Eleusinian Mysteries.

The word mysteries signifies something not commonly known. The Mysteries of Eleusis seems to have been an institution resembling modern Masonry, in the particular of secrecy at least. *Initiated persons*—that is, those who were admitted to be present at the ceremonies at Eleusis, were strictly forbidden to divulge what they saw there.

Persons of both sexes were admitted by the high priest, called the Hierophant, to the mysteries of Eleusis. It was pretended that those who enjoyed this privilege were under the immediate protection of the goddess, and not only in this life, but after death. Those who broke the vow to conceal what they were instructed in, in these mysteries, were accounted *execrable.*

Execration was a sentence which forbade all people to dwell in the same house, to enter the same ship, to drink from the same vessel, to buy and sell, or to converse with the person considered *sacrilegious.* The sentence of execration permitted any one to put the supposed criminal to death as a public offender.

The mysteries of Eleusis are believed to have consisted of certain spectacles, sometimes brilliant, and sometimes frightful. Splendid fireworks, succeeded by complete darkness, artificial thunder and lightning, and pretended forms of spirits.

The first introduction to these exhibitions was the *initiation*. What these mysteries really signified is unknown. The garments worn at the *initiation* were accounted holy, and preserved as *charms*, that is, as being preventives to accidents and diseases, or malevolence of enemies.

Who was Ceres ?

What is the primitive condition of mankind ?

What favour did Ceres probably confer, and what was she called by the Egyptians ?

How was Ceres represented ?

In what verses is her worship described ?

What honours were offered to Ceres at Eleusis ?

What are Mysteries ?

How were persons admitted to the mysteries of Eleusis regarded ?

What was execration ?

What spectacles were exhibited at Eleusis ?

What superstition is related concerning the initiation ?

PROSERPINE.

See plate, page 65.

ONE of the prettiest fictions of the mythology is the story of Proserpine. Proserpine was the beloved daughter of Ceres. The favourite residence of Ceres was the beautiful and fertile island of Sicily. In Sicily the young Proserpine was bred up, and her innocent and happy occupation was to wander over the valley of Enna, where, attended by companions as lovely as herself, she delighted in gathering flowers.

One day as Proserpine, with the daughters of
Oceanus, was diverting herself in the pleasant fields
of Enna, Pluto, the king of the infernal regions,
appeared in his chariot drawn by two fine horses,
black as ebony.

Admiring the beauty of Proserpine, Pluto was
resolved to make her his queen, and had come to
carry her off with him.

The young virgins saw him, and one of them,
says a modern poet, in terror exclaimed,

> 'Tis he, 'tis he, he comes to us
> From the depths of Tartarus.
> For what of evil doth he roam
> From his red and gloomy home,
> In the centre of the world,
> Where the sinful dead are hurled?
> Mark him as he moves along,
> Drawn by horses black and strong,
> Such as may belong to night
> Ere she takes her morning flight.

> Now the chariot stops: the god
> On our grassy world has trod;
> Like a Titan steppeth he,
> Yet full of his divinity.
> On his mighty shoulders lie
> Raven locks, and in his eye
> A cruel beauty, such as none
> Of us may wisely look upon.　　*Barry Cornwall.*

It appears, however, that Pluto had nothing frightful in the apprehension of Proserpine, and that she
was taken without much resistance. The ground
opened upon the occasion, the ebon coursers descended, and where the earth closed over the car of
Pluto and Proserpine a fountain gushed out. This
fountain was called Cyane, and thither the Sicilians
would afterwards resort, and celebrate the descent
of Proserpine in annual festivals.

Ceres, alarmed at the absence of Proserpine,

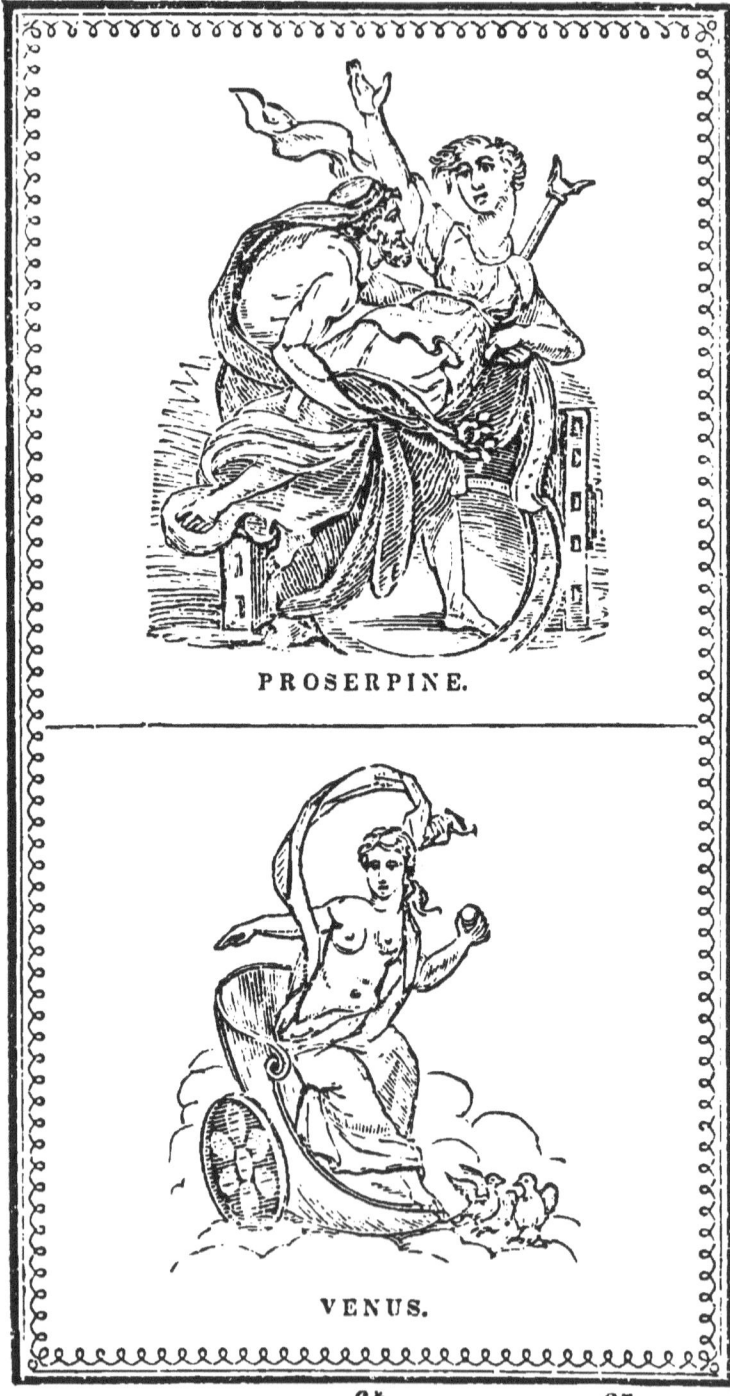

PROSERPINE.

VENUS.

sought for her among the flowers of Enna, but she only found her daughter's veil. It is related of Ceres, that in her distress she kindled a torch at the flames of Mount Ætna, and carrying it in her hand, to light her in all dark places, went over the world in search of her lost child.

Ceres, after a while, discovered whither Proserpine had been carried. Angry and grieved at this act of violence, Ceres supplicated Jupiter that Proserpine by his supreme authority might be restored to earth. Jupiter, to comfort and appease Ceres, consented, on condition that Proserpine had not tasted any thing in hell.

Ceres, upon this, descended to the dark dominions of Pluto, and was welcomed by Proserpine, who gladly prepared to return to earth with her mother. Pluto, however, was not to be deceived ; he had employed a spy called Ascalaphus to watch Proserpine, and when she was about to depart Ascalaphus declared that he had seen her eating a pomegranate. Therefore Proserpine was detained, and Ceres compelled to leave her.

Again Ceres entreated Jupiter, and he consented that Proserpine should divide the year between earth and hell. She was to spend six months with her mother, and the other six months with Pluto. The mythologists say this signifies that Proserpine represented corn, which lies during winter, in its seed state, below the surface of the earth, and then rises to the upper air and adorns the fields

Minerva, the goddess of wisdom, is usually drawn with an owl by her side. This owl is no other than Ascalaphus. When Proserpine heard him inform Pluto that she had eaten the pomegranate, in her anger she sprinkled water of Phlegethon upon his head, and metamorphosed him into an owl, which Minerva afterwards took for her attendant.

The owl is not accounted a sagacious bird but his faculty of seeing in darkness, when others cannot see, represents the vigilance of Ascalaphus, who watched Proserpine when he was not himself observed. It is suitable to wisdom, which discerns where the careless are blind, to take such a bird as her emblem.

Who was Proserpine, and how did she employ herself?
Who carried off Proserpine to the infernal regions?
What did one of her companions exclaim?
What happened on the descent of Pluto and Proserp ne?
What did Ceres when she lost her daughter?
Of whom did Ceres entreat relief?
Was Proserpine restored to earth?
Did Ceres offer a second petition to Jupiter, and what is re presented by this part of the fable of Proserpine?
What became of Ascalaphus?
Is the owl a proper attendant of Minerva?

VENUS AND CUPID.

The froth-born Venus, ravishing to sight,
Rose from the ample sea to upper light,
And on her head the flower of summer swelled,
And blushed all lovely, and like Eden smelled.
A garland of the rose; and a white pair
Of doves about her flickered in the air;
There her son Cupid stood before her feet,
Two wings upon his shoulders, fair and fleet;
And blind as night, as he is often seen,
A bow he bare, and arrows bright and keen.
No goddess she, commissioned to the field,
Like Pallas, dreadful with her sable shield,
Or fierce Bellona thundering at the wall,
While flames ascend, and mighty ruins fall.
To the soft Cyprian shores she graceful moves,
To visit Paphos and her blooming groves;
While to her power a hundred altars rise,
And grateful incense meets the balmy skies.

VENUS.

See plate, page 65.

VENUS was the personification of female beauty
The poets represented her as having sprung from
the foam of the sea. She first appeared upon the
surface of the waves in a sea-shell, and was gently
wafted to the foot of mount Cythera, and when she
set her feet upon the land, flowers sprung up beneath them. The *rosy Hours*, who were intrusted
with her education, received her, and conducted her
to heaven.

The Romans sometimes called Venus, Cythera,
from the island to which she was borne, and sometimes she was called Dione. Her favourite residence
was in the island of Cyprus, where she was worshipped at the city of Paphos. Venus, from her
vivacity and happy disposition, is often styled the
laughter-loving goddess. That she was intrusted
to the Hours and conveyed by them to heaven, only
signifies that she passed her time happily :

> Young Dione, nursed beneath the waves,
> And rocked by Nereids in their coral caves,
> Charmed the *blue* sisterhood* with playful wiles,
> Lisped her sweet tones, and tried her tender smiles.
> Then, on her beryl throne, by Tritons borne,
> Bright rose the goddess like the star of morn.
> With rosy fingers, as uncurled they hung
> Round her fair brow, her golden locks she wrung ;
> O'er the smooth surge in silver sandals stood,
> And looked enchantment on the dazzled flood.
> The bright drops rolling from her lifted arms,
> In slow meanders wander o'er her charms,
> See round her snowy neck their lucid track,
> Pearl her white shoulders, gem her ivory back,

* The Nereids were represented in the mythology to have
blue hair. Milton says, " blue-haired deities." See *Comus*

Round her fine waist and swelling bosom swim,
And star with glittering brine each crystal limb.
—And beauty blazed to heaven and earth unveiled.

Botanic Garden.

She is often represented in her sea-shell sporting
upon the ocean, the sea-nymphs, called Nereides,
and dolphins, and Cupids, surrounding her. When
she ascended to heaven her chariot was drawn by
doves and swans, accompanied by Cupid and the
Graces. She guided her doves by a golden chain
She was clothed in slight and graceful apparel,
bound round the waist by a girdle called the *cestus.*
The cestus was supposed to make Venus a thousand
times more graceful and beautiful than she was with
out it.

The temples of Venus were numerous in the heathen world; those of Paphos, Cythera, and Idalia
were the most celebrated. In some places incense
only was offered to this goddess. The dove and
the swan, the rose and the myrtle, the most graceful
of birds, and the sweetest and most odorous of
plants, were sacred to Venus.

In ancient times the Greeks regarded fine hair as
the greatest natural ornament of the female sex.
The ladies preserved their hair carefully, and ar-
ranged it in a very tasteful and becoming manner;
they often consecrated it to Venus.

Some instances are related of beautiful ladies who
had grown old, and no longer could take pleasure in
the reflection of their own faces, who would send
the mirror they had been accustomed to use, and
hang it up in the temple of Venus, as if they had
said, Time has robbed me of my beauty; I only
see in this mirror that I am no longer young; I will
bestow it upon her whose beauty never fades, and
whose youth is immortal.

ADONIS.

ADONIS was a beautiful youth, and beloved by Venus. His favourite occupation was hunting Venus often cautioned him against exposing his life to the violence of wild beasts, but he did not attend to her counsels, and died of the wound which a wild boar whom he pursued gave him.

Venus mourned him excessively, and transformed him to the flower called Anemone, or wind-flower. Proserpine offered to restore him to life if he would spend half the year with her in the infernal regions. This fable has the same meaning with that of Proserpine herself. Proserpine spent half the year with her mother on earth, and the other half with Pluto in hell. These allegories signify that the seeds and roots of plants are interred beneath the soil in winter, and rise to the light and adorn the earth in summer.

The feasts of Adonis were celebrated in Greece and Syria. They commenced with mourning for his death, and concluded with expressions of joy for their renovation. The Syrians called Adonis, Thammuz. The prophet Ezekiel reproves the idolatrous women for weeping for Thammuz ; that is, for joining in the funeral procession with which the Syrians celebrated his memory.

> On Lebanon's sequestered height
> The fair Adonis left the realms of light,
> Bowed his bright locks, and, fated from his birth
> To change eternal, mingled with the earth ;
> With darker horror shook the conscious wood,
> Groaned the sad gales, and rivers blushed with blood.
> And *Beauty's goddess* bending o'er his bier,
> Breathed the soft sigh, and poured the tender tear.
> Admiring *Proserpine*, through dusky glades,
> Led the fair phantom to Elysian shades,
> Clad with new form, with finer sense combined,
> And lit with purer flame the ethereal mind.

Erewhile emerging from infernal night,
The youth immortal rises to the light,
Leaves the drear chambers of the insatiate tomb,
And shines and charms with renovated bloom.

Botanic Garden, Canto II.

In what verses are Venus and Cupid described?
What did Venus personify?
What were the appellations of Venus?
In what verses is her rising from the sea described?
Where, and how was Venus worshipped?
What personal ornament did the Greek ladies particularly value?
What use did the Greek ladies sometimes make of a mirror?
What is the story of Adonis?
In what verses is Adonis described?

CUPID.

CUPID was the son of Venus, and was the emblem of *love*. He was generally painted as a beautiful winged boy, with a bow and arrows, and very often with a bandage over his eyes.

Ancient statues sometimes represent him bestriding the back of a lion, and playing on a lyre, whilst the fierce savage, turning his head, seems to listen to its harmonious chords.

Sometimes he appears mounted on a dolphin; and sometimes he is represented as breaking the winged thunderbolt of Jove. He was the son of Venus; his wife was Psyche—a Greek word, signifying spirit, or soul.

The love of Cupid for Psyche was an allegory intended to show that all true affection is towards the mind. The most beautiful object in nature without *life* cannot be loved. The gift of life to an intelligent being is only of value according to the degree of understanding, sensibility, and goodness which he possesses. We can only be beloved by

CUPID.

DIANA.

the intelligent and good, according to the goodness, the ability, and the generous sympathies of our nature.

THE GRACES.

THE Graces were three beautiful females, daughters of Venus, and often attendant upon her. The Graces were supposed to be beautiful and amiable, and to represent the sweetness, civility, and purity which are proper to delicate, elegant, and accomplished persons.

The names of the Graces were Aglaia, Thalia, and Euphrosyne ; they are usually represented in a group, naked, and adorned with flowers on their heads. The *Graces*, properly Charities or Virtues, were represented hand in hand, to show that virtues, though different, belong to each other, and that they are not found single but united. The Graces were *beautiful*, to signify that kind affections and good actions are pleasing and winning. They were exhibited unadorned and unclothed, because gentleness of manners and kindness of heart are sufficient, without disguise or art, to gain good will.

Who was Cupid ?
What is signified by the story of Cupid and Psyche ?
What were the Graces, and what were their attributes ?

DIANA.
See plate, page 73.

DIANA was the twin sister of Apollo. Juno, being offended at Latona, drove her from heaven, and forbade the earth to afford her an asylum. Old Ocean was more compassionate. Neptune, in pity of her desolate condition, raised the island of Delos from the Egean sea, and gave it to Latona. In Delos,

Apollo and Diana were born. The Greeks held Delos in reverence as the birthplace of these divinities. Apollo and Diana are commonly regarded as representatives of the sun and moon.

The Egyptians called her Isis. Among the Greeks Diana or Phebe was honoured under three different characters, as a goddess of heaven, earth, and hell, and was therefore called the triform goddess. As a celestial divinity she was Luna, the Moon ; as a terrestrial goddess, Diana ; and in the infernal regions, Hecate.

Diana was the goddess of chastity, of the chase, and of woods. In *heaven*, she was supposed to enlighten by her rays; on *earth*, to restrain the wild animals by her bow and dart; and in the *realms below*, to keep in awe the shadowy multitudes of ghosts.

Diana was represented under the figure of a very tall and beautiful young virgin, in a hunting dress ; a bow in her hand, a quiver of arrows suspended across her shoulders, and her forehead ornamented with a silver crescent. Sometimes she appears in a chariot of silver, drawn by hinds.

Diana had two temples famous in history. The first was that of Ephesus, one of the seven wonders of the world. This was burnt to the ground the very day on which Alexander the Great was born. A man named Erostratus, wishing to make his name immortal, set fire to this magnificent temple, imagining that such an action would necessarily transmit his name to posterity.

Diana was worshipped with peculiar reverence at Ephesus. When St. Paul preached the gospel there, the word of God grew mightily and prevailed. A man named Demetrius, who made "silver shrines for Diana," that is, little altars and images of the goddess, and models of the great temple, (probably for the embellishment of houses,) being in fear that the goddess would fall into contempt, thus admonished the Ephesians :

"Not alone at Ephesus, but almost throughout *all Asia*, (all the Greek cities of Asia,) this Paul hath persuaded and turned away much people, saying, that they be no gods which are made with hands: so that not only this our craft is in danger to be set at naught, but also that the temple of the great goddess Diana should be despised, and her magnificence should be destroyed, whom all Asia and the world worshippeth."

The citizens of Ephesus then raised a great clamour against Paul, but one of the town officers, a friend of the old superstition, appeased them, saying, " Ye men of Ephesus, what man is there that knoweth not that the city of the Ephesians is a worshipper of the great goddess Diana, and of the image which fell down from Jupiter ? Seeing that these things cannot be spoken against, ye ought to be quiet, and to do nothing rashly."—*Acts*, ch. xix.

From this time, however, the phantoms of Paganism faded before the light of Christianity, and the religion of Paul has been diffused all over the world, while that of the heathens has passed away like a dream of the night.

The second celebrated temple of Diana was that of Taunica Chersonesus, or the modern Crimea. This was in the ancient Scythia, which comprehended parts of modern Russia and Tartary. The Scythians there worshipped Diana with barbarous rites, offering to her human sacrifices.

Who was Diana?
What were Diana's several characters?
What were Diana's offices ?
How is Diana represented ?
Where was the most celebrated temple of Diana?

7*

How was the preaching of Paul received at Ephesus?
What was the admonition of the shrine-maker at Ephesus?
How were the Ephesians appeased?
What has taken place in the world in regard to Paganism?
Where was another temple of Diana?

THE MUSES.

THE Muses are the favourite goddesses of the poets. The ancients used often to begin their verses by *invoking* the muse, that is, by a short address or prayer to one of the Muses, entreating her to *inspire* the poet—to give him some portion of celestial intelligence, that his poetry might be worthy of the favour of the goddess, and of the esteem of mankind.

The Muses were daughters of Jupiter and Mnemosyne, or memory; mistresses of the science, patronesses of poetry and music, companions of Apollo, directresses of the feasts of the gods.

They are represented as nine beautiful virgins, sometimes dancing in a ring, around Apollo, sometimes playing on various musical instruments, or engaged in scientific pursuits. They are called Muses, from a Greek word, signifying to meditate, to inquire.

The Muses had each a name derived from some particular accomplishment of mind, or branch of science.

The first of the Muses, Clio, derives her name from the Greek word, signifying *glory, renown.* She presided over *History.* She was supposed to have invented the lyre, which she is frequently depicted as holding in her hand, together with the plectrum, the instrument with which the ancients struck their harp or lyre.

Thalia presided over *comedy.* Her name signifies, *the blooming*. She is represented reclining on a pillar, holding in her hand a mask.

Melpomene presided over *tragedy*. She is generally seen with her hand resting upon the club of Hercules ; because the object of tragedy was to represent the brilliant actions and the misfortunes of heroes.

Euterpe was the patroness of *instrumental music*. Her name signifies *the agreeable*. She is always depicted as surrounded with various instruments of music.

Terpsichore, or *the amusing*, presided over the dance. She has always a smiling countenance : and one foot lightly touching the earth, while the other sports in air.

Erato. Her name is derived from the Greek word signifying *love*. She is the inspirer of light poetry, and of the triumphs and complaints of lovers.

Polyhymnia, whose name signifies *many songs*, presides over miscellaneous poetry, and the ode.

Urania, or *the heavenly*, was esteemed the inventress of *astronomy*. In her hands she holds a globe, which sometimes appears placed on a tripod, and then she grasps a scale, or a pair of compasses.

Calliope owes her name to the majesty of her voice. She presided over *rhetoric* and *epic poetry*.

The Muses had favourite haunts in Greece,—the vale of Tempe in Thessaly, Mount Parnassus in Phocis, Pieria in Thrace, the country Aonia, and Mount Helicon in Bœotia. Their fountains were Hippocrene, and Castalia at the foot of Parnassus. Their horse had wings, and was called Pegasus— when Pegasus struck the earth forcibly with his foot the fountain Hippocrene sprung out.

The Muses are frequently represented surrounding Apollo on Mount Parnassus or Helicon ; while

Pegasus, with extended wings, springs forward into the air.

Who were the Muses?

How were they represented?

From what were their names derived?

What was the office of Clio; of Thalia; of Melpomene; of Euterpe; of Terpsichore; of Erato; of Polyhymnia; of Urania; of Calliope?

Where were the favourite haunts of the Muses?

DIVINITIES

OF

THE SEA AND RIVERS.

THE heathens deified the ocean, and believed that not only the sea itself, but every fountain and river had its peculiar divinities. Oceanus and Nereus both represented the ocean. Nereus was the son of Oceanus. Oceanus had seventy-two daughters, called the Oceanides, and Nereus had fifty, these were the Nereides. There were a great multitude of sea-nymphs besides the Oceanides and Nereides.

The names of the Nereides, in Greek, express waves, tempests, calms, rocks, ports, &c. The Nereides, who were the attendants on Neptune were esteemed very handsome. In ancient monuments the Nereides are represented sometimes with an entire human body, and sometimes with the tail of a fish. They are sometimes pictured riding in the sea upon Tritons, and sometimes upon sea-horses.

How did the heathens regard the ocean?

What do the names of the Nereides express, and how did they appear?

NEPTUNE.

Neptune was the brother of Jupiter. In the division of their father's kingdom the empire of the seas fell to his share. He was worshipped as the god of the seas. Amphitrite was his wife. He was represented with black hair and blue eyes, standing erect in a chariot formed of a vast shell drawn by sea-horses; clothed in an azure mantle, and holding in his hand the trident which commanded the waves. Around him played the sea-nymphs, and the Tritons sounding their trumpet of shells.

He was the ruler of the waters, the god of ships and of all maritime affairs, and his supreme command could raise the stormy waves, or calm the wildest fury of the tempest.

The Isthmean games, which were celebrated at Corinth in Greece, were in honour of Neptune That city being the centre of the Greek commerce, derived its wealth from the sea, and therefore held

Neptune in more grateful estimation than the other states.

Who was Neptune, and how was he represented?
What were Neptune's attributes?
Why was Neptune worshipped with peculiar rites at Corinth?

POLYPHEMUS.

POLYPHEMUS was a son of Neptune, a giant who, like the Cyclops had but one eye. He kept sheep in the island of Sicily, and lived by violence and murder, devouring human beings whenever they fell in his way. Polyphemus surprised Ulyssus when he was driven to the island of Sicily and devoured several of his companions. Ulysses contrived to intoxicate Polyphemus, and while he was asleep extinguished his only eye. Phorcus, father of the Gorgons and of Proteus, and Triton, were sons of Neptune.

THE TRITONS were imaginary sea animals, the upper part of whose bodies was supposed to resemble that of man; the lower part that of the dolphin. The first of them was the son of Neptune and Amphitrite. This Triton, being the trumpeter of Neptune, terrified the giants in their war with the gods, by the sound of his instrument.

THE SIRENS were sea nymphs of rare beauty, who dwelt upon the coast of Sicily; their names were Parthenope, Ligeia, and Leucosia. In the neighbourhood of the Sirens lived the enchantress Circe. They were all admirable singers, and lured mariners, whom they detained from prosecuting their voyage, to visit them

Circe metamorphosed men to brutes.

Milton, the British poet describes the effect of their music thus :

> Circe and the sirens three,
> Amid the flowery kirtled Naiades
> Culling their potent herbs and baleful drugs ;
> Who, as they sung, would take the prisoned soul
> And lap it in Elysium ; Scylla wept
> And chid her barking waves into attention,
> And fell Charybdis murmured soft applause.

SCYLLA AND CHARYBDIS.

Scylla, daughter of Phorcus, was a beautiful woman, whom Circe hated because she was beloved by Glaucus, whom Circe desired for herself. The mischievous Circe infected the water in which Scylla bathed, so that she was metamorphosed into a monster, retaining the female form, but having six dogs' heads ; some say she was changed to a rock on the coast of Sicily.

Scylla was, in fact, a rock, and the table of the dogs' heads was derived from the supposed resemblance between the dashing of the waves and the howling of dogs. Opposite to Scylla was a whirlpool called Charybdis. Charybdis was supposed to have been a female robber killed by Hercules.

It was said that the rock Scylla and the whirlpool Charybdis, were so near to each other in the strait of Messina, that a ship, when it would steer clear of Charybdis, struck upon Scylla, and, if it would avoid Scylla, it was swallowed up by Charybdis. Hence the proverb, *when we shun Scylla we are lost in Charybdis*, signifying, one of two dangers is inevitable.

The Halcyones were sea-birds, who were supposed to build their nests upon the waves, and to calm their violence by their presence. Halcyone, wife of Ceyx, King of Trachinia, seeing the corpse of her husband driven on shore by the tide, who had been shipwrecked on his return from consulting the oracle of Delphi, threw herself into the sea. The gods, pitying the unhappy fate of Ceyx and Halcyone, changed them into the birds called Halcyones, and imparted to them the power of stilling the waves.

The Halcyon of the ancients is supposed to be the king-fisher, an aquatic bird, which makes its appearance immediately upon the abatement of storms; thus they were ignorantly presumed to be the cause of allaying tempests.

———

PROTEUS was a son of Neptune, who was intrusted with the care of his flocks, consisting of sea-calves, (phocæ, or seals,) and other marine animals. He is represented by the poets as possessing the faculty of changing himself into whatever forms he chose. Hence, a fickle person is frequently called Proteus. History makes mention of a Proteus King of Egypt, about the time of the Trojan war, who was illustrious for his secrecy, wisdom, and foresight.

Proteus was a prophet. When Menelaus was detained on the coast of Africa on his return from Troy, he wished to consult Proteus; Proteus, however, would not attend to him, so Menelaus and his companions covered themselves with seal skins, and appeared to Proteus to be of his flock. In that way they succeeded in securing him, though he assumed sundry forms in order to escape.

> Now thronging quick, to bask in open air,
> The flocks of ocean to the strand repair.
> Couched on the sunny sand the monsters sleep ·
> Then Proteus mounting from the hoary deep,

Surveys his charge unknowing of deceit,
Pleased with the false review secure he lies,
And leaden slumbers press his drooping eyes.
   Shouting we* seize the god; our force to evade,
His various arts he summons to his aid.
   A lion now he curls a surgy mane;
Sudden our bands a spotted pard retain;
Then armed with tusks, and lightning in his eyes,
A boar's obscener shape the god belies.
On spiry volumes, there, a dragon rides;
Here, from our strict embrace a stream he glides.
And last, sublime, his stately growth he rears
A tree, and well dissembled foliage wears.

Pope's Homer's Odyssey.

HARPIES, certain disgusting demons mentioned by Virgil. The Harpies had human faces, but bodies of vultures, with long claws like the talons of carnivorous birds. The Harpies not only injured but defiled whatever they lighted upon. They were represented as rapacious and cruel, and destroying for the mere pleasure of destruction.

These subordinate deities were not all which mythology has recorded. There were various tribes of nymphs: those who presided over rivers and waters, were named Naiades; those who resided in marshes, Lymniades. The wood nymphs were called Dryades and Hamadryades. The nymphs of the mountains, Oreades. Milk, honey, oil, and sometimes goats, were sacrificed to their honour.

Who was Polyphemus?
Who were the Tritons?
Who were the Sirens?
How does Milton describe the music of the Sirens?
Who was Scylla?
What does the fable of Scylla signify, and who was Charybdis?
   What proverb is derived from the fable of Scylla and Charybdis, and what is its meaning?

---

   * Menelaus and his associates.

What were the Halcyones?
What is the truth concerning the Halcyones?
Who was Proteus?
What is Homer's description of Proteus?
Were there other inferior deities who presided over different
parts of nature?
Who were the Harpies, and what was their character?
Who presided over the waters and the woods?

RURAL DEITIES.

· BACCHUS.

Bacchus, that first from out the purple grape,
Crushed the sweet poison of misused wine.
                    Milton's Comus.

Bacchus was probably some ancient conqueror
and civilian of the Eastern nations. The mythologists say that Bacchus was born in Egypt and educated at Nysa in Arabia; that he taught the culture of
the grape, and the art of converting its juice to
wine, and the preparation of honey: and that he subdued India, Phrygia, Egypt, and Syria. The conquests of Bacchus seem to have been of a pacific nature. They represented the triumph of the useful
arts over brute force.

Bacchus, drawn by wild beasts, subject to his
will, attended by rural deities,—Pan, Silenus, and
the Satyrs, and making a peaceable progress from
one country to another, exhibits a benefactor and not
a disturber of nations. The fir, the ivy, the fig, and
the vine, were sacred to Bacchus. The goat was
slain in his sacrifices, because that animal is injuri-
ous to vines.

The festivals of Bacchus were celebrated in the
woods. Women were his principal worshippers
His priestesses were called Bacchæ, Bacchantes, and

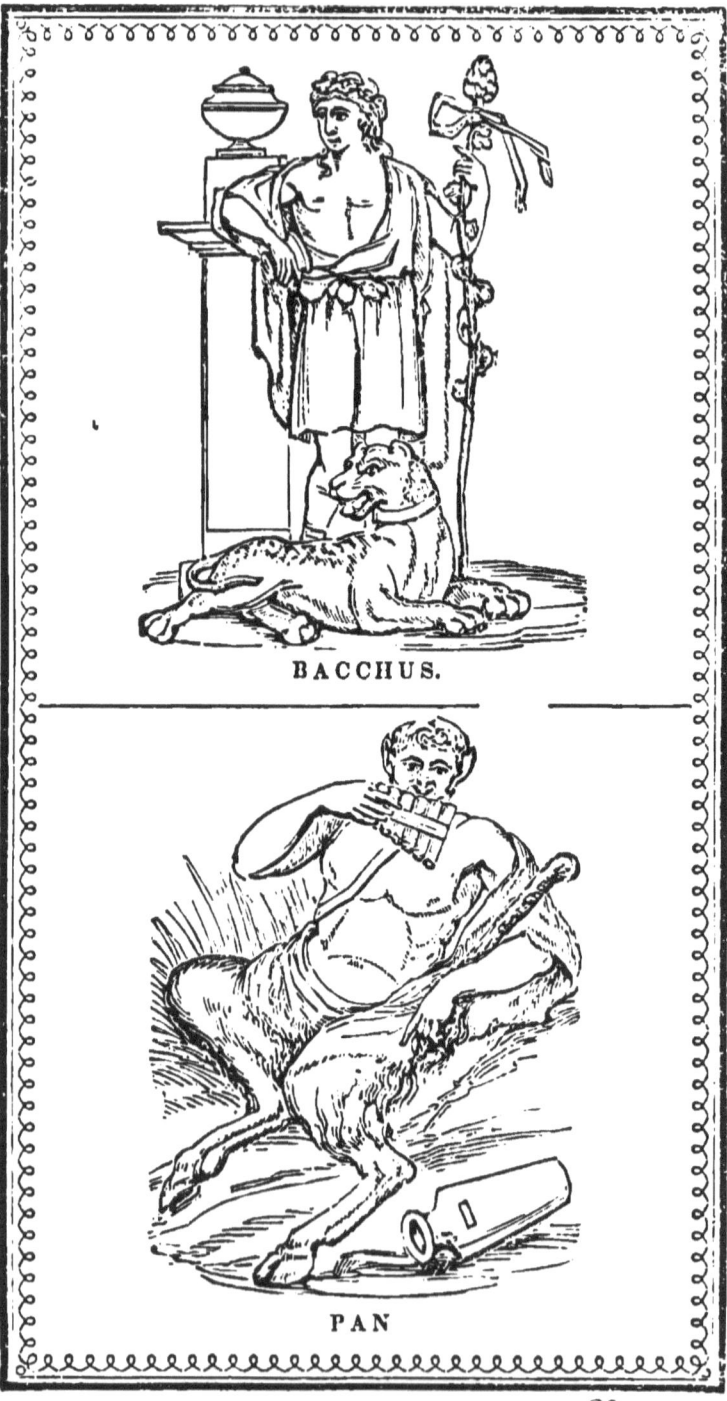

BACCHUS.

PAN

Menades, the Bacchæ ran about disguised in the skins of beasts with dishevelled hair, bearing torches in their hands, and waving the thyrsus, and sometimes bearing upon their shoulders young kids for the sacrifice.

The feasts of Bacchus were sometimes noisy, and those who attended them were often intoxicated. These feasts were called Bachanalia, Revels, and Orgies. Riotous meetings of those who drink much wine and keep late hours are now often called *orgies.* The Bacchæ hung little images of Bacchus upon the pine trees when they went into the woods to celebrate his worship.

TO BACCHUS.

Bacchus, on thee we call, in hymns divine,
And hang thy statues on the lofty pine.
Hence plenty ev'ry laughing vineyard fills,
Through the deep valleys and the sloping hills
Where'er the god inclines his lovely face,
More luscious fruits the rich plantations grace.
Then let us Bacchus's praises duly sing,
And consecrated cakes and chargers bring;
Dragg'd by their horns let victim goats expire,
And roast on hazel spits before the sacred fire.
Come, sacred sire, with luscious clusters crowned,
Let all the riches of thy reign abound;
Each field replete, with blushing autumn, glow,
And in deep tides, by thee, the foaming vintage flow.
Pitt's Virgil.

In the Medici gallery, at Florence, is a fine statue of Bacchus by Michel Angelo. He is crowned with ivy and vine tendrils, and holds in his right hand a cup, and in his left a bunch or cluster of grapes, of which a little satyr, covered with a goat skin, is endeavouring to get a taste.

Who was Bacchus?
Was Bacchus a hostile conqueror?
What do the conquests of Bacchus exhibit?
Where, and by whom were the feasts of Bacchus celebrated?

What was the character of the rites of Bacchus ?
How did Virgil praise Bacchus ?

FLORA was the wife of Zephyrus, the goddess of flowers; in honour of whom the Romans celebrated games.

Flora was celebrated at Rome in certain festivals. called the Floral Games. Her head was adorned with a chaplet of roses. She carried in her arms a profusion of flowers, and was young and fair, as became " the queen of all the flowers."

POMONA was the goddess of orchards, married to Vertumnus. The supposed skill of this goddess in the cultivation of fruit-trees and gardens, procured for her great reputation among the Romans, who placed her in the Pantheon, or temple of all the gods. Pomona was represented under the form of a beautiful young woman sitting upon a basket of fruit; and near her stood Vertumnus, in the figure of a young man, holding fruit in one hand, and in the other the horn of plenty.

PRIAPUS was considered as the god of gardens. He was accounted the son of Venus and Bacchus; and his image, a most hideous mis-shapen figure, was set up to frighten away birds and thieves. The eastern nations worshipped him under the name of Baal-Peor.

PALES was the goddess of shepherds and protect-ress of flocks. Her feasts, called Parilia, were cele-trated in the month of April, on which occasion no victim was killed, and nothing offered but the fruits of the earth. The shepherds purified their flocks with the smoke of sulphur, olive wood, box, laurel, and rosemary. They then made a fire of straw, round which they danced; and, afterwards, present-ed to the goddess, milk, cheese, prepared wine, and

millet cakes. It was during this feast they celebrated the founding of Rome.

Other rural deities were Anna-Perenna, nearly the
same as Pales; Bubona, goddess of herdsmen;
Mellona, of bees; Seisa, protectress of corn when
in the ground; Segesta, during the harvest; Tute-
lina, when stored; and Robigus, who was invoked
to preserve it from the mildew. Populonia protected the fruits of the earth from hail and lightning.
Pilumnus presided over the grinding of corn, and
Picumnus over the manuring of lands.

Hippona was the goddess of horses and stables ;
and Collina of hills: while Jugatinus presided over
hillocks. These were all invented by the Romans,
and are not to be met with among the Grecian deities.

The Satyrs, and Fauns were rural divinities, supposed to inhabit forests and mountains. They were
represented as half men and half goats.

Terminus was a Roman deity. Numa, finding
the laws which he had established for the security
of property insufficient, persuaded the Romans that
there existed a god, the guardian of boundaries, and
the avenger of usurpation. Numa built a temple to
him upon the Tarpeian mountain, instituted feasts
to his honour, and prescribed the form of his worship. He was represented under the form of an
immovable rock. Milk, cakes, and fruit were offered to him, and his image was crowned with flowers
and rubbed with oil.

Æolus was a son of Jupiter; god of the winds
and tempests ; which he was supposed to retain in
a vast cave, or to set at liberty at his own will, or at
the command of his father.

His children were Boreas, the north wind ; Aus-
ter, the south ; Eurus, the east ; and Zephyrus, the
west wind.

Æolus lived in the time of the Trojan war, and reigned over the Æolian islands, called, before, the Vulcanian. Æolus, possessing penetration and foresight superior to his contemporaries, by frequently foretelling the approach of storms, seemed to them to be something more than mortal. By attentively observing the direction in which the smoke of volcanoes was driven by the winds, he learnt to distinguish those which blew most violently, and were of longest duration. The descendants of Æolus sent colonies into Asia Minor, and afterwards passed over into Italy. Æolia may be seen in Asia Minor.

Who was Flora?
Who was Pomona?
Who was Priapus?
Who was Pales?
Who were other rural deities?
Who were the Fauns and Satyrs?
Who was Terminus?
Who were Æolus and his children?
What fact in history is connected with Æolus?

PAN.

See plate, page 87.

THE god Pan held a principal place among the most ancient divinities. By the poets, he is said to be the son of Jupiter and Calista. He was represented under the form of a satyr, half man and half goat, holding in his hand the rural pipe, invented by him, and called Syrinx. He was generally venerated by the Arcadians, as the head of all the rural deities. In the month of February, the Romans celebrated his feasts, which they called Lupercalia, from the place consecrated to him being supposed to be the same where Romulus and Remus were suckled by a wolf, in Latin *lupus*. The priests of Pan, at Rome, were called Luperci.

Pan was regarded as the inspirer of sudden un-
founded terror; *more* especially of the consternation
which sometimes turned armies to flight. These
frights are called *Panics.* The Athenians had a statue of him, like that of Mars. And in some antique
gems and sculptures, his figure is nearly as frightful
as that of Medusa.

The real origin of Pan was extremely ancient.
The Egyptians worshipped the sun as Osiris, and
the moon as Isis, and the several parts of the universe under various names, and they adored the
whole collectively, under a figure of half man and
half other animals. To this deity the Greeks gave
the appellation of Pan, that is, in their language, *the
whole.*

The poets relate that Pan successively loved the
nymphs Echo, Syrinx, and Pithys. Echo preferred
the beautiful Narcissus; who, seeing his own image in
a fountain, was so captivated with it that he remained
gazing there, till he languished and died. Echo
pined away with grief for the loss of Narcissus, but
being immortal preserved her voice, repeating every
sound which reached her.

Syrinx was a nymph in the train of Diana, and,
when pursued by Pan, fled for refuge to the river
Ladon, her father, who changed her into a reed. Pan
observing that the reeds, when agitated by the wind,
emitted a pleasing sound, connected some of them
together, formed of them a rural pipe, and named it
Syrinx.

Pithys was favourable to the god, but Boreas being jealous of this preference, with his powerful
blast precipitated her from a rock. While falling,
she was changed into a pine tree, which was afterwards sacred to Pan. Milk and honey were offered
to this deity.

Who was Pan?

Was Pan regarded as the inspirer of false fear?
What was the Egyptian Pan?
Whom did Pan love, and what became of Echo?
What was the origin of Pan's pipe the Syrinx?
Who transformed Pithys?

SILENUS.

SILENUS was the chief of the Satyrs, the foster-father of Bacchus. They represented him as an old man with a bald head, a flat nose, large ears, and every mark of intemperance. He was generally seen accompanying Bacchus, riding upon an ass, but so intoxicated, as to be almost incapable of keeping his seat. Historians give a different account of him. They say that he was a philosopher of great wisdom and learning, who accompanied Bacchus in his expedition to India, and was his principal counsellor.

Who was Silenus?

DOMESTIC DIVINITIES.
LARES AND PENATES.

THE Lares and Penates were Roman gods, who presided over empires, cities, highways, houses, and individuals. Among these divinities, were ranked the souls of them who had faithfully served the state; and families placed among them the spirits of their departed friends and relations. They were esteemed as the guardians of houses; were worshipped by the Romans under the figure of small images of human form, and were kept in the most retired part of the edifices. Lamps, the symbols of vigilance, were consecrated to them, and that faithful domestic animal, the dog, was sacrificed to them When infants quitted one of their first ornaments

called the Bulla, it was deposited before the feet of
these domestic deities. During the public feasts of
these Lares and Penates, small waxen images of
them were suspended in the streets.

The Lares and Penates were represented as young
boys, covered with dog-skins, and at their feet was
placed the image of a dog. The dog is the emblem
of faithful attachment and watchful care, and he is
more the friend and guard of man than any brute animal; therefore he was a proper companion of the
domestic gods.

The Lares were placed on a hearth in the hall;
and on festivals they were crowned with garlands,
and sacrifices were offered to them.

The other household gods, the Penates, were
worshipped only in an interior apartment called the
Penetralia. They were held so sacred by the Romans, that the expression of driving a man from his
Penates, signified that he was expelled from his
home, his country, and from all that he loved.

GENII were invisible spirits, regarded as the intimate companions of man's thoughts, governing and
disposing his mind and his conduct. Every man
was supposed to have two Genii. His evil genius
disposed him to wrong conduct, and led him to
misery—his good genius inspired him with virtuous
sentiments, and instructed him in what is excellent
in action.

They were represented as young men, holding,
in one hand, a drinking vessel, and in the other, a
horn of plenty. Sometimes they were depicted under the form of serpents.

The Genii presided over the birth and life of men.
Each spot had a *local genius*—one of the place.
Cities, groves, fountains, and hills, were provided
with these guardians.

It was the custom of the Romans to invoke these

Genii on birth-days. The ground was strewed with flowers, and wine was offered to them in cups.

The opinion prevailed, that the universe abounded in spirits, presiding over its various parts and movements. Plato, the Greek philosopher, speaks of Gnomes, Sylphs, and Salamanders; the first inhabiting the earth; the second, the air; the third, fire.

Who were the Lares and Penates?
How were the Lares represented?
How were the Penates worshipped?
Who were the Genii?
Did the Genii preside over places as well as persons?
How were the Genii worshipped, and what was the opinion of the ancients respecting spirits?

AURORA.

AURORA was the goddess of morning, and the mother of the winds and the stars. She was represented seated in a light car, drawn by white horses. The clouds dispersed at her coming, and she "sprinkled with rosy light the dewy lawn;" Nox and Somnus (*night* and *sleep*) fled before her, and the constellations vanished in the heavens as she advanced from the east.

Aurora married Tithonus, and a prince of Troy, and a mortal. Tithonus entreated of his wife to bestow upon him the gift of immortality, and the goddess obtained it for him from the Destinies. But when Aurora presented her petition, she forgot to ask for perpetual youth, and Tithonus, though he continued to live for ages, was in such a *state of dotage*, that is of infirm old age, that he wished rather to die than live.

Tithonus, according to fabulous history, was transformed to a grasshopper, an insect which the ancients considered as peculiarly happy and long-lived. The

AURORA.

ZEPHYR.

Greek poet Anacreon wrote some pretty verses to the grasshopper, which have been translated by Thomas Moore.

Oh thou, of all creation blest,
Sweet insect! that delight'st to rest
Upon the wild wood's leafy tops,
To drink the dew that morning drops,
And chirp thy song with such a glee,
That happiest kings may envy thee!
　　Whatever decks the velvet field,
Whate'er the circling seasons yield,
Whatever buds, whatever blows,
For thee it buds, for thee it grows.
Nor yet art thou the peasant's fear,
To him thy friendly notes are dear;
For thou art mild as matin dew,
And still, when summer's flowery hue
Begins to paint the bloomy plain,
We hear thy sweet prophetic strain,
Thy sweet prophetic strain we hear,
And bless the notes and thee revere!
　　The muses love thy shrilly tone;
Apollo calls thee all his own;
'Twas he who gave that voice to thee,
'Twas he who tunes thy minstrelsy.
Unworn by age's dim decline,
The fadeless blooms of youth are thine.
　　Melodious insect! child of earth!
In wisdom mirthful, wise in mirth;
Exempt from every weak decay,
That withers vulgar frames away;
With not a drop of blood to stain
The current of thy purer vein;
So blest an age is past by thee,
Thou seemest—a little deity!

Who was Aurora, and how is she represented?
What is the history of Tithonus?
How was Tithonus transformed, and who wrote verses to the grasshopper?

ZEPHYR.

See plate, page 97.

ZEPHYR or Zephyrus was the west wind. He was represented as a beautiful youth, with butterfly's wings. He cooled the air by the fanning of his wings during the heat of the summer, and revived the flowers when they fainted under the sun's rays.

Zephyr was married to Flora, the goddess of flowers. He was represented in the octagon temple of Athens, which is called the Temple of the Winds. Zephyr loved young Hyacinth, who was also beloved by the nymph Echo, and by Apollo. Hyacinth preferred Apollo, but the envious Zephyr applied his strongest breath to a *discus* which Apollo was throwing, and killed Hyacinth.

Who was Zephyr?
To whom was Zephyrus married, and whom did he love?

INFERNAL REGIONS.

PLUTO.

PLUTO, the supreme ruler of the infernal regions, sometimes called Dis, was the third son of Saturn and Ops. He was represented seated on a throne, surrounded with gloomy darkness, his countenance severe and frowning; in his hand a two-pronged fork, or a key, denoting the impossibility of return-ing from his dominions; his head crowned with the flowers of the narcissus, or with cypress or ebony. Sometimes he was seen in a chariot drawn by black horses, with a helmet on his head, which had the power of rendering him invisible. The victims offered to him generally were black sheep.

The wife of Pluto was Proserpine; her history is related with that of her mother, Ceres. The follow-ing verses describe the rape of Proserpine prettily.

PLUTO.

TANTALUS.

╲——In Sicilia's ever-blooming shade,
When playful Proserpine from Ceres strayed,
Led with unwary steps her virgin trains,
O'er Etna's steeps, and Enna's golden plains;
Plucked with fair hand the silver blossomed bower
And purple mead—herself a fairer flower;
Sudden, unseen amid the twilight shade,
Rushed gloomy Dis, and seized the trembling maid.

   Her starting damsels sprung from mossy seats,
Dropped from their gauzy laps their gathered sweets,
Clung round the struggling nymph, with piercing cries
Pursued the chariot and invoked the skies.

   Pleased as he grasps her in his iron arms,
Frights with soft sighs, with tender accents charms.
The wheels descending rolled in smoky rings;
Infernal Cupids flapped their demon wings;
Earth with deep yawn received the fair, amazed,
And far in night celestial beauty blazed.

Botanic Garden, Canto IV.

Who was the presiding deity of hell, and how was he represented?
Who was Pluto's wife, and how is she described?

———

At hell's dread mouth a thousand monsters wait;
Grief weeps, and Vengeance bellows in the gate:
Base Want, low Fear, and Famine's lawless rage,
And pale Disease, and slow repining Age.
Fierce, formidable fiends, the portal keep;
With Pain, Toil, Death, and Death's half-brother, Sleep.
There, Joys, embittered with Remorse, appear;
Daughters of Guilt! here storms destructive War;
Mad Discord there, her snaky tresses tore;
Here, stretched on iron beds, the Furies roar.

THE Infernal Regions was the place of reception for souls who had lived upon the earth. Immediately upon death, according to the notions of the Greeks spirits were conveyed by Mercury to the care of Charon, who transported them across the river Achen, to the shore of eternity. They then proceeded to the tribunal of the judges of the dead, and were sentenced according to their past conduct, either to heaven or hell.

It was a superstition of the Greeks that the souls of the uninterred, or neglected dead, wandered about for a whole century without being admitted to the joys of heaven. On this account they were anxious to pay respect to their departed friends. When they died at home, the survivors sometimes interred the deceased, and sometimes they erected a pyre, or pile of wood, upon which the body was laid and consumed to ashes. These ashes were committed to an urn, and deposited with the remains of others of the same family. When a man perished at sea, or in an unknown spot, his friends would erect some monument in honour of him to satisfy his *manes*, or parted soul.

The entrance to the infernal regions was called Avernus. Before it was stationed a multitude of frightful forms, which produce misery and death. These were Diseases, Old Age, Terror, Hunger, Discord, and the Furies, terrible women, with snakes for hair, and whips of scorpions in their hands. The palace of Pluto, the sovereign of these dreary realms, was guarded by Cerberus, an enormous dog with three heads, one of which was always upon the watch.

Not far from the abode of Pluto was the tribunal, or judgment-seat of Minos, Eacus, and Rhadamanthus, who pronounced sentence upon the dead. Tartarus was an immense and gloomy prison, to which the wicked were doomed. It was surrounded by triple walls of solid brass, beneath which rolled the fiery waves of Phlegethon ; and further distant, was the stagnant marsh of Cocytus. In this forlorn region were the river Styx, whose waters were of inky blackness, and Lethe, *the stream of oblivion, or forgetfulness.* To drink of Lethe made one forget all that was past.

It was believed by many that the departed were
liberated from a state of punishment after a thousand
years, that they drank of Lethe, forgot their sufferings, and were removed by the gods to some happy
state of existence.

The poet Virgil describes the descent of the hero
Eneas into hell, and thus it appears to him.

Now to the left Eneas darts his eyes,
Where lofty walls with triple ramparts rise.
There rolls fierce Phlegethon, with thundering sound,
His broken rocks, and whirls his surges round,
On mighty columns raised sublime, are hung
The massy gates, impenetrably strong.
In vain would men, in vain would gods essay,
To hew the beams of adamant away.
　Here rose an iron tower : before the gate,
By night and day a watchful Fury sate,
The pale Tisiphone ;* a robe she wore,
With all the pomp of horror, dyed in gore.
Here the loud scourge, and louder voice of pain,
The crashing fetter, and the rattling chain,
Strike the great hero with the frightful sound,
The hoarse, rough, mingled din, that thunders round.
Pitt's Virgil.

What were the infernal regions ?
What did the ancients believe respecting funeral honours ?
Who stood at the entrance of hell ?
What were Tartarus and the rivers of hell ?
Did the ancients presume that the punishment of the wicked
was eternal ?
How has Virgil described Hades, or Hell ?

JUDGES OF THE DEAD.

High on a throne, tremendous to behold,
Stern Minos waves a mace of burnished gold ;
Around ten thousand thousand spectres stand,
Through the wide dome of Dis, a trembling band.
Still as they plead, the fatal lots he rolls,
Absolves the just and dooms the guilty souls.

* One of the Furies.

THE judges of the dead, Minos, Rhadamanthus, and Eacus, held their tribunal in a place called the Field of Truth, where no falsehood could be heard, and no misrepresentations deceive. The judges were reputed to have been men—kings, who ruled upon the earth with such integrity and wisdom, that it pleased the supreme deity to appoint them judges of the dead.

The probable history of Minos is, that he was a king of the island of Crete, and was contemporary with Moses. He governed his kingdom with such eminent skill and justice, that his laws became celebrated all over Greece, and continued in operation for centuries after his death.

Who were the judges of the dead?
What is the probable history of Minos?

THE FURIES.

THE Furies were supposed to be ministers of the vengeance of the gods, especially employed in punishing the wicked upon earth, and after death. The Furies were women, commonly represented with torches in their hands, and also carrying whips of scorpions.

Tisiphone, Megæra, and Alecto were the names of these avengers: they were daughters of Acheron and Night; their names signify rage, slaughter, and envy. The Greeks called them Diræ, and sometimes Erinnes, disturbers of the mind.

The afflictions which we suffer come from God: " Vengeance is mine; I will repay, saith the Lord;" but the same Scripture also says, " whom he loveth he chasteneth:" "He does not willingly afflict or grieve the children of men." The Greeks had notions of this divine justice, tempered with mercy.

and they represented the Furies as having a double office—one which inflicted all the miseries of violent passions and a guilty conscience—the other, which imposed those lesser evils that softer. the heart and make us better.

When the Furies punished men with obvious compassion, they were called *Eumenides*, or the Mild. In this case they were supposed to be appeased by Minerva, as it would be the part of wisdom to say, The guilty who are punished suffer enough; comfort them, give them opportunity to reform. The pain which their guilt has caused is sufficient to induce them to be virtuous hereafter.

Besides the Furies, Nemesis may be reckoned among the avenging deities. She presided over the punishment of guilt. She is represented as traversing the earth with great diligence, in search of the wicked; furnished with wings, a helm, and a chariot wheel, to signify that no place could secure the guilty from her pursuit. As a daughter of Astrea, or Justice, she rewarded virtue, while she punished vice with unrelenting severity.

Who were the Furies?
What were the names of the Furies?
Had the Greeks any notions of God's government like those expressed in the Scriptures?
What were the Furies sometimes called?
Who was Nemesis?

THE FATES.

THE Fates, or Destinies, sometimes called the Parcæ, and the Fatal Sisters, were, like the Furies, three in number, Clotho, Lachesis, and Atropos. They were supposed to preside over the life of man, from his birth to his death, and to put an end to his life by cutting off a thread.

Stern *Clotho* weaves the checkered thread of life
Hour after hour the growing line extends,
The cradle and the coffin bound its ends.

Clotho held the distaff; Lachesis turned the spin
dle; Atropos cut the thread. Happy days were
spun out of gold and silver, while the thread of sor
row was of black worsted. The Fates were repre
sented as three women bending under the weight of
years. Clotho wore a robe of various colours, and
a crown composed of seven stars. The robe of
Lachesis was spangled with stars, and near her lay
a number of spindles. Atropos, clothed in black,
held the fatal shears, ready to cut the thread of life.

Besides those which have been enumerated as
infernal deities, were Nox or Night, Death, and
"*Death's half-brother*, Sleep."

Nox, or Night, was the daughter of Chaos. She
was represented in a long black veil spangled with
stars, traversing the expanse of the firmament in a
chariot of ebony.

Mors, or Death, was a daughter of Nox, depicted
in the form of a skeleton, wearing a black robe co
vered with stars; having wings of an enormous
length; her fleshless arms supporting a scythe.

To these terrible deities no altars were ever
raised. Trenches were cut in the earth, into which
was poured the blood of black sheep or heifers.
During the prayers, the priest lowered his hands to
wards the earth, instead of raising them towards
heaven. Being regarded as implacable, these deities were objects of great terror. No hymns were
composed to their honour, and no temples were dedicated to them.

Who were the Fates?
Who was Nox?
Who was Mors?
What was the worship paid to the infernal deities?

CRIMINALS PUNISHED
IN THE
INFERNAL REGIONS.

AMONG the most memorable of the criminals punished in the infernal regions, were the Titans. They were represented as being precipitated into Tartarus for having made war against Jupiter and the gods; they were Atlas, Briareus, Gyges, Iapetus, Hyperion, and Oceanus. Some poets speak of them as whelmed beneath Sicily; and pretend that the dreadful eruptions of Etna are occasioned by their violent struggles.

SISYPHUS.

SISYPHUS, for having attempted to deceive Pluto, was condemned to the never-ceasing labour of rolling an enormous rock up to the summit of a steep mountain.

With many a weary step, and many a groan,
Up the high hill he heaves a huge, round stone,
The huge, round stone, resulting with a bound,
Thunders impetuous down, and smokes along the ground.
Again the restless orb his toil renews,
Dust mounts in clouds, and sweat descends in dews.

PHLEGYAS.

PHLEGYAS, a son of Mars, for having set fire to the temple of Apollo, at Delphi, was sentenced to hell, and was placed under a vast stone, which was suspended over his head, perpetually threatening to fall and crush him beneath its weight.

TITYUS.

THE giant Titvus, a son of Jupiter, whose body covers nine acres, was slain by the arrow of Apollo.

because he dared to insult Diana, and was thrown
into Tartarus, where vultures unceasingly prey
upon his liver, which is continually renewed.

> There Tityus, large and long, in fetters bound,
> O'erspreads nine acres of Infernal ground;
> Two ravenous vultures, furious for their food,
> Scream o'er the fiend and riot in his blood;
> Incessant, gore the liver in his breast;
> The immortal liver grows, and gives the immortal feast.

IXION.

Ixion, who offended Jupiter by an insult offered
to Juno, was bound to a wheel surrounded with serpents, and perpetually turning over a river of fire.

TANTALUS.

See plate, page 101.

Tantalus, King of Phrygia, for having savagely
murdered his own son, Pelops, and served up his
body at a banquet of the gods, was condemned to
the ever-enduring pain of parching thirst, and ra-
venous hunger.   He was plunged in water, and surrounded with delicious food, yet he was not permitted to reach either.

" I saw," said Ulysses, as Homer makes him describe the infernal regions, " the severe punishment
of Tantalus.   In a lake whose waters approached to
his lips, he stood burning with thirst without the
power to drink.   Whenever he inclined his head to
the stream, some deity commanded it to be dry and
the dark earth appeared at his feet.   Around him
lofty trees spread their fruits to view ; the pear, the
pomegranate, and the apple : the green olive and the
luscious fig quivered before him, which, whenever
he extended his hand to seize them, were snatched

by the winds into clouds and obscurity."—*Translation.—Rambler*, No. 163.

> There, Tantalus, along the Stygian bound,
> Pours out deep groans; his groans through hell resound·
> E'en in the circling floods, refreshment craves,
> And pines with thirst, amidst a sea of waves.
> When to the water, he his lip applies,
> Back from his lip the treacherous water flies.
> Above, beneath, around his hapless head,
> Trees of all kinds delicious fruitage spread.
> The fruit he strives to seize; but blasts arise,
> Toss it on high, and whirl it to the skies.

THE DANAIDES.

THE Danaides were the fifty daughters of an Egyptian prince. Danaus emigrated from Egypt to Argos in Peloponnesus; thither he was followed by the fifty sons of his brother Egyptus, who married the daughters of their uncle. For some cause, not precisely told by the mythologists, Danaus ordered his daughters to murder their husbands. They all, except one, obeyed this inhuman order, and as a punishment for their crime, were sentenced to the continued toil of filling with water vessels which had no bottom.

Who were the more remarkable criminals punished in the infernal regions?
Who was Phlegyas?
Who was Tityas?
Who was Ixion?
Who was Tantalus?
Who were the Danaides?

CERBERUS.

CERBERUS was a dreadful three-headed mastiff, placed as a sentinel before the gates of hell. At the entrance of Pluto's palace, the tremendous keeper of these gloomy abodes was stationed. He fawned upon those who entered, but tore all who attempted to return.

Hercules was commanded to bring Cerberus into upper air, and descended to hell for that object. Cerberus, at sight of Hercules, crouched under the throne of Pluto, but the hero was permitted to take him. From the foam of his mouth, which dropped upon the earth, sprung deadly poison, *aconite.*

What was Cerberus ?
Who dragged Cerberus from hell ?

ELYSIUM.

WE know that we are composed of the soul and the body. " When our friends die, and are laid in the cold ground," we naturally ask, is this the last of them—is there no better world to which they are removed—is the *mind* lost? All hope that those they love still exist after death ; and they hope to be reunited to their departed friends in another state of existence. This prolonged life is called the *immortality of the soul.*

Those of the heathens who believed in the immortality of the soul, could not believe that the good and the bad could associate together in another world, so they conceived that the gods would appoint them separate abodes—one a happy and glorious place suitable to virtuous men; the other a region of grief and horror, proper for the punishment of those who had made themselves vile.

Notwithstanding the heathens generally believed in the immortality of the soul, and in a future state of rewards and punishments, these truths were not established till Christ came into the world. Christ declared that men should live after the present life, and they should receive in the next life, according to the deeds done in the body—punishment and pain to the wicked glory, honour, and immortality to good and faithful servants of God.

The heathens *hoped* that the doctrine of immortality might be true—Christians *know* it is true. We trust in it because Christ declared it; but we have it proved by his resurrection and ascension. He died, and lived again, and he departed from earth in the presence of multitudes, thereby assuring us, that we, like him, shall have everlasting life. "He came," says the Scriptures, "*to bring life and immortality to light.*"

The heathen heaven was called the Elysian Fields. The Elysian Fields were the final abode of virtuous men and women.

> Patriots, who perished for their country's right,
> Or nobly triumphed in the field of fight:
> There holy priests, and sacred poets stood,
> Who sang with all the raptures of a god:
> Worthies, who life by useful arts refined;
> With those, who leave a deathless name behind,
> Friends of the world, and fathers of mankind.

Elysium was represented to be a beautiful country, in which perfect peace prevailed. The air was delicious, and never disturbed by storms. The sunshine was unclouded, and delicious fruits and odorous flowers constantly regaled the happy inhabitants. These were gratified by the society of each other, and by those occupations that had been agreeable to them during their lives.

Whence is the notion of immortality derived?

Did the heathens believe in a future state of rewards and punishments?

Who established the doctrine of immortality?

What particular *facts* prove the immortality of the soul?

What was the heathen heaven called, and who were admitted to it?

How was Elysium represented?

10*

PLUTUS was the god of riches. He was represented as blind, to signify that wealth is dispensed to the good and bad indifferently.

FORTUNE was a goddess, who distributed her favours without judgment. She was represented with a bandage over her eyes.

The ancients personified many virtues and blessings, and erected temples to these *abstractions*.

Virtue, Good Fortune, Hope, Eternity, Concord, Time, Thought, Filial Piety, Compassion, Fidelity, Liberty, Silence, Licentiousness, Modesty, Justice, Providence, Opportunity, Fear, Flight, Paleness, Discord; all these were personified, and honoured under their respective *emblems*, or appropriate representations.

COMUS and MOMUS were social divinities. The English poet Milton has made all readers of poetry acquainted with Comus. Milton's Mask of Comus describes him as the son of the enchantress Circe. The god of low pleasure, who transformed men to brutes, though they remained ignorant of their transformation.

Men are indeed no better than brutes, if to eat, drink, and be merry, is all that they live for. To be cheerful, modest, and moderate in our recreations, and in them to regard the improvement and happiness of others, is to be at once rational, sympathetic, and benevolent, and is the nature of true and lasting pleasure. Momus was the god of gay conversation, and of wit.

ESCULAPIUS was the son of Apollo and Coronis, the god of physic. Being exposed upon a mountain immediately after his birth, he was nourished by a goat. A shepherd discovering him, surrounded by

rays of light, carried him home, and committed him
to the care of his wife. He was afterwards placed
under the tuition of Chiron, the Centaur. At Epi-
daurus, he was worshipped under the form of a serpent, and sometimes under that of an old man, holding a staff encircled by a serpent.

Esculapius was, probably, only an excellent physician, but ignorant men mistook his skill for a
supernatural power, and exalted him to the rank of
a god.

Who was the god of riches ?

How was Fortune represented ?

Who were Comus and Momus ?

What really changes the nature of men to that of brute animals ?

Who was Esculapius reputed to be ?

What is the probable account of Esculapius ?

ECHO.

Echo was the daughter of Air and Earth. Juno
condemned her to repeat the last syllable of all she
should hear said. Echo loved the beautiful Narcissus, but he despised her. Echo was so afflicted at
the treatment she received from Narcissus, that she
pined entirely away, nothing of her remaining but her
voice. She still haunts rocks and solitary places,
and still repeats the last words of others.

The nymphs, companions of Echo, entreated
Love to punish Narcissus for his contempt to her.
The god granted their prayer, and conducted Narcissus to a fountain side. In the fountain, Narcissus beheld the reflection of his own face and form ;
it was more lovely than any object he had ever seen ;
he desired above all things, to possess the beautiful
image—it was but a shadow—he died of grief, because he could not obtain the reality of so charming
a figure.

Who was Echo?
Was Narcissus punished for his contempt of her?

MORPHEUS, the minister of Somnus or Sleep, is
represented with the wings of a butterfly, to express
his lightness.   He holds in his hand a bunch of poppies, which he shakes over the eyelids of those whom
he would put to sleep.

———

DREAMS were the children of Somnus.   The poets
imagined that dreams were *good* or *evil, true* or *de·
ceitful*.   *True dreams* were supposed to pass from
the cave of Somnus through gates of horn, to an-
nounce future blessings, or to warn men of impend-
ing dangers.   *False dreams* passed through a gate
of ivory, and suggested imaginary evils.   False
dreams are represented as hunting the couch of the
slumberer, and were known by bat's wings, of a
black colour.

Who was Morpheus?
What were dreams supposed to be?

———

THEMIS AND NEMESIS.

THEMIS, or ASTREA, is the personification of *Justice*.   She was the daughter of Heaven and Earth.
The figure of Justice ordinarily bears a balance in
one hand, and a sword in the other, and her eyes
were covered with a bandage.

These emblems express the attributes of Justice
Public justice decides which of two parties are right.
She punishes the guilty, and acquits and relieves him
who is innocent and falsely accused.   The *balance*
which Justice bears, intimates that she *weighs*, or de-
liberates upon all that two parties claim for themselves; the *sword* shows her power to punish the

guilty; and the *bandage*, and her consequent blind-ness, express that she cannot see the *bribes* or the *supplications* of those who might dispose her to be partial.

ASTREA descended from heaven in the Golden Age, that she might dwell among men ; but, says the my-thology, she has sometimes been driven into soli-tudes, and now comes among men not only as a friend, but an avenger.

NEMESIS, the goddess of divine vengeance, or *re-tributive justice*, punishes those who are ungrate-ful to Providence ; who neglect their own minds ; who abuse the blessings which they possess ; who are hard-hearted, and who persevere without com-punction in evil courses. The character and office of Nemesis show, that the ancients admitted the moral government of the world by a superior power.

Who was Astrea ?
What do the emblems which the figure of Justice bears ex-press ?
When did Justice descend from heaven ?
Who was Nemesis, and what were her attributes ?

FAME.

FAME is the report men make of actions good or bad. The celebrity or praise of greatness is *renown*. Fame, or Renown, is the messenger of Jove. Poets represent her as a female with innumerable wings, and as many voices. She flew in every direction, she repeated ten thousand times the *truth* or the *falsehood* she designed to spread abroad. It was equally her office to delight and to deceive mankind Fame carried a trumpet in her hand, to denote the loudness of her report. A figure of Fame was often fixed to the triumphal car of the Roman warriors.

FORTUNE.

WEALTH and poverty are variously distributed in the world. Some men abound with superfluities, others suffer want. The ancients thought that a blind goddess dispensed or denied riches to whom she pleased; and that she gave to the good or bad equally, without regard to the merit of either, what she pleased. They represented Fortune, as they called this blind goddess, turning a wheel, which raised up some persons, and threw down others at the same time.

ENVY AND DISCORD.

ENVY was personified by the poets of antiquity. She was a frightful woman, repining always at the happiness of others, and endeavouring to injure those she hated. Envy was the daughter of Night. Her girdle was a serpent, and snakes hissed in her hair.

DISCORD was a malevolent female deity, who excited quarrels and wars. Jupiter banished her from heaven, because she created ill will and contention among the gods.

HEALTH.

THE Greeks worshipped health under the name of Hygeia. The Romans call her Salus. She had a temple at Rome, and her priests offered up supplications to her for the health of all people. The Romans regarded this deity with high respect.

SOMNUS.

Somnus, the god of sleep, son of Nox, was represented as a child in a profound sleep, holding in his hand poppies, which serve also for his pillow.

Somnus, or sleep, is called by Homer, "Death's half-brother, Sleep." One of the ancients called Sleep, the happy king of gods and men, because he supposed the immortals, except Jupiter, like men, forgot their existence and refreshed their powers in salutary sleep.

Ovid represents the cave or dwelling of Somnus, to be in the country of Cimmeria. Into this cave the sun never shone, and perfect stillness prevailed, except the soft murmuring of the river Lethe ; poppies and somniferous herbs grew at its entrance. Here on a bed of black plumes, Somnus reclined, and hence he despatched true or false dreams, to comfort or disturb mankind as pleased him.

What is Fame, and how is she represented ?
How did the ancients represent Fortune ?
Under what forms were Envy and Discord personified ?
By what nations, and under what names was Health worshipped ?
Who was Somnus ?

DEMI-GODS.

Besides the divinities already described, the Greeks offered worship to heroes, or men who had rendered eminent services to society. In what manner they were led to this worship is told in the following article—the history of Hercules.

Hercules was the principal hero of the Greek Fabulous History. The early history of all nations is poetical, a mixture of facts and fables ; and the history of these heroes or *demi-gods* is recorded principally by the poets of Greece and Rome.

HERCULES.

I_N_ *an early stage of society,* that is when men, in small numbers, inhabit large tracts of country ; when their houses are only rude cabins, and where there are no considerable towns, nor many cultivated fields the forests which surround the abodes of human be-ings are filled with ferocious animals, which subsist on others weaker than themselves.

When the predaceous animals learn by their in-stincts, that their own domain, the wild woods, is shared with new occupants ; that men and their do mestic animals have come within their range, they immediately enter the slight enclosure where the flocks and herds are confined, and bear them off, an easy prey, sometimes attacking and destroying their helpless owners also.

When weak men, and weaker women, hear the roar of the lion, and the yell of the tiger ; when they see their cattle strangled by the bloodthirsty panther, and their little children dragged from the cradle by the rapacious wolf, their terror and despair cannot be ex-pressed.

If, in this state of peril, some man of a more power-ful body, and a more courageous spirit than others of these small communities, encourages his affright ed associates, arms himself with a strong club; in-vents snares to entrap the invaders ; kills them when they come near the habitations of men : seeks out their retreats : sets fire to their dens ; strangles their little ones ; and, at last, by his fearlessness, ingenuity, and perseverance, clears the country of these ravagers, he becomes the greatest benefactor of society.

Men who are delivered from danger and fear, feel lively gratitude to their deliverer; they admire his

HERCULES.

CENTAUR.

generosity and courage ; he has exposed his life for their security ; he has endangered himself, but he has preserved them. They delight to remember his extraordinary exploits, and to speak of all his goodness. When he is dead they relate his sufferings and his triumphs, and observe days to commemorate him. At first, they say the gods assisted him, but after many years, those who *hear* of his achievements declare that he was a *god* who accomplished these services to mankind. And so heroes come to be " as *gods* revered."

Hercules, one of the most renowned of the heroes of antiquity, was reputed to be the son of Jupiter and Alcmena. From his birth Hercules was favoured with extraordinary abilities: but notwithstanding his strength, courage, and accomplishments, he was destined by the will of Jupiter to be subject to Eurystheus, King of Argos and Mycenæ.

The first exploit which is related of the infant Hercules was the strangling of two serpents while he was in his cradle. Juno, who hated Hercules, sent the serpents to destroy him, but when they aimed at him their dreadful stings, the fearless babe, with his little hands, squeezed them to death, while his elder brother, Iphiclus, who saw the deed, ran about shrieking through fright.

Hercules was early instructed in the arts practised in that obscure age, (perhaps twelve centuries before Christ.) Castor, the son of Tyndarus, taught him how to fight ; Eurytus instructed him to shoot with the bow and arrow ; Antylocus, to swim ; Linus, to play upon the harp ; and Eumolpus, to sing. Like some of his illustrious contemporaries, his education was finished under Chiron the Centaur.

Hercules was bred up at Thebes, and at the age of eighteen killed a furious lion, which devastated the country round Mount Cithron. He next killed Erginus, who demanded of the Thebans tne tribute of a hundred oxen, because a Theban had slain his father. These public services induced Creon, King of Thebes, to bestow upon him his daughter in marriage, and to intrust him with the government of his kingdom.

When Eurystheus heard that Hercules was thus exalted, he commanded him to appear at Mycenæ and perform twelve most arduous labours, Eurystheus reminding him at the same time that Jupiter had given him the power to command him. Hercules upon this lost his senses, but Apollo restored to him his reason, and admonished him to submit to the will of the gods.

Thus instructed, Hercules resolved to bear with fortitude whatever trial gods or men should impose upon him. When he undertook the enterprises commanded by Eurystheus, the gods armed him for his labours. Minerva gave him a helmet and coat of mail; Mercury, a sword; Neptune, a horse; Jupiter, a shield; Apollo, a bow and arrow; and Vulcan, a golden cuirass, and brazen buskins.

The *first labour* of Hercules was the killing of the lion of Nemea, which ravaged the neighbourhood of Mycenæ. Hercules, not able to kill this lion with his club, pursued him to his den, and choked him to death. Hercules ever after clothed himself in the skin of the Nemean lion.

The *second labour* of Hercules was the destruction of the Hydra of the Lake of Lerna, a monster with a multitude of heads. As soon as one of these heads was struck off, two others immediately sprung up. But Hercules was enabled by the assistance of his friend Iolas to despatch the enemy. As fast as Hercules struck off a head, Iolas seared the place with a hot iron, and soon killed the Hydra. Hercules afterwards dipped the points of his arrows in the gall of the Hydra, which was a mortal poison and caused the wounds inflicted by the arrows to produce instant death.

The *third labour* was to take, and bring alive to Eurystheus, a stag consecrated to Diana. This stag had golden horns, and brazen feet, and was of incredible swiftness. After a chase of a year, Hercules succeeded in taking it. Diana reproved Hercules for this act : but he pleaded the command of a severe task-master, and the goddess forgave him.

The *fourth labour* of this hero, was also to take alive a wild boar. This boar ravaged Erymanthus in Arcadia, and Hercules succeeded in seizing him in a snow bank.

The *fifth labour* was the cleansing of the stables of Augias, where 3,000 oxen had been confined many years. This was effected by turning a river through the stable.

For his *sixth labour* Hercules was ordered to kill some carnivorous birds which devoured human flesh, and haunted the neighbourhood of Lake Stymphalus in Arcadia. This being accomplished, the *seventh labour* was the taking of a wild bull of Crete.

The *eighth labour* of Hercules was to obtain the mares of Diomedes, who preyed upon men. Hercules secured these animals, and gave them Diomedes for a repast.

The *ninth labour* was to get possession of a girdle belonging to Hippolyte, a formidable queen of the Amazons, a nation of warlike females. After Hippolyte was conquered, Hercules presented her to Theseus, King of Athens, for a wife.

The *tenth labour* was to kill Geryon, King of Gades, in Spain, and to bring his flock to Eurystheus.

The *eleventh labour* was to obtain golden apples from the garden of the Hesperides. The Hesperides were nymphs intrusted by Jupiter with the care of some golden apples which were guarded by a dragon. Hercules repaired to Atlas, the giant, for information concerning these apples, and took from him the burden of the earth which he bore upon his shoulders, while Atlas procured the apples.

The *twelfth* and *last labour* of Hercules was to bring up to earth the three-headed dog Cerberus, which guarded the entrance of hell.

The *Twelve Labours* are not the only exploits of Hercules; many others are related of him. When Hercules was driving the herds of Geryon through Italy, Cacus, a formidable robber, stole some of the cows, and concealed them in a cave; but the cows replied to the lowing of Hercules' oxen, so that Hercules discovered the theft, pursued Cacus, broke into his retreat, and strangled him, though the latter vomited fire and smoke.

Hercules delivered Hesione, daughter of Laomedon, King of Troy, from a sea monster, which would have devoured her.

It is related that the Achelous, a river of Epirus, which divides Acarnia from Etolia, was once transformed to an ox, and encountered Hercules as an adversary. Hercules conquered Achelous, and broke off his horn. This horn was picked up by the nymphs, filled with fruits and flowers, and presented to Plenty, as her emblem.

This allegory signifies that Hercules checked the inundation of a river, and that when the waters had subsided, the soil, which had been overflowed, produced fruits and flowers.

Before the time of Hercules, the ancients pretended that the Mediterranean was an immense lake but that Hercules tore open the western extremity, at the present strait of Gibraltar, and formed a communication between the Mediterranean and Atlantic.

The disunited coasts were called the Pillars of Hercules, and were separated by a space of eighteen miles. The promontory of Africa thus produced, was Mount Abyla; that of Spain, where Gibraltar now stands, Mount Calpe.

Hercules killed Antæas, a giant of Lybia, a son of the Earth. He was a powerful wrestler, and was assisted by Terra, but Hercules lifted him up from the ground, and strangled him.

Hercules wished to marry the Princess Iole, but her father Eurytus refused her to him. He then once more lost his reason, and showing some disrespect to the Pythia, at Delphi, Apollo caused him to be sold as a slave to Omphale, Queen of Lydia. In the service of Omphale, it is said, that Hercules forgot his former habits, and, confining himself to the conversation of Omphale, used to employ himself in spinning.

When Hercules returned to Peloponnesus, he married Dejanira, a princess of Etolia. Having accidentally killed a man at the court of his father-in-law, Hercules was obliged to leave the place, and he took with him his wife. On his journey, being obliged to swim across the river Evenus, he placed Dejanira on the back of the centaur Nessus. When they reached the shore, Nessus offered to carry off Dejanira, but Hercules aimed at him one of his poisoned arrows, and killed him. The dying Nessus, unobserved by Hercules, offered a poisoned robe to Dejanira, telling her, that if her husband should ever cease to love her, if she could contrive to put that garment upon him, it would revive his attachment to her.

After that time, Hercules, remembering that the

father of Iole had refused him his daughter, took
upon himself to make war upon that king, and killed
him and his three sons. Iole, therefore, fell into the
hands of her father's murderer, and was carried by
him to his house as a domestic slave.

Hercules soon preferred Iole to Dejanira, and the
latter, grieved to be deprived of her husband's affections, bethought herself of the robe of Nessus. By
some artifice Dejanira prevailed upon her husband
to put on this robe; but no sooner was he arrayed
in it than the poison penetrated his body, and threw
him into mortal agonies.

Tortured by a slow but fatal disease, Hercules
prayed to Jupiter, and prepared himself for death.
He gave his bow and arrows to Philoctetes, pulled
up trees by the roots, and erected for himself a funeral pile upon Mount Œta. He then spread his
lion's skin upon his pile, sustained himself upon his
club, and demanding of Philoctetes to set fire to the
pile, he expired in the flames, and was received by
the gods in heaven. Hercules is sometimes called
Alcides.

Hercules was worshipped after his death. He
was often invoked by people who wanted assistance in their weakness, as by the wagoner in
Æsop's fables.

It is represented by the historian Xenophon, that
when Hercules was young, two females once appeared to him,—one was Virtue, who proposed his
arduous duties; the other was Pleasure, who offered to his acceptance an easy and indolent life; but
he chose rather to perform the part of a deliverer of
mankind.

The fables which are related concerning Hercules,
are only disguises of eminent services rendered by
some good and powerful man to his fellow-creatures.
Eurystheus, probably represents the dictates of his

conscience, which commanded him to severe toils in the service of society—and Omphale, may be the *love of pleasure*, which sometimes made him remit his exertions, and indulge himself for a time in repose and amusement. It was said, that Omphale sometimes put on the armour of Hercules, and ridiculed him as he sat at her distaff.

It has been mentioned that one of the exploits of Hercules, was taking the girdle of Hyppolite, queen of the Amazons. The Amazons were reputed to be a nation of masculine females, who lived near the river Thermodon in Cappadocia of Asia Minor.

The Amazons admitted no men into their society. All their life was employed in war and martial exercises. The story of the Amazons is probably a fiction but the frequent mention of them in various books makes it necessary to understand what is meant by the Amazons. At the present time, by *an Amazon*, we express the idea of a bold woman, without any sexlike refinement

What is meant by an early stage of society?
When are men exposed to incursions of wild beasts?
What is the effect of danger and fear?
Who are the first deliverers from predaceous animals?
What respect do men show to the memory of heroes?
Who was Hercules?
What was the education of Hercules?
What was the first exploit of Hercules?
How did Hercules next distinguish himself?
Who imposed twelve labours upon Hercules?
Who enabled Hercules to achieve his labours?
What was the first labour of Hercules? The second? The third? The fourth? The fifth? The sixth? The seventh? The eighth? The ninth? The tenth? The eleventh? The twelfth?
Were the twelve labours the only toils of Hercules?
What was the transformation of Achelous?
What does this signify?
What did the ancients say of the Mediterranean?

What were the disunited rocks called?

Who was Antæus?

Was Hercules worshipped?

What is related of Hercules by Xenophon?

Whom did Hercules wish to marry, and to whom was he sold as a slave?

Whom did Hercules marry?

What did Nessus give to Dejanira?

With whom did Hercules make war, and what was the result of that war?

Whom did Hercules prefer to Dejanira, and what was the consequence of his preference?

How did Hercules die?

LABOURS OF HERCULES.

The mighty Hercules o'er many a clime
Waved his vast mace in virtue's cause sublime,
Unmeasured strength with early art combined,
Awed, served, protected, and amazed mankind.
 First, two dread snakes, at Juno's vengeful nod,
Climbed round the cradle of the sleeping god;
Waked by the shrilling hiss and rustling sound,
And shrieks of fair attendants trembling round,
Their gasping throats with clinching hands he holds;
And death untwists their convoluted folds.
 Next in red torrents from her sevenfold heads
Fell Hydra's blood on Lerna's lake he sheds;
 Grasps Achelous with resistless force
And drags the rolling river to his course;
 Binds with loud bellowing, and with hideous yell
The monster Bull, and threefold Dog of hell.

Then where Nemea's howling forests wave,
He drives the lion to his dusky cave;
Seized by the throat, the growling fiend disarms;
And tears his gaping jaws with sinewy arms;
 Lifts proud Antæus from his mother plains,
And with strong grasp the struggling giant strains;
Back falls his fainting head, and clammy hair,
Writhe his weak limbs, and flits his life in air;
By steps reverted, o'er the blood-dropped fen
He tracks huge Cacus to his murderous den.

Where, breathing flames through brazen lips, he fled,
And shook the rock-roofed cavern o'er his head.
Last, with wide arms the solid earth he tears,
Piles rock on rock, on mountain mountain rears;
Heaves up huge Abyla on Afric's sand,
Crowns with high Calpe, Europe's salient strand;
Crests with opposing towers the splendid scene:
And pours from urns immense the sea between.
  Loud o'er her whirling flood Charybdis roars,
Affrighted Scylla bellows round his shores:
Vesuvius groans through all his echoing caves,
And Ætna thunders o'er the insurgent waves.
Botanic Garden, Canto L

What verses describe the labours of Hercules?

CENTAUR.

See plate, page 121.

CHIRON, the preceptor of Hercules, of Achilles and others of their class, was one of a fabulous race, the Centaurs. The Centaurs were represented to have the head and body of a man, terminated by the body and limbs of a horse.

This fable represents the people of Thessaly, who first bestrode the horse, and made him serviceable to man. Rude and ignorant people, when they first behold a man and horse thus coupled, imagine them to be one being. From a misconception of this sort, arose the fable of the Centaurs.

How were the Centaurs represented?
What is the origin of the false ideas concerning the Centaurs?

JASON.

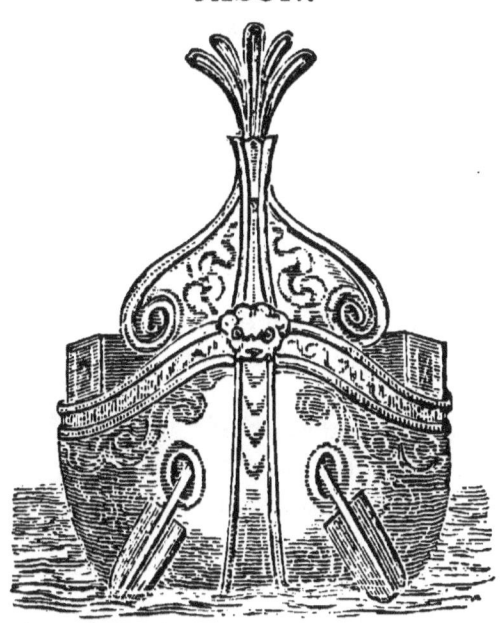

JASON is chiefly known as the chief of the Argo-nautic expedition, which took place, according to common chronology, B. C. 1243. This expedition was probably the first considerable voyage under-taken by the Greeks to buy and sell: to exchange the commodities of their own with those of a distant country.

The voyage of Jason was from Aulis in Thessaly to Colchis on the Euxine sea, and he was accom-panied by many young and adventurous Greeks. Jason's ship was called the Argo, and his compa-nions the Argonauts.

The history of Jason is the following. He was the son of Eson, King of Iolchos, in upper Greece. Eson died, and his kingdom was usurped by Pelias, and the young Jason driven from his country. Chi-ron, the preceptor of Achilles, likewise educated Jason, who acquired all the accomplishments of that rude age.

When Jason became a man, he was instructed by an oracle to go back to Iolchos Pelias, when he saw the rightful heir to the throne returned, in order to remove him from his sight, advised him to undertake the recovery of the Golden Fleece ; and Jason was prevailed upon to engage in that enterprise, with many others as fearless and full of hope as himself.

A certain king of Thebes, had a son and daughter, named Phryxus and Helle, who were persecuted by Ino, one of their father's wives.   Phryxus and Helle, to escape from Ino, who had determined to offer them as sacrifices to some god, resolved to put themselves under the protection of Etes, King of Colchis The poets relate, that just as they were about to be offered, a winged ram, with a *golden fleece*, took them upon his back, and flew away to Colchis through the air.

Helle on the way fell off, and was precipitated into the strait, thence called Hellespont. When Phryxus arrived at Colchis, he sacrificed the ram to Jupiter, as an expression of gratitude for his preservation, and dedicated the fleece to the god.   Etes envied Phryxus the possession of the fleece, and murdered him in order to obtain it.

When Jason demanded his inheritance of Pelias, the latter promised it to him, provided he would bring him the golden fleece ; which was, perhaps, if Jason would pay him a certain sum, which he might gain in a voyage of traffic, though such a one had never been before attempted by any Greeks.

After stopping at some islands of the Egean, and sundry ports of the Euxine sea, Jason arrived at the capital of Colchis, and demanded the fleece of Etes Etes then required of him to tame 'two ferocious bulls, to tie them to a plough, and with them to plough a field, never before cultivated. He wa next to kill an ever-watchful dragon that guarded th fleece; to pluck out his teeth, and sow the plain; armed men were to spring from these teeth, and Jason was to kill them all.

These conditions appeared to be so many impossibilities; but Medea, the daughter of Etes, a sorceress, offered her magic aid to Jason. Medea gave him a *somniferous* draught, which he poured into the dragon's gaping jaws, and then assisted him in taming the bulls, &c. The fleece being thus obtained, Jason, as he had promised, took Medea for his wife, and returned in triumph to his native country.

The return of the Argonauts was celebrated with every demonstration of joy in Thessaly. This voyage of the Argonauts was, in fact, an expedition of discovery; it opened a new channel for trade, and new sources of wealth to the people of Greece, and they afterwards carried on a productive commerce, and established colonies upon the Asiatic border of the Euxine.

For ten years, says the fable, Jason loved Medea, and they lived happily together; but at length, he attached himself to another female, and the wretched Medea, to revenge herself upon him, killed their children. This is a frightful story, but it was made very affecting by Euripides, who wrote a tragedy called Medea, which is exceedingly admired by those who understand the Greek literature.

It is said that Jason lived a melancholy and unsettled life, after he was separated from Medea; and that going one day to the water-side to look at the Argo, a beam fell on his head, and he was thus killed.

Who was Jason?
From what place did Jason embark?
Who was Jason's father and his preceptor?
What induced Jason to undertake the voyage to Colchis?
Who were Phryxus and Helle?
To whom did Phryxus offer the ram with the golden fleece?
What offer did Pelias make to Jason?

Upon what condition did Etes offer Jason the fleece ?

Who assisted Jason in procuring the golden fleece ?

How were the Argonauts received on their return to Thessaly ?

Did Jason remain faithful to Medea ?

How is it supposed that Jason was killed ?

THESEUS.

THESEUS was a king of Athens, yet he is also ranked among fabulous heroes; for it is sometimes said of him that he went with Jason to the Argonautic expedition, and sometimes that he was the friend of Hercules. The father of Theseus was Ægeus, King of Athens, and his mother was Æthra, daughter of Pittheus, King of Trœzene.

The parents of Theseus did not live together, and Æthra bred up her son in the court of her father. The deeds of Hercules were reported to Trœzene, and were related to Theseus. When Theseus heard of the achievements of Hercules, he longed to resemble that renowned hero. Robbers, too many for Hercules alone to contend with, ravaged Peloponnesus, and Theseus resolved to expel them.

Æthra, during his youth, had never informed Theseus that his father was King of Athens, but when he was grown to be a man, she thought proper to send him to Ægeus. Æthra one day, previously to the departure of Theseus, took him along with her to a spot where a large stone was fixed, and commanded her son to raise it; and though it was exceedingly heavy, the vigorous Theseus lifted it, and saw beneath it a sword.

" This sword, my son," said Æthra, addressing herself to Theseus, " belonged to your father, who is Ægeus, King of Athens ; whenever you shall present it to him, he will remember that it was left in my possession, and he will acknowledge you as his

son. Depart, but do not venture the perils of a land
journey; robbers will surprise you, and you will be
cut off by their cruel hands; a sea voyage is safe
and short, and you will soon reach Athens." The
aged Pittheus joined Æthra in her entreaties that
Theseus would not expose himself to the lawless
men who infested the then untravelled ways of
Greece; nevertheless, Theseus ventured, and soon
distinguished himself.

On his road to Athens, Theseus met three famous robbers. The first, Sinis, used to dart out
from his haunts, sieze the unwary passer-by, and
having stripped him, would tie his limbs to the
branches of trees, which, having been bent down,
suddenly would spring up, and tear the unhappy
sufferer in pieces. The second, Sciron, occupied a
narrow foot-path along the sea-side, and having robbed the passenger, who could not escape, afterwards
precipitated him into the sea. The third, Procrustes, in the wantonness of his cruelty, had invented a bed into which he forced his victims ; and,
if they were too tall for its length he would cut off
their limbs to fit the bed ; or, if they were too short,
by dreadful tortures, he stretched them to its extent.
This *bed of Procrustes*, is now often spoken of to
illustrate some cruel or foolish contrivance, designed
to alter what is properly unalterable. According to
the fable, Theseus attacked and killed all these
wretches.

When Theseus arrived at Athens, Ægeus was an
old man, and having no acknowledged son, the
Pallantidæ, a powerful family at Athens, expected
that one of themselves would succeed to the throne
Theseus did not immediately declare himself the
king's son, but the people flocked to see the destroyer of the robbers, and treated him as a deliverer
and a benefactor. Ægeus also was pleased with

the young stranger, and was particularly kind to him.

The Pallantidæ saw that Ægeus loved Theseus. They said, " He will adopt him for his son, and will leave him the kingdom. We then shall be no more than the subjects of this upstart: let us kill him." The Pallantidæ soon induced Ægeus to hate the young stranger, and even persuaded him to offer Theseus a cup of poison, with his own hand. Before this wicked project was executed, Theseus appeared to his father with the sword which Æthra had given him. Ægeus knew the sword, and readily believed Theseus when he related what his mother had told him.

Ægeus was delighted with his new-found son, and the Athenians were rejoiced to find that the brave stranger was to be their future monarch. The Pallantidæ, however, were disappointed and enraged, and did not give up their purpose of killing Theseus; but in this they did not succeed. Theseus knew their malice, and put them to death.

Some years before the appearance of Theseus at Athens, Minos, King of Crete, accused the Athenians of having killed his son, Androgeus, and demanded of them, as a satisfaction, a certain number of Athenian youths and maidens, who were to be sent periodically to Minos, at Crete. Some writers say these young persons were destined to become slaves; and others, that they were to be eaten up by a frightful monster called the Minotaur.

It is a curious fact, that all partially civilized people, and all savages, require the life of one person to be given for that of another, which has been treacherously taken. In the Hebrew law, it is said, " An eye for an eye, and a tooth for a tooth;" which means, if a man violently strike out another's eye or tooth, the injured person was permitted to strike out the eye or tooth of his adversary. The Athenians admitted such a law to be just, and Minos demanded many lives, as a compensation for the single life of his son, because in those days people pretended to think a prince was of more value than a hundred ordinary persons. We know better at the present time.

The young persons who were to be sent to Crete were chosen by lot out of a large number, and they were doomed to slavery or death. On the day when the choice was made, all Athens was in tears. The parents were distracted to lose their children, and the children were afflicted beyond measure to be torn from their affectionate parents. Theseus witnessed this melancholy scene. At once he determined to free his country from this odious tribute, and comforted the distressed parents who were about to give up their children, by offering to go with them to Crete, and promising to restore them in safety.

The fable says, that Theseus went with the Athenian youths to Crete, and when he got there, learned they were to be devoured by a monster which was half a man and half a beast, that was kept in a curious building called the *Labyrinth*. This Labyrinth was built by the famous architect Dædalus. The Labyrinth was so artfully constructed that no person could get in and out again without a guide ; but the daughter of King Minos, the beautiful Ariadne, gave Theseus a *clew*, or thread, which ran along through all the windings of the Labyrinth, so that he was enabled to find the Minotaur, which he killed, and he afterwards induced Minos to give up the exaction of the tribute. It is probable the truth is nothing more, than that the two princes peaceably agreed that this bad custom should cease.

Theseus married Ariadne, and promised to take her with him to Athens, but being arrived at the

.sland of Naxos, he left her there alone, and in the utmost grief. Poets and painters, when they would describe a beautiful and unhappy lady, represent the forsaken Ariadne. It is related that one of the sails of Theseus' vessels was black, and that when he left Athens he promised his father, should he return successful, that he would displace the black sail and put up a white one. About the time that he expected Theseus, Ægeus used to go to a promontory that overlooked the sea, to watch his approach : at length the vessel appeared in sight, and with it the fatal black sail. Theseus had forgotten to remove it.

As soon as Ægeus saw the black sail, he apprehended that some misfortune had happened to his son, and, in his despair, precipitated himself into the sea. From this circumstance it is said that the Archipelago was called the Ægean Sea.

Who was Theseus?
Whose achievements excited the ambition of Theseus?
Who acquainted Theseus of his parentage?
What counsel did Æthra give Theseus?
What robbers did Theseus encounter on the way to Athens?
How was Theseus received at Athens?
What enemies did Theseus meet at Athens, and how did his father learn who he was?
How did Theseus treat the Pallantidæ?
What did Minos exact of the Athenians?
What custom prevails among the half-civilized people?
How did the Athenians regard the tribute of Minos?
What were the adventures of Theseus in Crete?
How did Theseus treat Ariadne, and how did Ægeus terminate his life?

The character of Theseus, as a king, belongs to true history. Cecrops, who led the first Egyptian colony into Attica, was the first civilizer of that country. Cecrops divided Attica into twelve little republics: all these acknowledged the King of Athens for their sovereign, but they chose their own chiefs and inferior magistrates among themselves. Until the time of Theseus, these petty states were always at war with each other.

When Theseus became King of Attica, he perceived that his subjects could not improve nor be happy, because they were always injuring each other, and always in fear. No man wishes to cultivate his field if he expects another to take away his harvest; nor will he plough and sow the soil, if he thinks he can go into the next field, and take from it the corn, and not expect to be punished.

In peaceable and prosperous society, every man must have his own property; every man must take care of his own, and no man must take what does not belong to himself; and if one should take what is not his own, that dishonest and violent conduct is punished by the magistrate, who learns from books of written laws what is to be done to the *criminal* or *the breakers of laws*. The right which a man has to keep his own property separately from others is political *security*. The security of property, and the punishment of all *outrages*, is a state of *political order*. Theseus found in Attica the entire want of political order.

As soon as Theseus became king, he travelled all over Attica, and told his people he was sorry to see them always quarrelling, and that if they would cultivate the earth, take care of their flocks, make comfortable garments, worship the gods, and leave off injuring one another, they would be happy and grow rich. Then they were poor and in want, because they did very little work, and ravaged each other's territory. He told them he was King of Athens. and would be general of an army, and command the soldiers: and when the army of any other state should come into Attica, he would be ready to punish such an enemy.

Theseus also said he would take advice of wise men in Athens, and they would make laws to govern all the people. He would sometimes call together *assemblies of the people*—that is, all the men who were respectable should come into one place, and deliberate upon what was best for the people to do; and if any man did wrong, he might be complained of; and there should be courts, and the judges should be taught the laws, and they should prevent bad men from doing wrong to others, by punishing the persons who were guilty; and the courts should be held in Athens; and the people all over the province of Attica, might come to the magistrates at Athens, to settle their disputes.

The subjects of Theseus consented to be governed in this manner, and they soon became so happy under his regulations, that peaceable people from other places where no wise government existed, went to reside in Attica, that they might live in safety and quiet. All these people were grateful to Theseus, for introducing this excellent civil order: and the people of all Greece heard of these regulations, and some of them adopted the same institutions.

Before the time of Theseus, Athens was a rude place, without any beautiful buildings, or any thing elegant: but Theseus caused new houses and temples, much better than the old ones, to be erected: and he showed much respect to religion: extended his dominions to the territory of Megara, and set up a column to show the boundary of his kingdom. On that side of the column which stood towards Peloponnesus, was written,

On this side is Peloponnesus.

On the other side the inscription was,

On this side is Ionia.

Ionia was a name of upper Greece.

It is to be lamented that a legislator so wise and
so successful in improving the condition of his subjects as Theseus, could not have spent his whole
life so honourably and usefully; but he became tired
of quiet; he remembered the days which he had
spent in hazardous enterprises; in killing robbers
and wild beasts; and as then there were no books
to read, he felt the want of something more to do, so
he left his people to govern themselves, and went
into the less civilized countries of Greece, to seek
new adventures.

One Peritheus, King of Thessaly, carried off some
flocks from Marathon, near Athens, and Theseus,
resolving to punish him as he deserved, followed
Peritheus.   But instead of punishing him, Theseus
became greatly delighted with Peritheus, and they
traversed Greece together, doing more harm than
good.   Among other violent acts, Theseus seized
the beautiful Helen, as she was dancing in the temple of Diana, and might have carried her to Athens,
but her brothers, Castor and Pollux, recovered her,
and took her home to her parents at Sparta.

Theseus and Peritheus next heard of a princess
of Epirus, Proserpine, daughter of Aidoneus, King
of Sparta, and they went to her father's court to
seize her; but Aidoneus suspected them, and drove
off Peritheus by means of some furious dogs, and
threw Theseus into prison.   Hercules, however,
prevailed upon Aidoneus to release Theseus, and at
length he returned to Athens.

The Athenians could no longer respect Theseus,
because he had abandoned his duty. and had shown
no regard to the rights of other princes, and they
banished him to the island of Scyros, where he died
and was buried.   In time, the Athenians forgot the
follies of Theseus, and honoured his memory.   Ci-
mon, about four centuries before Christ, took up the

remains of Theseus, had them removed to Athens,
and there buried. Over the place of his interment a
monument was erected ; and a beautiful temple, the
temple of Theseus, still remaining in Athens, was
raised in honour of this hero.

What was the character of Theseus as a king, and in what
condition was Attica when he began to reign?

Why could not the people of Attica be happy ?

What is a state of *civil order ?*

What admonition did Theseus give his subjects?

What measures did Theseus propose in order to improve the
state of society in Attica ?

What effect did the institutions of Theseus produce ?

What was the state of Athens previous to the time of Theseus, and how did he improve it ?

Was the conduct of Theseus uniformly wise and honourable?

Who attended Theseus in search of new adventures, and
what was his conduct to Helen ?

How were Theseus and his companion received by Aidoneus?

How did the Athenians afterwards regard Theseus?

ŒDIPUS.

AMONG the fables of antiquity there is not one
more sad than the story of Œdipus. Œdipus, King
of Thebes, in Bœotia, was the son Laius. Laius
was descended from Venus, say the mythologists,
and Juno hated Venus, and all who belonged to her ;
so Juno always persecuted the posterity of Venus,
and she pronounced a curse upon the descendants
of Labducus, the father of Laius.

Laius was married to Jocasta, and an oracle foretold to them that the former should be killed by his
son. As soon as Jocasta had a son, Laius commanded her to kill him ; but no mother could be so
cruel, so she gave the infant to her servant, and ordered him to destroy it. The man, not willing to
kill him with his own hands, carried the child to the

woods, bored his heels and hung him upon a tree on Mount Citheron.

The infant would soon have died, but one of the shepherds of Polybus, King of Corinth, found him and took him to the palace of the king.

The Queen of Corinth, Peribœa, had no child. and she soon loved the little Œdipus, as the foundling was called, as well as if he had been her own son; as well as the Egyptian princess loved Moses: and she instructed him in all the accomplishments known at that time to the Corinthians.

The companions of Œdipus envied his talents, and told him he was some low-born stranger, and not the son of Peribœa. When Œdipus heard this, he begged his supposed mother to tell who were his real parents: Peribœa did not herself know, but she comforted Œdipus as well as she could. Afterwards the poor young man, in order to learn what he wished to know, went to the oracle at Delphi.

When he inquired concerning his parents, the oracle answered Œdipus, that he must not go *home*, for if he did, he would murder his father, and marry his mother. Œdipus did not know what to do: he had no home but the house of Polybus, and he resolved not to go back to Corinth, lest the prediction of the oracle should be accomplished.

Œdipus, uncertain whither he should go, took the road to Phocis, but he had not proceeded far, when he met on the way a chariot, on which was Laius, King of Thebes, and his armour-bearer. The road was narrow, and Laius ordered Œdipus to make way for him to pass. Œdipus refused; the two parties began to fight, and soon Laius and his attendant were killed. In that rude age it does not appear that people set much value upon life. Œdipus did not care whom he had killed, but went on towards Phocis .

At that time a terrible monster, called the Sphinx, ravaged the neighbourhood of Thebes. This monster was, perhaps, a robber. The Sphinx had proposed a riddle, and it was said, whoever should expound it, would be able to kill him. The riddle was, " What animal walks on four feet in the morning, on two feet at noon, and upon three in the evening!"

When Œdipus heard the riddle, he instantly perceived its meaning, and explained it thus :—Man, in the morning of life, walks upon his hands and feet; when he has grown to maturity, which is the noon or middle of the day of life, he walks on his feet only : and, in the evening of his days, when he is very old, he uses a staff in addition to his own limbs. The monster, upon hearing this, dashed his head on a rock and killed himself.

While the Sphinx was terrifying and tormenting the people about Thebes, Creon, the queen's brother, proclaimed that the man who would destroy that monster, should marry the queen, and govern the kingdom; accordingly Œdipus married his mother. But in a few years a terrible *pestilence*, or mortal disease, prevailed at Thebes, and the Thebans inquired of an oracle what could be done to put a stop to the fatal plague. The oracle answered that the plague would cease when the murderer of Laius should be discovered and punished.

Œdipus loved his people, and forgetting that he had ever killed a man himself, resolved upon discovering the concealed murderer. He spared no pains, and soon learned that he was himself the man whom he sought. When this fact was proved, Jocasta killed herself; and Œdipus, in his distress, tore out his own eyes. Œdipus had four children: two sons and two daughters: the sons were Eteocles and Polynices, and the daughters, Antigone and Ismene. The oracle had pronounced that Œdipus should not die in Thebes, so, blind as he was, and led by his daughter, Antigone, he wandered into Attica. Arrived at Mount Colonos, Œdipus took refuge in a grove sacred to the Furies. Theseus, King of Attica, being informed that Œdipus was at Mount Colonos, went thither and found the fugitive king attended by Antigone. As soon as Theseus approached him, Œdipus exclaimed that the gods had appointed that spot on which he stood for his burial place, and instantly expired.

What melancholy story is told of a king of Thebes ?
What happened to Œdipus in his infancy ?
Who educated Œdipus ?
On what account did Œdipus consult the oracle of Delphi ?
What was the answer of the oracle ?
What unhappy circumstance soon occurred to Œdipus ?
What was the Sphinx, and what was his riddle ?
How did Œdipus expound the riddle of the Sphinx ?
Whom did Œdipus marry, and what public calamity followed at Thebes ?
What discovery did Œdipus make concerning himself ?
What was the death of Œdipus ?

THE THEBAN PAIR.

AFTER Œdipus left Thebes, his two sons Eteocles and Polynices, agreed to reign one year, each, alternately. Eteocles reigned over Thebes, the first year, and then his brother demanded the throne. Eteocles refused to relinquish the kingdom, and Polynices went into Argos, and asked aid in procuring his right, from Adrastus, King of Argos.

Seven chiefs, princes of Peloponnessus, at the head of their troops, marched against Thebes, and stationed themselves at the seven gates of the city. Here they meant to attack the forces of Eteocles, but the two brothers agreed to end the quarrel by single combat, and each killed the other. These brothers hated each other with such perfect hatred, that it was said, when their dead bodies lay upon one pyre, the flames from each refused to unite in the same blaze. Hence the expression—*hatred*, like that of the *Theban pair*.

Another story is related concerning Polynices; it is, that his uncle Creon refused to allow him to be buried, and threatened to punish with death any person who should offer to inter him. According to the notions of the ancients, to permit the dead to remain unburied, was an act of the greatest indignity and cruelty. Antigone, the sister of Polynices, resolved to perform this office for her brother: and she entreated her sister Ismene to help her in this sad duty; but Ismene had less courage, and dared not comply with Antigone's request.

Antigone, who was pious and affectionate, could not refrain from this duty, and in despite of the orders of Creon, she buried Polynices in the night. Creon being informed that Antigone had disobeyed him, ordered her to be buried alive. Hæmon, the son of Creon, loved the virtuous Antigone, and when he learned her cruel fate killed himself.

Sophocles wrote a tragedy on the death of Antigone. This tragedy was exceedingly admired by the Athenians, and their admiration of it shows a just moral taste in that people, for Antigone is a beautiful example of female excellence. Her constant attendance upon her afflicted father, her heroic love for her brother, and her strong sense of her duty, which she performed at the loss of her life, exhibit exalted virtues—a beautiful specimen of character among the Greek women, at once domestic and heroic. Ismene was, in fact, scarcely less heroic than Antigone, the former through timidity, refused to assist in the obsequies of Polynices, but when Creon accused Antigone of disobeying his commands, Ismene urged that she was equally guilty, and urged that she might be equally punished, which the gene-rous Antigone as strongly resisted.

Ten years after the first Theban war, the sons and descendants of the chiefs who engaged in behalf of the brothers, renewed their hostilities, and carried on a second war. The Argives, or chiefs from Pe-loponnesus were called the Epigoni, and they were finally defeated.

Did the sons of Œdipus peaceably succeed to their father?

Who took the part of Polynices; and what was the occasion of his death?

Who resolved to bury Polynices?

What was the end of Antigone?

Who has celebrated the death and character of Antigone?

Was the Theban war renewed after the death of Eteocles and Polynices!

... ...

ORPHEUS.

ORPHEUS was the son of Apollo and the muse Calliope. Apollo gave a lyre to Orpheus, and the fable says, he sung and played so sweetly, that beasts and trees, as well as men danced to his music. Eurydice was the wife of Orpheus; he loved her dearly: but another man, one Aristæus, loved her also. The Greeks of that age had never heard of the commandment, " Thou shalt not covet thy neighbour's wife," and often stole each other's wives.

Aristæus one day ran after Eurydice; she fled from him, and as she was running, a serpent in the grass stung her to death; so she went to the dark dominions of Pluto and Proserpine. Orpheus in his grief at the loss of Eurydice, thought he could persuade Pluto to restore her to him, and with his lyre in his hand, he descended to the infernal regions,

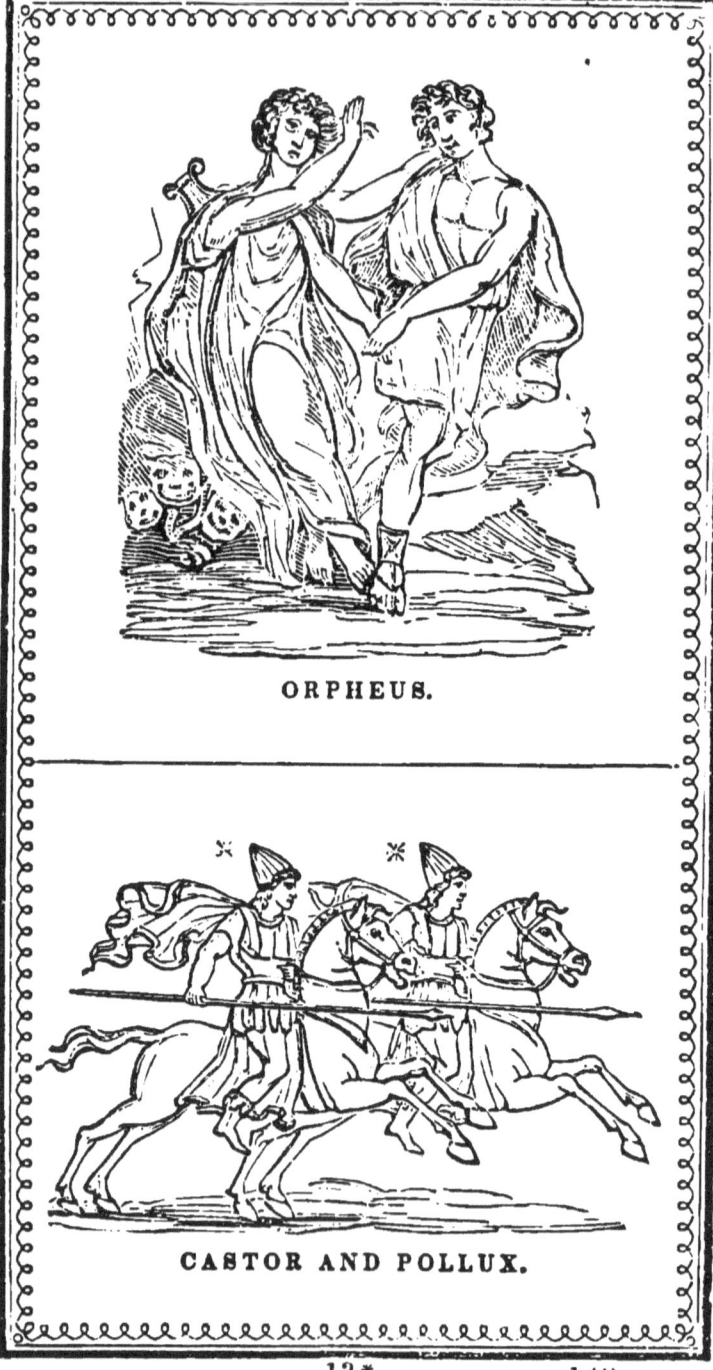

ORPHEUS.

CASTOR AND POLLUX.

and played most delightfully when he had entered the domain of "gloomy Dis."

At the sound of this music, say the poets, the wheel of Ixion stopped, the stone of Sisyphus stood still, Tantalus forgot his thirst, and even the Furies relented. Pluto and his queen, charmed with the music, and pitying the affliction of Orpheus, consented that Eurydice should return to earth, if her husband would refrain from looking at her till she should be come to upper air.

Orpheus thus satisfied, proceeded to the region of day, and Eurydice followed ; but before he had set his foot upon earth, Orpheus forgot the command of the god, and turned about to look at Eurydice ; he saw her, but she vanished directly from his eyes. Thus deprived of Eurydice forever, Orpheus consoled himself for the loss of her by playing upon his lyre as he wandered about Mount Rhodope, in the rude country of Thrace.

Orpheus never more liked the society of females, and they conceived a dislike for him. Some of the Bacchæ are reported, in their drunken revelry, to have torn him to pieces, and thrown his head into the Hebrus, a river of Thrace. The floating head was carried down to the Egean sea, the lips uttering the sad sound, Eurydice ! Eurydice !

The philosophers of antiquity pronounced the existence of Orpheus to be an entire fable.

——

AMPHION was another musical prodigy, who raised the walls of the city of Thebes by his lyre, as Apollo raised those of Troy, perhaps persuading the people to raise the walls, or encouraging them during their labours in erecting them.

——

ARION was also a famous poet and musician, who acquired wealth by his talents, and being on a voy-

age to Lesbos was thrown overboard by the sailors,
who wanted his money.   Arion was playing on his
lyre when his murderers precipitated him into the
sea, and so charmed were the dolphins that they
gathered round the ship to hear the music, and one
taking Arion on his back, conveyed him to Cape Te-
narus.

What miracle was produced by Orpheus?
What caused the death of Eurydice?
What effect had the music of Orpheus in the Infernal
Regions?
Upon what condition was Eurydice restored to Orpheus?
What was the reputed death of Orpheus?
Who was Amphion?
Who was Arion?

CASTOR AND POLLUX.

See plate, page 149.

CASTOR AND POLLUX were twin brothers of Helen
and Clytemnestra.   When Helen first took a view
of the Grecian host at Troy, she did not perceive her
brothers, she exclaims, that

> ———" two are wanting of the numerous train,
> Whom long my eyes have sought but sought in vain ;
> Castor and Pollux, first in martial force,
> One bold on foot, and one renowned for horse,
> My brothers these ; the same our native shore,
> One house contained us as one mother bore.
> *   *   *   *   *   *
> So spoke the fair, nor knew her brothers' doom,
> Wrapt in the cold embraces of the tomb ;
> Adorned with honours on their native shore,
> Silent they slept, and heard of wars no more.

Castor and Pollux were among the Argonauts,
and they recovered Helen from Theseus.   They
were probably roving adventurers, who did as much
wrong as right.   It is related in their history, that
Leucippus, a prince who was uncle to these adven-

turers, had two daughters, Phœbe and Talaria; these young women were to be married to two friends, Lynceus and Ilas, and Castor and Pollux were invited to attend their wedding.

As soon as the brothers saw the brides, they felt a desire to possess them, and laid a plan to carry them off, but Lynceus and Ilas, perceiving their purpose, a battle ensued. Castor killed Lynceus, and Ilas killed Pollux. Castor, being a son of Jupiter, for the children of Leda were all called Jupiter s, was immortal, but Castor begged that his brother might share his undying existence, and that they might be alive and dead alternately, whether for a day each, or for six months, the mythology does not determine.

Castor and Pollux were worshipped by the Greeks and Romans. Among the Romans reports often prevailed that Castor and Pollux made their appearance in their armies, mounted on white steeds. They were generally represented on white horses, armed with spears, riding side by side, their heads covered with a *petasus*, on the top of which glittered a star. Castor and Pollux are constellations, one never appears with the other, but when one rises the other sets.

Who were the brothers of Helen ?
Were Castor and Pollux good men ?
Of what violent act were Castor and Pollux guilty ?
Who worshipped Castor and Pollux, and how are they represented ?

DÆDALUS.
See plate, page 159

DÆDALUS was a celebrated mechanician of antiquity. An Athenian descended from Erechtheus, a king of Athens. Dædalus was the most ingenious man of his time and was the reputed inventor of the wedge, the lever, the axe, and the sails of ships. It is said that Talus, a nephew of Dæda lus, discovered as much inventive talent as his uncle and that the latter, through envy, killed the young artist.

After the murder of Talus, Dædalus, with his son Icarus, fled from Athens to Crete, where they were welcomed by Minos. Dædalus constructed the Labyrinth of Crete, but Minos afterwards, being offended at Dædalus, confined him and Icarus in that edifice. Dædalus contrived wings of wax and of feathers, for himself and his son, and they took their flight towards Italy. Icarus mounted too high, fell into the sea, and was drowned, but his father was more fortunate, getting safe into Sicily, where he is supposed to have built certain temples.

The wings of Dædalus are supposed to have signified ships.

Who was Dædalus, and what were his inventions ?

Why did Dædalus quit Athens, who received him, and how did he escape from Crete ?

THE LAPITHÆ.

THE Centaurs were a people of Thessaly, who first tamed and used the horse. The battle of the Centaurs and of the Lapithæ was famous. The Lapithæ were some chiefs, Perithous, and others, descended from Lapithus. When Perithous was to be married to Hippodamia, the Centaurs were invited to the marriage ; but they became intoxicated with wine, and were rude to some of the females present, and the Lapithæ, justly provoked at this brutality, punished it by killing some, and driving others into banishment.

THE WAR OF TROY.

TROY was a city of Asia Minor. Troy was not far from the Hellespont. near the Promontory of Si

gæum, between the river Simois and Scamander, at
the distance of four miles from the sea shore. Near
to Troy was a range of mountains called Ida. It is
said that three several kings of this city gave names
to it: the kings were Dardanus, Tros, and Illus, and
hence the city is sometimes called Dardania, Troja,
and Ilio or Ilium. Homer's description of the war
of Troy, is thence called the Iliad.

The ancients declared that Neptune built Troy,
and that its walls were raised by the music of Apollo.
This can only mean that Tory was a maritime city,
and that its site was fixed upon as being a convenient abode for seafaring men ; and the fable of
Apollo's music must signify, that while men laboured
in building the wall, their toil was beguiled by music.

Priam, son of Laomedon, was the last king of
Troy ; his wife was Hecuba, and he had according
to the story, fifty children ; the most remarkable of
these were Hector, Paris, and Cassandra. It was
foretold to Priam, that the last-born of his children
should cause the destruction of Troy. Priam, on the
birth of Paris, effectually to prevent the accomplishment of the prophecy, ordered a slave to destroy the
infant.

The man employed in this inhuman service, did
not kill the child, but left him to his fate in the soli-
tude of Mount Ida. There he was found by a shepherd of the neighbourhood, and the poor man, touched with compassion, took home the foundling, and
reared him as his son. Paris, though educated
among peasants, soon exhibited much courage,
beauty, and grace ; and so boldly did he defend the
flocks of Ida from wild beasts, that he was called the
deliverer, and he might have passed his life in rural
quiet and honour, if the deities themselves had not
intruded upon his peaceful obscurity.

Peleus, a prince of Thessaly, was married to the

sea-nymph Thetis, and certain goddesses attended the wedding.   Venus, Minerva, and Juno were there, and *Discord* came also among them : that is, the goddesses contended with each other, which of the three was the most beautiful.   Discord, says the fable, threw a golden apple among them, on which was written " *To the fairest.*"   Each claimed the apple, and each demanded it of the gods.   To settle the question, the three disputants were referred to Paris.

The goddesses then repaired to Mount Ida, and found Paris.   They instantly related the matter of contention, and entreated him to bestow the apple upon her, who was truly the most beautiful ; but they all offered him a *bribe*, Juno promised him a kingdom ; Minerva victory and glory when he should engage in war ; and Venus, the most beautiful woman in the world for his wife.   Venus obtained the apple, and the beautiful woman promised to Paris, was Helen, the wife of Menelaus, King of Sparta.

Soon after Priam proposed a contest to the princes of Troy, and promised that the most beautiful bull in his dominions should be given as a price to the victorious combatant.   This rare animal was found in the herd of Paris on Mount Ida.   On receiving intelligence of the intended combat, Paris repaired to Troy, and offered himself among the candidates, and so gracefully and skilfully did he acquit himself in the contest, that he defeated all his competitors, and obtained the prize.

His sister Cassandra, a woman of rare sagacity, perceived in the beautiful stranger a resemblance to her family.   She inquired his history, finally discovered that he was her brother, and introduced him to their father as his son.   Priam forgot the disastrous prophecy, and affectionately acknowledged Paris.

Some years before this event, Hercules had carried

off Hesione, the sister of Priam, and married her to a prince of Peloponnesus, and now Priam resolved to recover her. Paris readily engaged to redeem Hesione, and set out for Greece for that object. His real design, however, was to obtain the princess whom Venus had promised him.

Paris visited Sparta, and Menelaus, the husband of Helen, treated him with hospitality and kindness: but Paris treacherously repaid him; for Menelaus being absent in Crete, Paris persuaded Helen to elope with him for Asia, and to take with her much of the treasure of her husband; nor did Priam and his family refuse to receive her.

When Helen was young, Theseus had carried her off, but she was recovered, and her numerous admirers, the princes of Greece, made a vow, if she should ever again be forced away, that they would unite to punish the person who should commit the outrage. The injured Menelaus remembered the promise of the princes, and demanded of them to assist him in punishing the Trojans, who had encouraged Paris in his perfidy.

Menelaus, with more forbearance than was common to that age, when princes in their quarrels sought revenge rather than right, sent ambassadors to Troy to demand the restoration of Helen: but Priam refused to comply with the demand, and war was mutually declared between the Greeks and Trojans. The Greek princes readily consented to aid Menelaus: and 1000 ships, and 100,000 warriors, according to the common estimate, engaged in the enterprise.

Where was ancient Troy, and whence were its names derived?

What is the fabulous origin of Troy?

Who was the last king of Troy, and who were the most memorable of his children?

Where was the early life of Paris spent ?
What created a dispute between three goddesses ?
What goddesses visited Paris, and for what purpose ?
What induced Paris to visit the court of Priam ?
Who discovered Paris to be the son of Priam ?
In what enterprise did Paris engage ?
How did Paris requite the hospitality of Menelaus?
Who had vowed to punish those who should carry off Helen !
Did Menelaus proceed rashly to the punishment of Paris ?

IPHIGENIA. ˙

The Greek princes having made suitable prepara-
tions for the siege of Troy, assembled with all their
forces at Aulis, a city opposite to Colchis, in Eu-
bœa. They chose Agamemnon, King of Mycenæ,
and brother of Menelaus, for their chief, and Calchas,
the soothsayer, for their priest.

> Calchas, the seer, whose comprehensive view,
> The past, the present, and the future knew.

But being assembled at Aulis, the host was prevented from sailing by contrary winds.

Calchas being consulted in this emergency, declared that Agamemnon had provoked Diana, by
killing her favourite stag, and that it was the pleasure
of the goddess to detain the Greeks by adverse
winds, until the king should sacrifice to her, his
daughter Iphigenia. At first, Agamemnon chose
rather to abandon the expedition, but the other
princes at length persuaded him to yield to the will
of Diana.

In obedience to this suggestion, the King of Mycenæ sent a message to his wife Clytemnestra, re-
questing her to bring to him Iphigenia, that he might
marry her to Achilles. Clytemnestra gladly obeyed
this summons, but nothing could exceed her grief and
indignation when she was informed of her daughter's
cruel destiny.

ICARUS, SON OF DÆDALUS.

IPHIGENIA.

Iphigenia saw the preparation for a sacrifice, and when she learned that she was the victim, she entreated her father to save her life ; but a fatal superstition hardened him against her supplications. Calchas took the knife in his hand, and was about to strike Iphigenia to the heart, when she suddenly disappeared, and a goat was found in her place, and sacrificed accordingly.

The mythologists explain this story thus: they say Diana had compassion upon the innocent virgin, and carried her away miraculously to her temple in Taurica, (the Crimea of modern geography,) where she made her a priestess. After this, the *Argive host*, as Homer often calls the Greeks, departed from Aulis, and had a favourable passage to Troy.

At Troy, the Grecian armament was encountered by a force sufficiently prepared to receive them. Hector, the valiant son of Priam, was the chief of the Trojans, and the neighbouring states sent large supplies of soldiers to them. The siege was begun, and a long conflict of ten years was carried on before Troy was taken by the Greeks. The Greeks did not confine their assaults to the city of Troy, but they ravaged the neighbourhood, and pillaged the towns and domains of the adjacent territory.

In the tenth year of the siege, the army of the Greeks was visited by a *pestilence* or plague, which destroyed many lives, and retarded the war, before Troy was taken. The loss was great on both sides ; the most valiant of the Trojans, and particularly of the sons of Priam, were slain ; indeed, so great was the slaughter, that the rivers of the country are represented as filled with dead bodies, and suits of armour. These rivers were so shallow as hardly to deserve the name, and are better known in Homer's verses, than in the topography of Troy.

The poetical account of the taking of Troy is this
14*

The Greeks, no being able to enter the city, pre
.ended to abandon the siege, and to return to their
ships, but instead, they built a wooden vessel, in the
form of a horse, into which several armed men entered and concealed themselves. How this was
done, without being observed by the Trojans, is not
well accounted for, but such is the story told by
Virgil.

The Trojans, looking down from their walls, and
perceiving the absence of the Greeks, and nothing
left but the wooden horse, went out of their gates to
examine the wonder, and afterwards had it drawn
within their walls. When the Greeks, concealed
within the horse, found themselves in Troy, they
took advantage of the night, got out of the horse,
forced open the gates of the city, and admitted the
Greek troops, who were concealed without; and thus
Troy was taken, after a siege of ten years.

Another story is told concerning the taking of
Troy. It is said that it had been decreed by the
gods that Troy should not fall till large numbers
of the Trojans should be slain by the arrows of
Hercules. These arrows had been dipped in the
blood of the Lernean Hydra, and communicated a
mortal poison. When Hercules was expiring, he
gave his bow and arrows to Philoctetes, and made
the latter swear that he would never reveal the place
where Hercules commanded him to inter his remains,
when his body should be consumed on the pile.

After the death of his friend, Philoctetes repaired
to Sparta, and Menelaus engaged him to go to the
siege of Troy. Philoctetes, in an unguarded moment, revealed to Ulysses the place where Hercules
was interred; and the gods, to punish his *perjury*,
suffered him to let fall one of the arrows upon
his foot, which inflicted a loathsome and incurable
wound.

While the fleet was sailing to Troy, the envenomed wound became so offensive to those about him, that Ulysses persuaded them to land on the island of Lemnos, and abandon Philoctetes while he slept.

During the ten years of the siege, Philoctetes remained alone upon the desolate island, suffering from his wound, and sustaining himself by the flesh of birds which he killed with his arrows. A soothsayer at that time told the Greeks that Troy never could be taken without the arrows of Hercules, and Ulysses immediately departed for Lemnos, where he found Philoctetes, and entreated him to follow him to Troy.

Philoctetes hated Ulysses for his treachery, and refused at first to accompany him, but at length he was persuaded, for Hercules appeared to him and commanded him to go with Ulysses. Philoctetes slew vast numbers of the Trojans with the fatal arrows, among others, Paris, who had caused the war. Sophocles has made a drama of the history of Philoctetes, at Lemnos; it is not unlike that of Robinson Crusoe, excepting that the latter was not lame, and was much the happier of the two. Philoctetes was cured of his wound by Machaon, the son of Esculapius, who was the most eminent physician of the Greeks.

What king commanded the Greek armies against Troy and what prophet attended them?

What detained the host at Aulis, and what remedy was proposed?

Did Agamemnon send for his daughter from Mycenæ?

Was Iphigenia sacrificed?

How do mythologists explain the story of Iphigenia?

How were the Greeks encountered at Troy?

How many years was the siege of Troy continued?

What stratagems did the Greeks invent to deceive the Trojans?

How was Troy taken at last?

What otner story is told concerning the fall of Troy?

On what account was Philoctetes permitted to wound himself?

What induced Ulysses to go to Lemnos?

What happened after the departure of Philectetes from
Lemnos?

AGAMEMNON.

Agamemnon and Menelaus were brothers. Agamemnon was King of Argos and Mycenæ; he married Clytemnestra, the sister of Helen, Queen of
Sparta. These princes in their youth were driven
away from Argos, by their uncle, Thyestes, who
usurped the kingdom, but Tyndarus, King of Sparta,
deposed Thyestes, and restored Agamemnon to the
sovereignty of Argos and Mycenæ; and, having
given his two daughters to the brothers, left his
own kingdom of Sparta to Menelaus.

When Agamemnon sacrificed his daughter Iphigenia, Clytemnestra was bitterly incensed against
him, and, soon after that event, wickedly attached
herself to Egisthus, son of the usurper Thyestes.
During the absence of Agamemnon, Egisthus and
Clytemnestra ruled together in his kingdom; and
when Agamemnon, after the taking of Troy, returned to Mycenæ, the guilty pair determined to kill
him.

Agamemnon brought with him Cassandra, the
daughter of Priam. Apollo had conferred upon Cassandra the gift of prophecy, but afterwards taking
offence at her, he ordained that though her predictions should be true, she should never be believed
Thus it was in vain that Cassandra foretold to Aga
memnon, that Clytemnestra would put him to death.
Agamemnon despised her warning, and entered his
palace without fear. Egisthus and Clytemnestra

soon contrived the murder of the king.   The latter,
being in need of refreshment, took a bath, and while
he was unarmed, the queen and Egisthus killed him.

Who were Agamemnon and Menelaus, and what happened
to both in early life ?

What incensed Clytemnestra against her husband, and how
did she injure him ?

Who forewarned Agamemnon of his fate, and how was his
destruction accomplished ?

ORESTES AND PYLADES.

BESIDES Iphigenia, Agamemnon had two children, a son and a daughter; these were Electra and
Orestes.   Electra is described by the Greek drama-
tists, Eschylus and Sophocles, to have been exceedingly good; abhorring the conduct of her mother ,
piously lamenting her father's murder, and anxiously
preserving the young Orestes.   On the death of
Agamemnon, Orestes was the proper successor to
the throne, and Electra knew that the usurper, Egisthus, feared that Orestes, when he should become a
man, would punish his perfidious conduct.

To save her brother's life, Electra sent him to
the care of Strophius, King of Phocis.   Strophius
had a son, whose name was Pylades, and so much
did Orestes and Pylades love each othei, that their
friendship has become a proverb.   *To love like
Pylades and Orestes*, expresses the most faithful
friendship.

When Orestes was grown to manhood, he conceived the design of punishing his mother and her
accomplice; and, to aid her brother's purpose, Electra
caused it to be reported that he had died in Phocis.
Clytemnestra and Egisthus rejoiced at this, and went
together to the temple of Apollo, to thank the god
for the young prince's death.   Orestes con ealed

himself near the temple, and, watching their approach killed his father's murderers, after they had reigned seven years.

After this horrid act, however cruel the provocation, Orestes was tormented by the Furies, and could not be happy anywhere. *To be tormented by the Furies*, means that he was sorry for what he had done; that he thought constantly of his murdered mother, and hated himself for his crime. Euripides, one of the Greek poets, says, that Orestes consulted the oracle of Apollo, to learn how he must make amends for his crime, and to escape from the vengeance of the Furies.

The oracle commanded him, in order to recover the peace of his mind, to go to Taurica Chersonesus,* and bring from thence the statue of Diana. This was a difficult undertaking, for the King of Chersonesus always sacrificed every stranger who entered his dominions. But Orestes was not intimidated, and, accompanied by his friend Pylades, set out for the dominions of the *barbarian†* king.

When the two friends arrived at Tauros, they were carried before Thoas the king, and he commanded them to be sacrificed to Diana. Iphigenia was the priestess, and assisted at all the sacrifices of the goddess. As soon as Iphigenia learned that the victims she was appointed to offer were Greeks, she thought of her far off country, and longed to see the strangers, and to converse with them.

Iphigenia was touched with pity at the sight of Pylades and Orestes, and she resolved to spare the life of one of them, though she could not so far disobey the king as to save both. She told them as she was a Greek, that she had friends in Greece, and

---

* Chersonesus is from the Greek, and signifies a peninsula.

† The Greeks called all nations who were not Greeks, *barbarians*.

that one or other of them should be permitted to return to their country, if he would take letters from
her to her friends.

Iphigenia did not determine which of the two
friends should be spared. Orestes declaring that he
was willing to die, entreated Pylades to be the bearer
of the letters, and to preserve his own life. Pylades,
in his turn, not to be outdone in generosity, begged
that Orestes might become the messenger of Iphigenia, and himself the victim. In the midst of this
generous strife, the letters of Iphigenia were produced. One was addressed to Orestes, Prince of
Mycenæ.

Orestes, upon this discovery, declared himself to
be the same individual. Iphigenia confessed that
she was that daughter of Agamemnon, who had miraculously escaped from Aulis, and she instantly resolved she would return with her brother and his
friend to Greece, and that they would take along
with them the statue of Diana.

Thoas soon discovered the flight of the priestess,
and of the intended victims of Diana, and he would
have followed, and brought them back to Scythia,
but Minerva informed him that all had been done according to the will of the gods. The three friends
in due time arrived at Argos, and were all kindly
welcomed by Electra. Pylades married that princess, and Orestes married his cousin, Hermione
the daughter of Menelaus and Helen. He afterwards reigned in peace and honour, at Argos, and
died in old age. Perhaps Iphigenia still continued a
priestess of Diana, and lived happily with her affectionate brother and sister.

Who were the children of Agamemnon, and what was the
character of Electra?

How did Electra preserve the life of Orestes?

Who killed the murderers of Agamemnon?

How was Orestes tormented?

What did the oracle of Apollo require of Orestes?

What sentence did the Scythian king pass upon Orestes and his friend?

How did Iphigenia treat the friends?

What generous strife took place between the friends?

What discovery was made by Iphigenia?

Did the lives of Orestes and Pylades end happily?

MENELAUS.

AGAMEMNON and Menelaus were called the Atridæ, or sons of Atreus. When Troy was taken, Helen was recovered, and Menelaus carried her back to Sparta. The voyage of Menelaus to Sparta is related in the fourth book of Homer's Odyssey. When Telemachus, the son of Ulysses, went to Sparta to inquire concerning his father, he found Menelaus and Helen living in much luxury and enjoyment. Menelaus relates to Telemachus, that his vessels were tossed about the Egean sea for eight long years, sometimes on the coast of Cyprus, and then along the shores of Phœnicia, till they were driven to the borders of Egypt and Lybia. Menelaus, in the Odyssey, says, this protracted voyage was owing to the displeasure of the gods on account of some neglect in the worship due to them.

> Long on the Egyptian coast by calms confined
> Heaven to my fleet refused a prosperous wind;
> No vows had we preferred, nor victim slain!
> *For this the gods each favouring gale restrain.*
> *Odyssey, Book* IV

A long and weary calm ensued,

> And the pale mariner at once deplores,
> His wasted vigour and exhausted stores.

But one day while some of his men were gone to the shore for provisions, and others were engaged in fishing, one of the sea nymphs, Eidothea, tne daughter of Proteus, appeared to Menelaus, and counselled him to apply to her father for instruction how to reconcile the offended deities.

Proteus was a sea-god capable of transforming himself into any shape he chose, and always endeavouring to elude those who asked any thing of him. Eidothea, however clothed Menelaus and three of his associates in the skins of Phocæ, or seals, which animals belonged to her father's sea-herds, laid them in the sands, and instructed them to take her father by surprise, and hold him till he should declare the will of the gods, of which he was informed.

Menelaus did as he was directed by Ediothea; and Proteus informed him by what religious services to appease the gods, and gain a prosperous voyage. Having received these instructions, Menelaus inquired of the seer concerning his companions in arms, Agamemnon, Ulysses, and Ajax. Proteus told him of the fate of his brother and of Ajax, and informed him that Ulysses still lived.

Menelaus, as soon as he knew the will of the gods, performed the ceremonies required, and erected a *cenotaph** to the memory of Agamemnon.

> These rights to piety and grief discharged,
> The friendly gods a springing gale enlarged:
> The fleet swift tilting o'er the surges flew
> Till Grecian cliffs appeared, a blissful view.

Who were the Atridæ, and in what book is their history related?

For what cause was the voyage of Menelaus prolonged?

Who appeared to Menelaus near the coast of Egypt, and what instructions were given him?

How did Menelaus deceive Proteus?

---

* Cenotaph, a monument, erected upon a spot where the remains of the dead are not interred.

What information did Proteus give to Menelaus?

Did Menelaus follow the directions of Proteus, and arrive safely in Greece?

AJAX.

AJAX, next to Achilles, was the most valiant of the Greeks, who went to the siege of Troy. Ajax was the son of Telamon, a king of the island of Salamis. During the war he engaged in single combat with Hector; neither was killed, and at parting they exchanged arms. On the death of Achilles, Ulysses and Ajax contended which should possess his armour, and because it was given to Ulysses, Ajax went mad. In his phrensy, he slew a flock of sheep, supposing them to be sons of Atreus, who had bestowed the armour upon Ulysses, and at length killed himself in despair.

Another AJAX was the son of Oileus, King of Locris. The night that Troy was taken, Ajax pursued Cassandra into the Temple of Minerva. Cassandra had fled thither as an *asylum*, a place where she might be secure from the ill treatment which soldiers in a moment of victory offer to the defenceless. Minerva was offended at the disrespect shown to her by Ajax, and resolved to punish him.

Minerva borrowed thunders from Jupiter, and tempests from Neptune, and destroyed the vessel in which Ajax was returning to Greece. Ajax swam to a rock, and declared himself safe, in despite of the gods. This impiety offended Neptune, who shook the rock with his trident, and precipitated Ajax into the sea, where he was drowned.

By Neptune rescued from Minerva's hate,
On Gyræ, safe, Oilean Ajax sate

His ship o'erwhelmed; but frowning on the floods,
Impious he roared defiance to the gods;
To his own prowess all the glory gave,
The power defrauding who vouchsafed to save.
This heard the raging ruler of the main;
His spear, indignant for such high disdain,
He launched, dividing with his forky mace
The aërial summit from its mighty base;
The rock rushed seaward with impetuous roar,
Ingulfed, and to the abyss the boaster bore.

Odyssey, Book IV.

Who, next to Achilles, was the bravest Greek at the siege of Troy?

Who was Ajax, sometimes called the *Less?*

How did Minerva and Neptune punish the impiety of Ajax?

What description of the death of Ajax is taken from Pope's Homer?

ULYSSES.

ULYSSES, King of Ithaca and Dulichium, two little islands near the western coast of Greece, was, of all the heroes of the Trojan war, most renowned for his eloquence and cunning. Ulysses was the son of Laertes, and the husband of Penelope. When Ulysses married, his father went into rural retirement, and left his kingdom to his son. Ulysses was very happy in his government, and in his family, for he tenderly loved Penelope, and their only child, the infant Telemachus.

When Ulysses was summoned to go to the war of Troy, he was unwilling to leave his wife and child, and pretended to be insane. To make his insanity probable, he yoked a horse and a bull together, and sowed a field with salt instead of barley. Palamedes, suspecting that Ulysses was not insane, placed the little Telemachus before the plough, and Ulysses, instantly turning it from the furrow, would not hurt the child. This proved that he was in a sound mind.

Being forced to go to the war, Ulysses performed the most eminent services, and received thanks and praises from all the Greeks. But on his return from Troy, he was exposed to many misfortunes. His vessel was first driven out of its course to the coast of Africa, and next to the island of Sicily, where he visited the Cyclops. Polyphemus, the King of the Cyclops, seized Ulysses and his companions, five of whom he devoured; but the King of Ithaca put out the eye of Polyphemus, and narrowly escaped with his life, by tying himself under the body of a sheep, which carried him out of the cave of Polyphemus.

In Æolia he met with a friendly reception, and Æolus, the wind-god, gave him all the adverse winds in bags, that he might have none but fair winds to carry him to Ithaca. But the companions of Ulysses were curious to know what the bags contained; so they opened them, and out rushed the blasts, carrying all before them, and the whole fleet was destroyed, except the ship carrying Ulysses.

Ulysses was next driven to the island of Circe, where the enchantress metamorphosed all his companions into hogs. The god Mercury had given Ulysses an herb called Moly, which preserved him from the effects of her arts, and he retained his human figure. Ulysses afterwards visited the infernal regions, and there he consulted the prophet Teresias, how he might return to Ithaca.

Ulysses had compelled Circe to restore his men to their natural form, and once more, with his single vessel, he embarked for Ithaca, but he was not destined yet to return. By the directions of Circe, he passed along the coasts of the Sirens unhurt, and escaped the whirlpools of Scylla and Charybdis. On the island of Sicily, the companions of Ulysses seized upon, and devoured, some cattle which were designed for victims to Apollo; this gave such offence to the god, that he sunk the vessel, drowned the mariners, and permitted Ulysses only to escape on a single plank.

Thus destitute and forlorn, Ulysses floated to the island of Calypso, where he was kindly received by that goddess. Calypso lived in a delicious spot, and was so much delighted with Ulysses, that she wished to detain him in her island as long as he should live; but after he had resided with her seven years, the gods commanded him to leave Calypso, and return to Ithaca. Mercury ordered Calypso to furnish Ulysses with every thing necessary for his voyage, and she obeyed him, and the hero departed once more for Ithaca.

He had almost reached Corcyra, when Neptune recollected that his son Polyphemus had had his single eye put out by Ulysses, and thought it just that he should suffer still more as a punishment for that act; so the god raised a storm and sunk Ulysses' ship, and the latter, not till he had suffered many perils, arrived safely at the island of the Phocians; there, though he was alone, and exposed to wild beasts, he laid himself down to rest and fell asleep.

While Ulysses was sleeping, Nausicaa, the daughter of Antinöus, King of the Phocians, came, with her attendants, to the spot where the stranger lay, and awakened him by their voices. Ulysses soon made his forlorn state known to these young women. They were moved with compassion for him; provided him with clothes, and directed him to apply to the king and queen for succour.

Ulysses found the king and queen of Phocia living in a sumptuous palace, surrounded with beautiful gardens. They were persons of amiable manners, and generous dispositions, and did all the * could to divert the unfortunate stranger; exhibiting towards him that generous hospitality which the ancients considered as the first of duties. At a convenient time, they persuaded him to relate his adventures. Ulysses readily complied, and afterwards Antinöus had him safely conveyed to his own kingdom, which he reached after an absence of twenty years.

When Ulysses found himself once more in Ithaca, he resolved to proceed to his palace in the disguise of an old beggar; but he first went to the cottage of one of his servants, Eumæus; who, though he did not know his master, entertained him kindly, and afterwards conducted him to his palace, where he asked charity of his son Telemachus, which the latter gave. As Ulysses approached his palace, his faithful dog Argus recognised him, and immediately fell dead at his feet.

During the absence of Ulysses, the neighbouring princes had severally importuned Penelope to marry one of them; but the queen, tenderly attached to the memory of her husband, and hoping that he still lived, denied them all. The *suitors*, as the princes were called, took up their abode in the palace of Ulysses, slaughtered his flocks, drank his wine, and insulted his son.

No sooner did Ulysses appear in Ithaca, and discover himself to his family, than the suitors were properly punished for their audacity and violence. Ulysses killed them all, and restored order and quiet in his dominions; rewarding Penelope for her fidelity, cherishing his son, and improving his people. The interesting story of Ulysses is related at length in the Odyssey. According to some opinions, he was a wise man, but he was certainly not very honest; and the want of honour is a blemish in his character, which diminishes esteem for him.

Who was Ulysses ?

How did Ulysses try to escape from going to the siege of Troy ?

What were the adventures of Ulysses on his return to Ithaca ?

What accident was caused to Ulysses by the gift of Æolus ?

Where were the companions of Ulysses metamorphosed ?

After Ulysses left Circe, what prevented his return to Ithaca ?

How long did Ulysses live with Calypso ?

On what island was Ulysses next landed ?

What princess relieved Ulysses ?

How was Ulysses treated by the king and queen of Phocia ?

In what character did Ulysses go to his palace ?

Who had taken possession of the palace of Ulysses in his absence ?

How did Ulysses conduct himself on his return to Ithaca, and what is the chief defect of his character ?

ACHILLES.

ACHILLES, the principal of the Greek heroes who went to the siege of Troy, was the son of Pelides, King of Thessaly, and of Thetis, a sea-nymph. To render his person *invulnerable*, (impenetrable to the darts of his enemies,) Thetis, in his infancy, dipped her son into the waters of the Styx. After this precaution, the heel only, the part by which his mother held him, was liable to be wounded.

Achilles was instructed by Chiron, the Centaur, in the arts of war and music, and by Phœnix in eloquence. When Menelaus was about to attack Troy, Chalcas, a diviner in whom the Greeks placed implicit confidence, declared that Troy could not be taken without the assistance of Achilles. Thetis, who foresaw that her son would perish in this enterprise, concealed him in female attire among the household of Lycomedes, King of Scyras Here he was discovered by Ulysses. That wily Greek, travelling about in the disguise of a merchant, exposed jewels and arms for sale to the maidens of Lycomedes' court. Achilles was among them; and, in despite of his habiliment, chose the armour, and thus discovered his sex.

Achilles then felt himself in honour compelled to engage in the cause of Menelaus, and led his *myrmidons*, the soldiers of Pythia, in fifty ships to Troy. Here he soon distinguished himself by his ravages in the neighbouring districts, his person being defended by a suit of impenetrable armour, which Thetis had procured to be made for him by Vulcan.

Among the captives taken by Achilles, in his predatory incursions, was Briseis, a beautiful female, upon whom Agamemnon set his affections. Agamemnon was the chief of the expedition, and the laws of war required that he should be obeyed. Even the fierce Achilles could not refuse submission to "the king of men," as Agamemnon was called, and he was forced to surrender the fair Briseis.

The displeasure of Achilles upon this occasion forms the principal subject of Homer's Iliad, which commences thus, in Pope's translation:

> *Achilles' wrath*, to Greece the direful spring
> Of woes unnumbered, heavenly goddess, sing."

Achilles withdrew himself from the battle, and after his separation, the Trojans prevailed.

Achilles had a friend whom he tenderly loved: this was Patroclus, who was slain by Hector, the chief hero of Troy. Indignant at this misfortune, Achilles determined to avenge the death of his friend by that of Hector. He therefore returned to the battle-ground, and they came to an engagement in which Achilles slew Hector, and dragged his lifeless body three times round the walls of Troy.

The manner of Achilles' death is variously related; the common tradition is, that he went into a temple with Polyxena, the daughter of Priam, to be married to her, and that her brother, Paris, there aimed an arrow at his defenceless heel, which caused his death. From this circumstance the tendon of the heel is called, by anatomists, the *tendon of Achilles.*

When Achilles was young, his mother asked him whether he preferred a long life, spent in obscurity and retirement, or a few years of military glory not being better instructed, he chose the latter, and Jupiter granted his desire. When Achilles was lamenting the loss of Briseis, he reminds his mother of his destiny.

> Oh ! parent goddess ! since in early bloom,
> Thy son must fall, by too severe a doom,
> Sure to so short a race of glory born ;
> Great Jove, in justice, should this span adorn ;
> Honour and fame, at least, the Thunderer owed,
> And ill he pays the promise of a god,
> If yon proud monarch thus thy son defies,
> Obscures my glory and resumes my prize.
> *Iliad, Book V.*

Achilles is supposed to have been buried near the promontory of Sigæum, not far from the site of ancient Troy. Some ages after the war of Troy, Alexander, as he was going into Persia, offered a sacrifice on the tomb of Achilles, to celebrate the hero, and the poet who had transmitted his fame to posterity.

Who was Achilles ?
What is the history of Achilles' early life ?
How was the person of Achilles defended ?
What was the cause of Achilles' displeasure against Agamemnon ?
What is the principal subject of Homer's Iliad ?
What incited Achilles to the destruction of Hector ?
What is the common tradition in respect to the death of Achilles ?

Did Achilles desire long life ?

Where was Achilles buried, and who offered sacrifices on his tomb ?

NESTOR.

Nestor, King of Pylos, a city of Messinia in Pe-loponnesus, went to the siege of Troy.   His character is more amiable than that of the heroes generally. Nestor was very old, having lived *three ages,*—that is supposed to signify three of thirty years, and he was consequently ninety years old.   Nestor, though a warrior, was a peace-maker.   When Achilles and Agamemnon, in the first book of the Iliad, had their fierce quarrel concerning the captive Briseis, the wise Nestor endeavoured to allay their mutual fury.

> To calm their passions with the words of age,
> Slow from his seat arose the Pylian sage,
> Experienced Nestor, in persuasion skilled,
> Words sweet as honey from his lips distilled.
> Two generations now had passed away,
> Wise by his rules and happy by his sway;
> Two ages in his native realm he reigned,
> And now the example of the third remained.
> All viewed with awe the venerable man.
>
> *Iliad, Book 1.*

Nestor returned from the war of Troy in safety to his own dominions and family in Messinia.   He lost his son Antilochus in the battles of Troy; but his old age is represented to have been passed in th. piety and peace, which the sovereign of a small and unwarlike state might be likely to enjoy without disturbance.

Who was Nestor, and what was his character ?

How does Homer describe Nestor ?

How was the old age of Nestor passed !

DIOMED.

DIOMED, the King of Etolia, was one of the bravest of the followers of Menelaus. Diomed is celebrated in Homer, for what is called his night adventure. This was entering during the night the city of Troy, in order to report to the Greeks the condition of the enemy.

> Is there, said he,* a chief so greatly brave
> His life to hazard, and his country save?
> Lives there a man who singly dares to go,
> To yonder camp, or seize some straggling foe?
> Or, favoured by the night, approach so near,
> Their speech, their counsels, their designs to hear?

None of the host answered to this appeal but Diomed.

> ———————— " Untaught to fear
> Tydides spoke—The man you seek is here.
> To yon black camps to bend my dangerous **way,**
> Some *god within* commands, and I obey.
> But let *some other chosen warrior* join,
> To raise my hopes and second my design."

This other " chosen warrior " was Ulysses. They proceeded together among the unwary Trojans, committed great slaughter, and returned to the Greek camp, having murdered Rhesus, King of Thrace, one of the allies of the Trojans, and bringing with them the famous horses of Rhesus,

> " Swift as the wind, and white as winter snow."

When Diomed returned to Etolia, he found his kingdom and family in the condition which any might presume upon, who should abandon his duties for ten years. His wife had married a stranger, and his subjects had become regardless of all laws ; so

* Nestor

he left his country and settled himself in Magna Grecia, where he died.

What was the character of Diomed ?

What proposal did Nestor make to the Greeks in the camp?

Who answered Nestor's appeal, and undertook the enter prise which he proposed ?

What became of Diomed ?

HECTOR.

HECTOR, the son of Priam and Hecuba, was the most valiant of the Trojans. His wife was Andromache, the daughter of Ætian, an Asiatic prince, and their only child was Astyanax. *The parting of Hector and Andromache* is justly accounted the most pathetic passage of the Iliad.

Hector killed Patroclus, the favourite friend of Achilles. After Achilles withdrew himself from the Greeks on account of his quarrel with Agamemnon, the Trojans gained perpetual advantages, and Patroclus entreated Achilles that he might be clothed in his armour and combat Hector. Achilles consented, and Patroclus fell.

Achilles, exasperated beyond measure at the loss of his friend, returned to the field, and renewed his attack upon the Trojans. Fear fell upon them as this mighty barbarian, instigated by his terrible passions, dealt death at every blow. Hector was not without terror at the thought of encountering so invincible a warrior; and his father, mother and friends, entreated him to avoid Achilles.

Hector was too proud to fly from an enemy; he met the ferocious Achilles, and died by his hand. Achilles afterwards fastened the dead body of Hector to his car, and dragged it ignominiously round the tomb of Patroclus. Priam afterwards went to the tent of Achilles, and begged his son's body

Achilles could not resist the supplications of the old man, and gave up the body.

By one of those miracles very common among the poets, the disfigured person of Hector was restored to its natural beauty, and when he was brought back to Troy, and received by his mother, wife, and sister, Hecuba exclaimed,

> " Yet glowest thou fresh with every living grace;
> No mark of pain or violence of face;
> Rosy and fair! as Phœbus' silver bow
> Dismissed thee gently to the shades below.

The amiable character of Hector was, perhaps, best described by Helen, who says, in Pope's Homer,

> "Yet was it ne'er my fate from thee to find,
> A deed ungentle or a word unkind;
> While *others cursed the authoress of their wo,*
> Thy pity checked my sorrows in their flow;
> If some proud brother eyed me with disdain,
> Or scornful sister with her sweeping train,
> Thy gentle accents softened all my pain ;
> For thee I mourn, and mourn myself in thee,
> The wretched source of all this misery.
>
> *Iliad, Book XIV.*

Hector feared that Andromache would be cruelly treated by whomsoever among the Greeks should make her his prisoner; he says,

> " I see thee weeping, trembling, captive led."

She fell to the share of Neoptolemus, son of Achilles. It is said that he married her. The infant Astyanax was killed by some of the barbarous conquerors of Troy.

When Priam entreated the body of Hector, Achilles for a moment was melted. The meeting between them was solemn and affecting. Old age in affliction touches the most obdurate heart. The wretched Priam kissed the hands that had been stained with the blood of his dear son, and supplicated the iron-hearted Achilles to restore his mangled form.

16

Achilles, implacable as he had shown himself, could not refuse a request so reasonable, and when he granted the body of Hector, he also allowed a *truce ;* a suspension of hostilities, that Priam might bury his son, and the funeral honours were paid according to the customs of the country.

When Troy was afterwards taken, the family of Priam fled to the altar of the gods for protection. Priam, in this last conflict, clothed himself in armour, and would have defended himself, but Hecuba detained him in the temple of Jupiter.   While Hecuba was thus endeavouring to save her aged husband, their son Polites entered the sanctuary ; Neoptolemus pursued him thither, and, disregarding the place, inflicted a mortal wound upon the youth, who fell dead at his parents' feet.

Priam lifted his spear against the murderer, but in vain ; his hand was feeble, opposed to the strong arm of the Greek.   The latter, without compassion or reverence, seized the gray hair of Priam, and severed his head from his body.   Hecuba was assigned, as a captive, to Ulysses, but that hero passing into Thrace, Hecuba made her escape from him, and lived and died in that barbarous land.   Cassandra was murdered by those who accomplished the death of Agamemnon, and thus ended the race of the Dardan kings.   So horrible are the details of war.

It is hardly probable that this story is exactly true, but it has certainly many parallels among nations not taught by the revelation of God, and some, alas ! among those who have been instructed in the gospel of peace.

Who was the most valiant of the Trojans?
What particularly exasperated Achilles against Hector ?
Was Hector afraid of Achilles, and what happened to him ?
How did the body of Hector appear when it was restored
Priam ?

How did Helen describe Hector?
What was the fate of Hector's wife and child?
What became of Priam and his family?
Is the history of Priam likely to be true?

ENEAS.

ENEAS was a prince of Troy, son of Anchises and the goddess Venus. When Troy was in flames, Eneas escaped with his life, taking upon his shoulders his aged father, Anchises, and in one hand his household gods, while he led, in his other hand, his young son, Ascanius. Creusa, the wife of Eneas, followed her husband and father, but she was unhappily lost in the crowd.

According to Virgil, the Roman poet, who has written the history of Eneas in the poem called the Eneid, Eneas attached followers to himself, and embarked upon the Mediterranean, in hopes to establish himself in some country more favoured than Troy. In his voyage, Eneas stopped at Delos, the Strophades, Crete, and Sicily. In Sicily, he buried his father; hence he would have continued his course to Italy, but he was driven upon the coast of Africa.

Carthage is commonly supposed to have been founded about eight hundred years before the Christian era, but Virgil pretends that it existed at the end of the war of Troy, 1184 B. C. This *anachronism* may be pardoned in a poet, for poets are not required to be accurate. Eneas, according to the fable, was driven to the city of Carthage, and kindly received by Dido.

Dido was a princess of Tyre, in Phœnicia. Her husband, Sichæus, was immensely rich, and Epymalion, a tyrannical king of Tyre, in order to possess himself of the wealth of Sichæus, murdered him. Dido, after the loss of her husband, in fear for her own life, escaped with a company of Tyrians to Africa, where she founded the city of Carthage.

According to Virgil, Dido wished to detain Eneas at Carthage, and to marry him, but he refused, and left her for Italy. In consequence of her grief for the departure of Eneas, Dido refused to live, and committed suicide. The readers of Virgil always pity her, because her sorrow and despair are described in an affecting manner.

In the passage from Carthage to Sicily, Eneas was driven ashore at Cumæ, and the Sibyl conducted him to the infernal regions, that he might learn the fate of himself, and his posterity. After a voyage of seven years, and the loss of thirteen ships, Eneas came to the Tiber. Here he was kindly received by Latinus, the king of the country, who gave him his daughter Lavinia, though she had been previously promised to Turnus, for a wife.

Eneas met also with a kind reception from Evander, a prince of Arcadia, who had brought a colony into Italy, had dispossessed the aborigines, or natives, of a little tract adjacent to Latium, and had established himself there. This prince gave Eneas an interesting account of the former state of Italy, of the golden age of Saturn, and the less happy days that followed.

Young persons are not to understand from the word *king*, as it is used in the history of ancient and pastoral people, the same idea as that of a king in modern times. Those *kings* who are mentioned in the history of Abraham, must have been the proprietors of small tracts of land, who exercised a patriarchal government over those who lived upon their domains, and who, like the nobles of Europe in the middle ages, called out their followers to fight their battles. A king of England or France, though he has not the absolute power of ancient kings, rules a large territory, and lives in a manner wholly different from Evander, or Chedorlaomer.

To prevent the marriage of Eneas and Lavinia, Turnus declared war against the former. Virgil related many battles which ensued between Eneas and Turnus; that Eneas was assisted by his mother, Venus, and by Evander, and that, being tired of fighting, the rivals at .ast, to finish the contest, agreed upon a single combat. Turnus was killed, and it may be that Eneas reigned peaceably in Latium.

Fabulous history does not relate with precision the death of Eneas, but it is somewhere said that he was drowned in the Numicus, a river of Italy, being weighed down by his armour; and that the Latins, as the Romans afterwards believed of Romulus, imagined their king was taken up into heaven. After this, the Latins honoured Eneas as a god, and offered sacrifices to him. To imagine a man to be a god, and to worship him as one, is the *apotheosis* of that man. This folly no longer exists in the world; men are now better instructed in the nature of God, and in the proper way to honour great men.

Who was Eneas, and what became of his family at the destruction of Troy?

Did Eneas immediately after his escape from Troy proceed to Italy?

Can it be a fact that Eneas was ever at Carthage?

Who is commonly supposed to be the foundress of Carthage?

What is Virgil's history of Dido's death?

How long was the voyage of Eneas before he reached Italy?

What king gave Eneas a hospitable reception?

What is to be understood by the word "king"?

What was the end of the war between Eneas and Turnus?

What was the reputed death of Eneas, and what is signified by the word *apotheosis?*

Besides the history of gods and demi-gods, compends of Mythology usually contain notices of cer tain eminent individuals of antiquity, who, by way of distinction, are called the Seven Wise Men of Greece—and to them is also added the tradition of certain monuments of art, now perished. The latter weie the Seven Wonders of the world. The common account of the celebrated men, and of the perished monuments, is the following.

SEVEN WISE MEN OF GREECE.

THOSE persons, called by way of eminence the Seven Wise Men of Greece, were Thales of Miletus, Solon of Athens, Chilo of Lacedemon, Pittacus of Mytilene, Bias of Priene, Cleobulus of Rhodes, and Periander of Corinth.

THALES was born at Miletus, in Ionia, about 640 B. C. At that time, the *means of knowledge,* schools, and colleges, did not abound for the instruction of the young. Those who felt the desire of improvement meditated upon what they saw about them, and sometimes travelled in search of knowledge from one country to another. In the age of Thales, the Greek cities of Asia Minor perhaps possessed as much knowledge, that is, had made as many discoveries in science, and had made as many useful inventions as the most intelligent of the European Greeks; but all the Greeks at that time looked to Egypt for instruction.

Thales, in his solicitude for improvement, repaired to Egypt, and by conversation with the philoso phers of that country, was initiated in their doctrines. On his return to Asia Minor, he discoursed to his countrymen on various subjects of theology, morals, and physical science, and founded what is called the *Ionian sect* in philosophy. Thales was the first of the Greeks who made discoveries in astronomy, and foretold eclipses.

Of his theology and morals, the following *tradition* is preserved ; for, if he *wrote* any thing, his treatises are lost. Thales maintained that the supreme God was eternal and uncreated ; that he made all things ; that the creation was perfect, being God's work, and that he continually sees the secret thoughts of every man's heart. He said that the most difficult thing in nature, is to know ourselves : the most easy to advise others ; the most sweet to accomplish our desires. He taught that in order to live virtuously we must avoid the faults we see in others ; that we should avoid saying any thing which another can repeat to our injury ; that we should live with our friends as if they might one day become our enemies, and that health is the felicity of the body, and knowledge that of the mind. Thales died at the age of ninety.

SOLON, the Athenian legislator, was born at Athens, and was a contemporary of Thales. During the life of Solon, the people of Athens were agitated by perpetual discords in respect to magistrates and laws. Draco, one of the archons, or chief magistrates of Athens, just before the time of Solon, had established laws, which the Athenians could not endure. These laws pretended to punish every offence with death. An idle man, or one who stole a cabbage, or an apple, suffered as severe a punishment as a capital offender.

The wise Solon was more just and humane, and his countrymen respected him so highly, that they called upon him to make a new body of laws, which they promised to observe. They gave him the regulation of the magistrates, the assemblies of the people, and the courts of justice. Solon discharged this trust with great ability, and gave the Athenians a republican government and many wise laws. These laws, called the *Institutions of Solon*, remained in force as long as the Athenians remained a free people.   Many of the laws of Solon were after-wards adopted by the Romans.   Solon died at the age of eighty.

CHILO, the Spartan, lived at the same time with Solon.   All that is recorded of him, are certain maxims.   " Three things," he was accustomed to say, " are most difficult.   To keep a secret—to employ one's time worthily—to bear injuries with patience."   It is said that he caused to be engraved in letters of gold in the temple of Apollo at Delphi, this aphorism, " Know thyself."—" Desire nothing too much," was often in his mouth.   Chilo had a beloved and accomplished son—the young man gained a victory at the Olympic games, and so overjoyed was the father by his son's success, that he expired in embracing him.

BIAS was a native of Priene, in Asia Minor.   Bias was contemporary with the wise men previously mentioned—like them he was a moral philosopher, though little more than his name now remains.   He is said to have died suddenly, while he was engaged in pleading the cause of an intimate friend.

PITTACUS was born in the city of Mytilene, in the island of Lesbos.   The Egean islands sometimes enjoyed independence, and had lawgivers and defenders of their own.   When Lesbos was attacked by the Athenians, Pittacus defended his countrymen and defeated their invaders.   In gratitude for his services, the people of Mytilene chose him for their king, and adopted laws which he gave them.   Pittacus died 579 B. C.

CLEOBULUS of Lindus, in the island of Rhodes, was a man of eminently good sense.   He loved the sciences, and particularly recommended the virtues of sincerity and gratitude.   He advised men to do good to their friends that they might preserve their friendship; and to be kind to their enemies, that they might make friends of them. Cleobulina, the daughter of Cleobulus, was celebrated for her wit and genius, but more for the sweetness of her temper Cleobulus died 560 B. C., aged seventy.

PERIANDER of Corinth was an *able*, rather than a wise man. Goodness and benevolence are essential parts of wisdom. Periander, tyrant of Corinth, knew how to govern so as to keep his subjects in order, and his enemies in fear. He caused to be built and equipped, a great number of ships, which carried on a great trade, and defended the maritime state of Corinth. Periander was a bad man; he is remembered as a skilful politician, not as the father of his people, or for his virtuous example. Periander died 588, B. C.

Who were the seven wise men of Greece?
To what country did the Greeks, six centuries before Christ, repair for instruction in the sciences?
What school of philosophy was founded by Thales?
What were the opinions of Thales in religion and morals?
Who was Solon, and what were the institutions of Draco?
Were the institutions of Solon humane and permanent?
Who was Chilo, and for what was he distinguished?
Who was Bias?
Who was Pittacus?
For what is Cleobulus memorable, and who was his daughter?
Was Periander of Corinth a virtuous man?

RELIGION OF THE HINDUS.

A PART of the people of Hindustan have received the religion of Mohammed, but another portio of the inhabitants of India retain their ancient mythology, though Europeans have introduced among them the doctrines of Christianity. The mythology of the ancients is of such high antiquity, that it is impossible to go back to its origin.

The doctrines of the Hindus are contained in a sacred book called the Vedas. The language in which they are written, is the *Sanscrit ;* the word Sanscrit signifies *to know.* According to the Hindu belief, these writings in the Sanscrit language, are true revealed knowledge. The sacred books of the Hindus are carefully preserved by their priests, called Bramins.

The Hindus acknowledge one supreme deity, called Brahma, or the great one ; and they acknowledge that he is uncreated and eternal, and infinitely too great to be comprehended by mortals ; as the Hebrew scriptures say, " Can man, by searching, find out God, or know the Almighty to perfection ?"

As the Greeks supposed three divine beings separately to preside over the heavens and the earth, the ocean, and the infernal regions ; the Hindus suppose that Brahma ought to have three names, and that he governs in three characters, when he is regarded as the *Preserver of the Universe, the Mover of the Waters,* and the *Destroyer or Changer of Forms.* The Preserver and Pervader, is Brahma ; the God of the Waters, Narayan ; and the Destroyer, Seva.

BRAHMA.

THE Hindus believe that the elements which form the material universe, were immersed in water before they were brought by Brahma to their present forms and order. They described the creation as Moses does in the book of Genesis. " In the beginning God created the heavens and the earth ; and the earth was without form and void, and darkness was upon the face of the deep, and the Spirit of God moved on the face of the waters."

The world being created, was divided into ten parts, each of which was committed to the care of a guar-

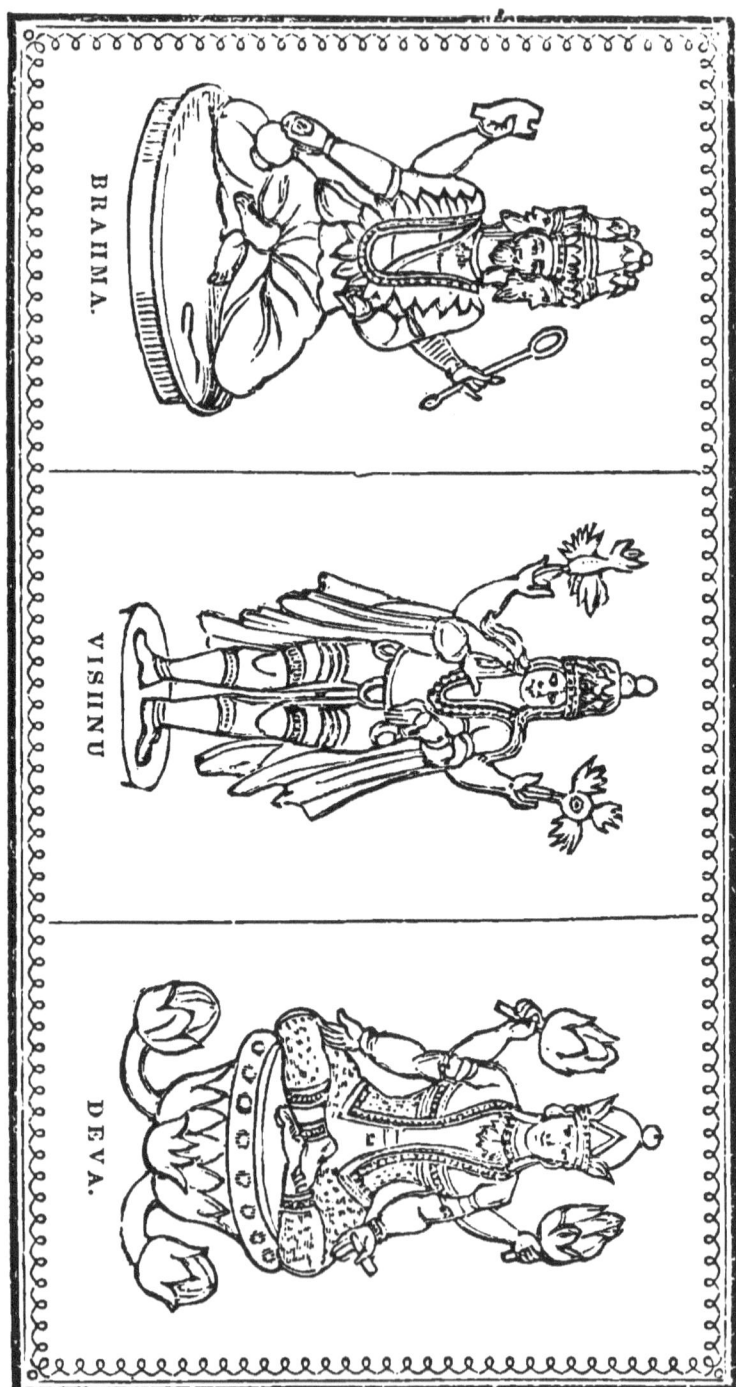

dian spirit. Besides Brahma in his three characters, and the guardian spirits, the Hindus believe in many inferior deities : the chief of these are,

Casgapa, the ancient god of the heavens, with Aditi his consort, parents of many of the inferior deities.

Ganesa, son of Seva, the god of wisdom, is depicted with an elephant's head, the symbol of sagacious discernment, and attended by a rat, which the Indians regarded as a wise and provident animal. All sacrifices and religious ceremonies ; addresses to superior gods ; serious writings, and worldly affairs of moment, are begun by pious Hindus, with an invocation of Ganesa. His image is set up in their streets and their high roads : and against their temples and houses. They daily sprinkle it with oil, and adorn it with flowers.

Menu, the lawgiver. Fourteen of this name are supposed by the Hindus to have existed successively.

Lachsmee, the goddess of abundance, who presides over agricultural labours, and is the wife of Vishnu. She is represented with a twisted cord under her arm, somewhat resembling the cornucopia, or horn of plenty, of the Grecian Ceres.

Indra the king ; the god of the heavens ; chief of the good spirits. His consort is named Sachi ; his celestial city, Amaravati ; his palace, Vaijayanta ; his garden, Nandana ; his chief elephant, Airavat ; his charioteer, Matali ; and his weapon, Vajra, or the thunderbolt. He is the master of the thunder ; the ruler of the winds and showers. His peculiar place of abode is Meru, or the North Pole, allegorically represented as a mountain of golden gems.

Seshanaga, the Sovereign of Patala, or the infernal regions ; the king of serpents. He is thus described in the Bhagavat, a sacred Hindu poem. His appearance is gorgeous and brilliant. He has a thousand heads ; and on each of them is a crown set with resplendent gems. His neck, tongues, and body, are black. His eyes gleam like torches. The skirts of his robes are yellow. A sparkling jewel is hung on each one of his ears. His arms are extended and adorned with rich bracelets. His hands bear the holy shell, the radiated weapon, the war-mace, and the lotos

Yama or Yamen, the god of death. He is esteemed to be a child of the sun : he is called also, King of Justice. He is distinguished as being the judge of departed souls ; for the Hindus believe that when a soul leaves its body, it is immediately conveyed to Yamapur, or the city of Yama ; where it receives a just sentence from him ; and thence, either ascends to Swerga, or the first heaven ; or is driven down to Narac, the region of serpents ; or assumes on earth, the form of some animal ; unless its offence had been so heinous as to merit a vegetable, or even a mineral prison.

Yamen is described under the double character of the Greek Furies. He is inexorably severe to the incorrigibly guilty ; but to the penitent he is gracious and relenting. And like the true God, though he is a "consuming fire," yet " he forgiveth iniquity, transgression, and sin."

> They, who polluted with offences come,
>   Behold him as the King
> Of terrors ; black of aspect, red of eye,
> Reflecting back upon the sinful mind
>   Its own inborn deformity.
> But to the righteous spirit, how benign,
>   His awful countenance!
> Where tempering justice with parental love,
>   Goodness and heavenly grace,
> And sweetest mercy shine. Yet is he still
> Himself *the same*, one form, one face, one will
> And these his twofold aspects are but one ;
>   And change is none

In him; for change in Yamen could not be,
The *immutable* is He.

Parvati is the consort of Seva, whose rites and emblems are shamefully immoral and indecent. Carticéya, the son of Parvati, leader of the celestial armies. He is represented as riding upon a peacock, clothed in a robe spangled with eyes, having six heads, and numerous hands, which grasp spears, sabres, and other weapons of war.

Seraswatti is the wife of Brahma, and emblem of his creative power, the patroness of the arts and sciences. She is depicted as holding in her hands the palmira leaf, and the reed for writing. Durga is the same goddess, when regarded as difficult of access, the severe, the majestic divinity of heroic virtue, the vanquisher of demons and giants.

Cama is the beautiful god of love, having a bow of cane, and shafts enwreathed with flowers. Suradevi, the goddess of wine, who arose from the ocean, when, after the deluge, it was disturbed by the gods, with the mountain Mandar, and forced to throw up the sacred things, and animals, and the water of life, which it had swallowed.

Varuna, the genius of the waters.

Agni, the genius of fire.

Agnastra, the fabricator of the heavenly arrows.

Pavan, the ruler of the winds.

Mariatale, the favouring goddess of the Parias, the lowest and miserably despised caste, or division of the Hindus; rejected by their countrymen, and condemned to perform all the most laborious and degrading offices of life.

What is the religious condition of Hindustan?

In what books are the doctrines of the Hindus contained?

Do the Hindus acknowledge any supreme deity?

Under what different characters do the Hindus represen Brahma?

What is the Hindu account of the creation ?
How was the world divided ?
Who is Casgapa ?
Who is Ganesa, and how is he worshipped?
Who is Menu ?
Who is Lachsmee ?
Who is Indra?
Who is Seshanga ?
Who is Yamen ?
Does Yamen appear in two forms ?
Who are Parvati and Carticeya ?
Who are Seraswatti and Durga ?
Who are Cama and Suradevi ?
Who are Varuna, Agni, and Agnastra, and Pavan?
Who is Maritale ?

———

The Hindus pay adoration to the Sun and Moon
The sun is adored under the name of Surya.
Surya is represented as riding in a chariot, drawn
by seven green horses, guided by his charioteer
Arun, or the dawn.   Temples, in honour of the sun,
now exist in India.   One of these is thus described :
" The walls were of red marble, interspersed with
streaks of gold.   On the pavement was an image of
the radiant divinity, hardly inferior to himself in
splendour ; his rays being imitated by a boundless
profusion of rubies, pearls, and diamonds, of inesti-
mable value."

Another temple of the sun at Juggernaut is of sur-
prising magnificence: It is surrounded by a high
wall, and has three entrances.   At the eastern gate
are two very fine figures of elephants, each with a
man upon his trunk.   On the west are two surpris-
ing figures of horsemen completely armed, who,
having killed two elephants, are seated upon them.
In front of that gate is an octagonal pillar of black
stone, fifty cubits* high.   Nine flights of steps lead
to an extensive enclosure, in which is a large dome,

* A cubit is eighteen inches.

constructed of stone, upon which are carved the sun and the stars ; and round them is a border on which is a variety of human figures, expressive of different passions ; some kneeling, others prostrate ; together with a number of strange imaginary animals.

The Hindu priests, at their first assuming the Zennar or sacred cord of three threads, the mystic symbol of their faith, learn the Gayteree, or invocation of praise to the sun.

The Hindus regard the moon as a male deity, to whom they give the name of Chandra, and whom their poets describe as sitting in a splendid chariot, drawn by two antelopes, and holding in the right hand a rabbit. Fountains are by them dedicated to this divinity.

VISHNU.

See plate, page 191.

The Hindus suppose that Vishnu takes upon himself different forms at different times, and is called by different names.

The different characters of Vishnu are called *manifestations of Vishnu.* When a god appears on earth in a human form, he is said to be *incarnate,* or clothed in flesh.

The Rama of the Hindus is an incarnate deity. He was a celebrated conqueror, who delivered his wife Sita from the giant Ravan, King of Lanca.

Chrishna is a manifestation of Vishnu. He is regarded by the Hindus as the god of shepherds ; of whose nature and actions, their sacred writings give the most extraordinary and strange representations. He is depicted as splendidly decorated, wearing a rich garland of wild flowers, and having his ankles adorned with strings of pearls. His complexion is dark blue, approaching to black, and hence, the large bee of that colour is often drawn fluttering over his head.   His character and attributes greatly resemble those of the Grecian Apollo.

DEVA.

See plate, page 191.

RAMA, Chrishna, and Budha, another beneficent deity, are sometimes called the Avatars. They came into the world to abolish human sacrifices, and to appoint in their place, the innocent oblation of fruits, flowers, and incense.

All the Avatars are painted with coronets of gems ; jewels in their ears ; necklaces ; garlands of flowers hanging down below their waists ; loose mantles of golden tissue, or coloured silk, with embroidered hems.   In their hands are placed the sacred shell, elliptical rings, and maces, or battle-axes.

In ancient times, not only sacrifices of beasts were common amongst the Hindus, but even of human beings.   Vestiges of this sanguinary superstition are still evident, in frequent instances of voluntary suicide ; and in the shocking practice of women burning themselves with their deceased husbands, which is yet encouraged by the Brahmins, and which civil authority has not been able effectually to check.

The Hindus offer religious services to certain animals.   They believe that Vishnu, who has already been incarnate nine times, in different forms, will appear once more in the figure of a horse, in order to put an end to all things here.   They are taught to practise most cruel, absurd, and impure rites ; and that it is meritorious to inflict on themselves severe penances ; such as wearing an iron collar, set with sharp points, about the neck ; dragging constantly along a heavy weight ; remaining for a long time in the most painful positions of body ; drowning themselves in the Ganges, or exposing themselves in its holy waters, to be devoured by tigers or alligators.

Of these wretched fanatics, the most disgusting are the Fakirs, who sometimes hang themselves upon spikes, and may be seen in this state till they expire, being a long time sustained by others infatuated like themselves, who bring them food.

Do the Hindus adore the Sun and Moon, and how is the temple of the Sun described?

Is the temple of Juggernaut of equal magnificence?

What homage do the Hindu priests offer to the Sun?

How do the Hindus regard the Moon?

Do the Hindus suppose Vishnu ever to appear in different characters?

Who is the Rama of the Hindus?

Who is Chrishna?

Who are the Avatars, and how are they represented?

Are human sacrifices still permitted?

Are brute animals revered by the Hindus?

What are the Fakirs?

HINDU TEMPLES.

ELEPHANTA.

THE Hindu temples of the highest antiquity are the subterranean temples at Salsette, and in the small isle of Elephanta near Bombay, which is thus denominated from the figure of a large elephant admirably well cut in the solid rock, of which the island is composed.

This astonishing cavern, which, as containing an assemblage of all the deified heroes and princes of India, may be called the Hindu Pantheon: is about half way up the steep side of the mountain, from whose stony bosom it is excavated. The temple is about one hundred and twenty feet square, and eighteen feet high. The enormous mass of solid rock which forms its roof, is supported by four rows of pillars, of beautiful proportion, and finely fluted. Over these columns runs a ridge of stone, so cut as to resemble a huge beam, which is richly adorned with carved work.

Along the sides of the cavern are ranged between forty and fifty statues, each, twelve or fifteen feet in height, of exact symmetry; but though round and prominent, yet not one of them is detached from the main rock. Some of these statues wear a kind of helmet; others, crowns richly ornamented with gems; whilst others display only large, bushy ringlets of curled or flowing hair. Many of them have four hands, and many six; grasping sceptres and shields; symbols of justice and religion; or war-weapons. Amongst them are conspicuous, the triform representation of Brahmé, and the frightful image of Sceva.

The principal Hindu temples of more modern date, are those of Juggernaut, Benares, Mattra, Tripetty, and Seringham. The Indian pagodas, in general, are commonly erected near the banks of the Ganges, the Kistna, or some other sacred river, for the benefit of ablution in the purifying stream. At the entrance of all the most considerable of them, is a portico, supported by rows of lofty columns, with handsome flights of stone steps. Under these porticoes, multitudes assemble at the rising of the sun, and having bathed in the stream below, await the opening of the gates, which universally front the east, to admit the first solar ray.

Of these temples, that of Juggernaut is the most celebrated. Juggernaut is the residence of the chief Brahmin of all India. The image of Juggernaut stands in the centre of the pagoda, upon an elevated altar, encompassed with iron rails, under a magnificent dome. So vast was the number of pilgrims who resorted to the Juggernaut, that the average annual amount of a tax of half-a-crown on each one of them, exacted by a Mohammedan prince of the country, was 750,000*l*.; and 8000*lbs*. weight of provisions were daily prepared for the use of the priests and the pilgrims. The priests of the temple of Seringham, with their families, composing a multitude of not less than 40,000 persons, were maintained by the liberality of the pilgrims frequenting its celebrated shrine.

The idol images in these temples are generally of the most monstrous forms that imagination can picture. Some have numerous heads and arms, the rude symbols of superhuman wisdom and gigantic power. Some have large horns branching from their heads; and others, huge tusks protruding from extended open mouths. Numbers of sacred hieroglyphical animals are sculptured on the walls. The bull of Sceva; the eagle of Vishnu; the elephant of Ganesa; the ram; the ape; the rhinoceros, are blended together in groups.

What are the most ancient temples of the Hindus?
What is found in the cavern of Elephanta?
Does the cave of Elephanta contain any statues?
What are the principal of the modern temples of the Hindus and where are they commonly erected?

Which is the most celebrated of the modern temples?
Who resort to the temple of Juggernaut?
Are the ornaments of Hindu temples in an elegant taste?

POLITICAL STATE OF THE HINDUS.

It is a singular fact, that in Asia, where the Hebrews dwelt, among whom a revelation of the true God existed from the age of Abraham to that of Christ, a period of nineteen centuries; and where our Saviour himself spent his days on earth, that a universal corruption of religion should exist,—that Mohammedanism or Paganism should universally prevail among the natives.

The Mohammedans compelled the people to embrace their religion, and instantly killed those who refused it; and the subjects of other religions, being unable for the most part to read at all, and being unfurnished with the Christian Scriptures, cannot know at present, and without instructions from European nations, the Christian doctrines. Besides the authority of their priests forbids them to receive new doctrines, and their political regulations also hinder them from learning from each other.

Among the Hindus a very remarkable political order exists, which effectually prevents the *progress of society;* that is, prevents one race of men from growing wiser and better than their fathers were— prevents any particular individual from endeavouring to improve his fellow-citizens. In the nistory of modern Europe, and of America, there are many instances of eminent persons who have spent their whole lives in the instruction of others, and who have particularly endeavoured to exalt the minds and raise the condition of the lower classes of the people: such as William Penn, John Wesley, and Dr. Franklin.

No such persons are allowed to exert themselves for the benefit of the unfortunate natives of Asia, except a few European missionaries, no native Hindu, in particular, is permitted to converse indiscriminately with persons of every degree and of every occupation. The custom and fixed law of the nation forbids it.

The regulation of society which forbids all improvement, is that of the people into orders or castes. The castes are hereditary, immutable divisions of the people, established in the earliest times, by their sacred laws. Of these there are four; that of the *priests*, or Brahmins; that of the *military;* that of the *agriculturists* and *traders;* and that of the *labourers* and *artisans.*

These are as much separated, and have as little mutual communication, as persons of a different nation, or a different species. They cannot intermarry, nor join in any common occupations, or remove from one caste to another.

Those of the superior castes regard those of the inferior with the utmost contempt: and consider themselves as polluted by their approach. Even the lowest Hindus refuse to eat with strangers of any class whatsoever. *The loss of caste*, that is, the breaking of any rule of the caste, degrades a Hindu to a most miserable condition; cuts him off from all society, and causes him to be regarded as an impure and detestable animal.

There is yet another class of persons, the Parias, who are accounted the vilest of all, and are subject to the extremest poverty, the lowest indignities, and the meanest services that can be imposed. It is easy to see why the Christian religion, which declares all men equal, should not be introduced among such a people.

The Brahmin caste holds all the others in the

most humiliating subjection. The Brahmins ab
stain entirely from animal food and fermented
liquors : and the other castes exercise an uncommon
degree of temperance and self-denial. The absti-
nence from animal food is occasioned by their belief
in the doctrine of the Metempsychosis, or transmigration of souls through various bodies. The Sanscrit, or sacred language, in which their books of religion are written, has long ceased to be a spoken
tongue ; and is understood only by the priests and
learned.

What singular fact exists in relation to the Paganism of
Asia.

Why did the Asiatics receive the doctrines of Mahomet, and
why do they not embrace Christianity ?

Does any remarkable social order exist among the Hindus,
and what is the effect of it ?

Into what classes are the Hindus divided ?

How do the Brahmins regard the other castes, and what are
their manners ?

SCANDINAVIAN MYTHOLOGY.

When the map of Europe is examined, its north
western section is seen nearly disparted from the
eastern portion. Beginning at the lakes in Russia,
proceeding to the gulf of Finland, continuing through
the Baltic Sea and its sounds to the North Sea, proceeding along the Atlantic shore of Norway to the
Arctic Ocean, and thence to the White Sea, we arrive once more at Russia. We have almost com-
pleted a circuit which includes a peninsula that contains Finland, Sweden, Norway—which countries,
comprehended under one name, ancient Scandinavia,
and were inhabited by people called the Scandinavian
nations.

The religion of the Scandinavians is contained in
two ancient books, the Edda and the Voluspa. Iceland

belonged to Scandinavia, and in that island the Edda was compiled. The Edda is filled with exploits of the supreme Scandinavian divinity Odin, or Wodin. The Voluspa is a book of prophecy, and consists of between two and three hundred lines. It was supposed to be the prophecy of Vola or Volo, a Scandinavian goddess.

The Voluspa begins with a description of Chaos; relates the formation of the world; the creation of its various inhabitants, giants, gods, men and dwarfs. It then proceeds to a description of the employments of the Destinies, called Nornies; the functions of the Deities; their most remarkable adventures, and their disputes with Loke, a Scandinavian goddess. It concludes with a representation of the final ruin of the world by a general conflagration.

The chief deities of Scandinavia were Odin, Frea, and Thor; besides these were a multitude of inferior deities, and the Scandinavians believed in spirits, elves and fairies, who did good or evil to mankind, as they chose.

According to Scandinavian mythology giants existed before the gods; who were supposed to be born, to reign, and to die, like earthly monarchs. Odin, or Wodin, was the greatest of their gods.

The particular abode of Odin was called Lidskialf, or the trembling gate. He was called the universal father; the father of battles; because he adopted as his children all those who died with arms in their hands. Odin took no nourishment but wine, and distributes to two wolves, named Geri and Ferki, the food served up to him at the celestial banquets.

It is probable that Odin was some formidable warrior, and that having subdued some of the barbarous tribes of northern Europe, he governed them wisely and improved their condition ; so that after his death they celebrated him equally as the god of war, and the giver of all good gifts. Temples were erected for the worship of Odin, and sacrifices were offered to him. The fourth day of the week was consecrated to him, and called Wodin's day, now corrupted into Wednesday.

The supposed actions of Odin are represented by the Scandinavian poets as most marvellous. In battle he slaughtered thousands at a blow. Odin is said, finally, to have retired into Sweden, and feeling the approach of death, and wishing to meet it, as he had often braved it in the field, he assembled his companions, and inflicted upon himself nine deep wounds with the point of his lance. As he was expiring he declared that he was going into Scythia to take his place amongst the other deities at the immortal banquet, where he would receive those who died with arms in their hands.

What was Scandinavia ?
In what books is the religion of Scandinavia described ?
What is contained in the Voluspa ?
What is the Edda, and what does it describe ?
Who were the chief deities of Scandinavia ?
What was the abode of Odin, and how was he attended ?
Who was Odin in reality ?
What actions did mythologists impute to Odin ?

FREA AND THOR.

FREA, or FRIGGA, the daughter of Niorder, goa of the winds and seas, was represented as the most amiable of the goddesses. She was the wife of Odin, accompanied him in battle, on horseback, and shared the dead with him. Frea was called Vanadis, goddess of hope. Frea inhabited a magnificent palace of heaven, named Fansal, the illustrious hode.

Virgins of high birth consecrated themselves to her service. In a temple at Upsal was seen her image reclining on cushions, adorned with the emblems of fertility and abundance. Under the name of Hertha, she was regarded as the earth. She was worshipped by most of the German tribes. To her was consecrated the sixth day of the week; which still bears her name, Frea's day, or Friday. She was attended by Fulla her handmaid, with long flowing hair, and a bandeau of gold.

THOR was esteemed to be the eldest and bravest of the sons of Odin and Frea. He was supposed to rule over the aërial regions; to launch the thunder; to point the lightning; to direct the meteors, winds, and storms. Prayers were addressed to him for favourable winds, refreshing rains, and fruitful seasons. The fifth day of the week was dedicated to him, and called after his name, Thor's day or Thursday.

The principal of the inferior deities of Scandinavia, were Niorder, &c.

NIORDER, who presided over the seas, navigation, hunting, and fishing. He espoused Skada, daughter of the giant Thiasse; who preferring the mountains of her father to the humid palace of her husband, prevailed with him to spend nine out of every twelve days in the hilly regions, while the other three were spent on the shores of the ocean. Niorder is supposed to have been a king of some part of Sweden, and high priest of Upsal.

BALDER, a son of Odin. He was represented as possessing a majestic, attractive beauty: light hair and dazzling eyes. He was mild and eloquent, uttering just and irrevocable decrees. Into his palace no impure person could enter; and upon its columns were engraven those Runic rhymes which were imagined to have power to revive the dead. He was killed unintentionally, by his blind brother, Hoder.

HEIMDAL, the guardian of the heavens. He was styled the powerful, the holy, the god with golden teeth. He was represented as posted in the celestial fortress, at one end of the bridge Bifrost, which reached from earth to heaven, and was evidently an emblem of the rainbow. There he defended he passage against the giants; taking less sleep than the birds; seeing a hundred leagues around him, by night as well as by day; hearing the grass growing on the ground, and the wool on the backs of the sheep. Heimdal held in his hand a trumpet, the sound of which might be heard throughout all worlds. He was esteemed to be the standard bearer of the gods; the judge and pacificator of combats and disputes. He was represented with a cock's crest upon his head.

To the gods just described, may be added several children of Odin: Hoder the blind; the silent Vidar, who walked the waters and the air; Vali the formidable archer; Uller, who presided over the trial by duel; and Forseti, who decided the differences between gods and men. Iduna, queen of youth; Saga, goddess of waterfalls; Vara, the witness of oaths; Lofen, the guardian of friendship; Synia, the avenger of broken faith.

Who was Frea, and how was she worshipped?
What were Thor's attributes and worship?
Who was Niorder?
Who was Balder?
Who was Heimdal?
Had Odin children?

NIFLHEIM.

THE Scandinavian hell was called Niflheim, and was represented as consisting of nine vast regions

of ice, situated under the north pole. Near its
eastern gate reposed the body of Vala, the pro-
phetess.

> Hard by the eastern gate of Hell
> In ancient time great Vala fell ;
> And there she lies in massive tomb,
> Shrouded by night's eternal gloom.
> Fairer than gods, and wiser, she
> Held the strange keys of destiny.
> She knew what chanced ere time began ;
> Ere worlds there were, or gods, or man ;
> No mortal tongue has ever said,
> What hand unknown laid Vala dead.
> But yet if rumour rightly tells,
> In her cold bones the Spirit dwells,
> And still if bold intruder come,
> Her voice unfolds his hidden doom.
> And oft the rugged ear of Hell
> Is soothed by some melodious spell,
> Slow breathing from the hollow stone
> In witching notes and solemn tone.
>
> *Herbert's Helga.*

The Dog of Darkness, similar to the Grecian Cerberus, guarded the entrance of Niflheim.

> Uprose the king of men with speed,
> And saddled straight his coal-black steed ;
> Down the yawning steep he rode,
> That leads to Hela's drear abode.
> Him the dog of darkness spied ;
> His shaggy throat he opened wide,
> While from his jaws, with carnage filled,
> Foam and human gore distilled.
> Hoarse he bays with hideous din,
> Eyes that glow, and fangs that grin.
>
> *Gray's Descent of Odin.*

In the Scandinavian Hell was the principal abode
of Loke, the cruel, cunning, and malicious enemy
of gods and men.   Here resided Hela, the dreadful
goddess of death, daughter of the evil genius Loke
and the giantess Angherbode, or messenger of ill

Hela was described as occupying an immense pa
lace; where her hall was Sorrow; her table, Famine; her knife, Hunger; her servants, Slowness
and Delay; her gate, Precipice; her vestibule, Lan-
guor; her bed, Malady and Leanness; her tent, Malediction. One half of her body was of the colour
of putrid, and the other of living flesh. In this region of horrors roamed the wolf Fenris, a monster
dreaded by the gods, as destined to be one instrument of their destruction; and the equally formidable serpent.

The Valkyries were maids of the god of war; the
goddesses of slaughter. It was their province to select those that were to fall in battle; to bear the in-
vitation of Odin to the most distinguished; to conduct the souls of heroes slain to Valhalla, his hall;
and there to pour out for them the beverage of the
gods.

> On steeds that seemed as fleet as light,
> Six maids in brilliant armour dight.
> Their chargers of ethereal birth,
> Pawed, with impatient hoof, the earth,
> And snorting fiercely 'gan to neigh,
> As if they heard the battle bray,
> And burned to join the bloody fray.
> But they unmoved and silent sate,
> With pensive brow and look sedate,
> Proudly each couched her glittering spear
> And seemed to know nor hope nor fear.
>   So mildly firm their placid air,
> So resolute, yet heavenly fair.
> But not one ray of pity's beam,
> From their dark eyelids seem to gleam;
> Nor gentle mercy's melting tear,
> Nor love might ever harbour there.
> Was never woman's beauteous face,
> So stern, and yet so passionless.   *Helga.*

What was the Scandinavian Hell?
Who es Vala?

Had the Scandinavians a dog like Cerberus?
What terrible goddess resided in Niflheim?
Who were the Valkyries?
What verses describe the Valkyries?

THE SONG OF VALA

[From Herbert's Helga.]

Silence, all ye sons of glory!
　Silence, all ye powers of light!
While I sing of ancient story,
　Wonders wrapt in mystic night.

I was rocked in giant's cradle,
　Giant's lore my wisdom gave;
I have known both good and evil,
　Now I lie in lowly grave.

Long before the birth of Odin,
　Mute was thunderous ocean's roar,
Stillness o'er the huge earth brooding,
　Strand was none, nor rocky shore.

Neither grass nor green tree growing,
　Vernal shower, nor wintry storm,
Nor those horses, bright and glowing,
　Dragged the Sun's refulgent form.

He who rules, by night, the heaven,
　Wist not where his beams to throw,
All to barren darkness given,
　There, confusion; Hell below.

Imir sat in lonely sadness,
　Watching o'er the fruitless globe;
Never morning beamed with gladness;
　Never eve with dewy robe.

Who are those in pride advancing,
　Through the barren tract of night?
Mark their steel divinely glancing,
　Imir falls in holy fight!

Of his bones, the rocks high swelling
　Of his flesh the glebe is made;

From his veins the tide is welling,
   And his locks are verdant shade.

Hark! his crest with gold adorning,
   Chanticleer on Odin calls.
Hark! another bird of morning
   Claps his wings in Hela's halls.

Nature shines in glory beaming;
   Elves are born, and man is formed,
Every hill with gladness teeming,
   Every shape with life is warmed.

Who is he by heaven's high portal,
   Beaming like the light of morn?
'Tis Heimdallar's form immortal,
   Shrill resounds his golden horn.

Say, proud warder, robed in glory,
   Are the foes of nature nigh?
Have they climbed the mountains hoary?
   Have they stormed the lofty sky?

On the wings of tempest riding,
   Surtur spreads his fiery spell;
Elves in secret caves are hiding;
   Odin meets the wolf of hell.

She must taste a second sorrow,
   She who wept when Balder bled,
Fate demands a nobler quarry;
   Death must light on Odin's head

See ye not yon silent stranger?
   Proud he moves with lowering eyes,
Odin, mark thy stern avenger!
   Slain the shaggy monster lies.

See the serpent weakly crawling;
   Thor has bruised its loathsome head!
Lo the stars from heaven are falling!
   Earth has sunk in ocean's bed!

Glorious Sun! thy beams are shrouded,
   Vapours dank around thee sail;
Nature's eye with mists is clouded;
   Shall the powers of ill prevail?

Say, shall earth with freshness teemi g
Once again from ocean rise ?
Shall the dawn of glory streaming
Wake us to immortal joys ?

He shall come in might eternal,
He whom eye hath never seen
Earth and heaven and powers infernal,
Mark his port and awful mien.

He shall judge, and he shall sever
Shame from glory, ill from good;
These shall live in light forever,
Those shall wade the chilling flood.

Dark to dwell in wo repining,
Far beyond the path of day,
In that bower, where serpents twining,
Loathsome spit their venomed spray.

This song of Vala contains a sort of abstract of the Voluspa. The third and fourth verses describe Chaos—the supposed state of the universe before the present order was commenced. The lines,

Nor those horses, bright and glowing,
Dragged the Sun's refulgent form,

remind the reader of Apollo's chariot.

The seventh stanza describes Imir, the supreme creator, sitting in "lonely sadness" because earth had no intelligent inhabitants. The ninth stanza supposes Imir to perish, and his substance to form the material world. The Scripture says, at creation, "the morning stars sang together, and all the sons of God shouted for joy." In the same way the Scandinavian mythology makes *birds of the morning* celebrate the day when "God saw all that he had made, and behold it was very good."

The eleventh stanza of the song of Vala supposes that evil spirits, *foes of nature*, begin to disturb the peace of the world, as the serpent entered

the garden of Eden. The powers of good and evil
contend, and Thor bruises the head of the serpent.
A good deity destroying evil and malignant beings
is a doctrine of the Scripture—Earth shall be destroyed and its beauty renewed. The Scriptures
say, these elements " shall wax old as a garment,"
but there shall be " *a new heaven* and *a new earth*."
The Christian doctrine of retribution is clear in this
verse,

> He shall judge, and he shall sever
>   Shame from glory, ill from good;
> These shall live in light forever,
>   Those shall wade the chilling flood.

These are a few of the parallels which may be
traced between the Bible and Scandinavian mythology.

CELTIC MYTHOLOGY.

THE Celtic nations consisted of the ancient Germans, Gauls, and Britons. These nations worshipped idols, and their priests were the Druids. The
Druids were held in such veneration that the people
under their influence dared not disobey them in any
thing.

The Druids had no letters nor any costly temples.
They composed poems which they sung, and which
were taught orally. They sometimes performed
their religious ceremonies in consecrated groves.
The oak was their favourite tree; and the mistletoe, or
parasitic plant which grows upon the oak, was used
in their worship.

The sacred groves were surrounded by a ditch or
mound. In their centre was a circular area, inclosed
with one or two rows of large stones. This was
their only temple. Close to that was the Cromlech

DRUIDS.

EGYPTIAN WORSHIP

or stone of sacrifice. Human victims were frequently offered by those who laboured under disease, or
were about to go to battle. Upon important public
occasions, the Druids constructed colossal images of
wicker work ; filled them with human beings, and
consumed them, together, by fire. Criminals were
deemed the offerings most acceptable to the gods ;
but when these were wanting, innocent persons were
frequently immolated.

When the Romans possessed themselves of Britain, they abolished the Druidical priesthood. The
poor conquered Britons were excessively grieved at
this : but if the Romans did not destroy the lives of
the Druids, they were right to abolish a worship
which permitted human sacrifices : besides the loss
of one religion made the Britons feel the want of another ; and, in the first or second century, perhaps,
the Roman soldiers first brought the Christian religion into Britain, where it was cordially received,
and where, either in the Catholic or Protestant form,
it has since been cherished.

The Hell of the Druids was a region of utter darkness, which no beam of the sun, no ray of light ever
visited. There serpents stung and hissed, wolves
devoured, and lions roared. Some nations considered hell, a " fire that is not quenched," but the Druids
represented it to be a region of thick-ribbed ice,
and called it *the isle of the cold land.*

Hela was goddess of the Goths. The northern
nations of Europe, in ancient times, were so warlike,
that they esteemed the attribute of ferocious courage
and the pursuit of military glory as the chief honour
of a man ; and they held those in contempt who preferred a quiet and peaceable life to one of violence
and depredation. They believed that those who fell
in war, were conveyed, after death, to Heaven, and
quaffed nectar from the skulls of their enemies, and

that those who had loved the chase upon earth, the shades of heroes, regaled themselves in hunting the shades of stags. These northern barbarians also believed that all those who died at home of disease, or old age, were conveyed to the abode of Hela, where they pined in endless hunger and want. Hela lay upon a bed called *Koer*, which signifies *wasting* and *sickness*, and the covering was *Blikande, malediction* or *cursing*.

Who were the Celtic nations?

Had the Druids letters, and what were some of their peculiarities?

What were their temples and sacrifices?

Who abolished the Druidical priesthood, and what religion succeeded it?

What was the Hell of the Druids?

Who was Hela?

SYRIAN MYTHOLOGY.

CANAANITES, Phœnicians, and Philistines may be comprehended with the inhabitants of their adjacent territory, the Syrians. These Syrian nations kept up frequent wars with their neighbours of Palestine, the Israelites; but the hostility which prevailed between the two nations did not prevent the Hebrews from imitating the idolatries of the Syrians. For many centuries, the Hebrews had but one place of worship, and most of them being far distant from that, they adopted the worship of idols on the ' high places," in the open air.

BAAL was the chief of Syrian gods; this name only signifies *lord*. MOLOCH was another name for this same imaginary deity. Moloch was the chief divinity of the Phœnicians and other neighbouring nations, in honour of whom, human victims, principally children, were immolated. *Adonis* or Thammuz was worshipped throughout Phrygia and Syria, and his supposed death by the tusks of a wild boar was annually lamented with solemn ceremonies. *Rimmon* and Astarte, queen of heaven, the Moon, distinguished by her silver crescent, were likewise objects of worship amongst those nations.

The chief god of the Philistines was Dagon, whose statue was a figure, of which the upper part resembled a man, and the lower extremity a fish. In Syria, besides Moloch, Chemos was worshipped.

The poet Milton, in Paradise Lost, describes these Syrian gods.

Next *Moloch*, horrid king, besmeared with blood
Of human sacrifice, and parents' tears ;
Though for the noise of drums and timbrels loud,
Their children's cries unheard ; that passed through fire
To his grim idol. Him the Ammonite
Worshipped in Rabba, and her watery plain.
　Next *Chemos*, the obscene dread of Moab's sons ;
Peor, his other name. With these, in troop,
Came *Astoreth*, whom the Phœnicians call
Astarte, queen of heaven, with crescent horns :
To whose bright image, nightly by the moon,
Sidonian virgins paid their vows and songs.
———————*Thammuz*, came next behind,
Whose annual wound, in Lebanon, allured
The Syrian damsels to lament his fate.
———————————Next, came one
Who mourned in earnest, when the captive ark
Maimed his brute image ; head and hands lopped off.
Dagon his name ; sea monster ; upward man,
And downward fish ; yet had his temple high,
Reared in Azotus dreaded through the coast
Of Palestine, in Gath and Ascalon.
Him followed *Rimmon*, whose delightful seat
Was fair Damascus, on the fertile banks,
Of Abana and Pharpar, lucid streams.
———————————*The captive ark
Maimed his brute image.*

These lines concerning Dagon and the ark refer to the fourth and fifth chapters of the first book of

Samuel   There it is mentioned, that in an engagement between the Philistines and the Israelites. the
latter were defeated, and the Philistines seized upon
and carried off " the ark of God !"   This *ark* was a
chest which contained the holy books of the Israelites, and the Israeiites held it in the highest veneration.

The Philistines deposited the ark in the temple
of Dagon, but on the following morning, Dagon was
broken from his pedestal, and lay upon the earth.
As soon as they saw it prostrate, his worshippers
replaced the image ; but it was not suffered to remain ; again it fell and was dashed in pieces.   So
terrified were the Philistines at this, that their priests
dared not enter Dagon's house, or temple, and
through fear they immediately restored the ark to
the Israelitish territory.

Who were the Syrian nations, and who imitated their idolatries ?

Who was Baal, and what was his worship ?

Who was Dagon, and the other principal gods of the Philistines ?

How has Milton noticed the Syrian gods ; Moloch ; Chemos ;
Thammuz ; Dagon ?

What does the passage *captive ark*, &c. refer to ?

What effect had the presence of the ark upon the statue of
Dagon, and what became of the ark ?

EGYPTIAN WORSHIP.

See plate, page 215.

THE rites of animal worship form a striking and
distinctive feature in the religion of the ancient Egyptians.   Those who visited Egypt approached with
delight its sacred groves and splendid temples, adorned with superb vestibules and lofty porticoes.   The
walls shone with gold and silver : they were adorn-

ed with amber, and sparkled with the gems of India and Ethiopia.

But, when the stranger entered the *penetralia*, the inner apartment of the temple, and inquired for the god in whose honour the fane had been built, one of the *pastophori*, an attendant of the temple, with a solemn air would draw aside a veil which concealed the image of the divinity, and behold, a crocodile, a cat, or a serpent—a fitter inhabitant for a cavern or a bog than for a temple.

The religion of ancient Egypt is wrapt in obscurity. It bears little relation to genuine history or to poetry, and is of little use to investigate. This religion appears to have been strangely compounded of degrading superstitions and sound philosophy. And much as the Egyptians excelled other nations in the wisdom of their laws, and the perfection of their arts, they equally surpassed them in all degrading idolatries.

The inhabitants of the Thebais, a region in Upper Egypt, were said to have worshipped only the immortal, uncreated God: and for this reason to have been exempted from contributing to the maintenance of the sacred animals, adored in Lower Egypt. The sun and moon appear to have been the chief objects of Egyptian worship, under various forms and names; but the crocodile, the dog, the cat, the cow, and ox, the ibis, wolf, and other animals, and even some inanimate substances, which were first used as hieroglyphics, finally came to be objects of adoration.

It is universally agreed that the ancient Egyptians believed the human soul to be immortal. While the bodies of their deified mortals were preserved in their sepulchres, their souls were imagined to be transferred to, and to shine forth in, different stars of heaven.

· The principal Egyptian deities were Osiris, Isis,

Horus, Typhon, Serapis, Anubir, Harpocrates, with many others, known as Grecian Deities, such as Mercury, Jupiter Ammon, and Juno.

ISIS.

Osiris, the great object of the adoration of the Egyptians, was sometimes regarded as some illustrious prince in a very early age of the world. He was the supposed author of all good; in constant opposition to Typhon, the author of evil. Osiris was adored under the form of the ox Apis.

Isis, the consort of Osiris, appears to have been an emblem of the moon. She was esteemed as the cause of abundance, and regarded, like Osiris, to be one of the sources of the inundation of the Nile. The cow was her symbol. Her image was usually in the form of a woman, with cows' horns on her head.

TYPHON was the imaginary author of evil who waged perpetual war against Osiris.

HORUS or Orus, was, as well as Osiris, an emblem of the Sun. This deity, the son of Osiris and Isis, was held in great veneration in Egypt. Three cities in the Thebais were named after him. Horus was considered as the supreme lord and regulator of time ; and therefore, he was represented as the star of day.

ANUBIS was the faithful companion of Osiris and Isis, represented under the figure of a man with a dog's head.

SERAPIS was worshipped under various names and attributes, as a tutelary god of Egypt in general, and as the patron of several of its principal cities.

His image was erected in a temple, built for that purpose at Alexandria, and called the Serapeum. It is said to have exceeded in magnificence all the other temples of that age, excepting that of the capitol at Rome. This edifice was, long afterwards, destroyed by order of the Emperor Theodosius. The celebrated statue of the god was broken to pieces, and its limbs borne in triumph through the city by the Christians, and then thrown into a fire kindled in the amphitheatre.

HARPOCRATES was the god of silence and meditation : a son of Isis. The Egyptians offered to him the first fruits of the lentils and pulse. The tree called Persea was consecrated to him, because its leaves were shaped like a tongue, and the fruit like a heart. He was depicted as a naked boy, crowned with an Egyptian mitre. He held in his left hand the horn of plenty, whilst a finger of his right hand was placed upon his lip, to denote silence.

What rites were peculiar to the religion of ancient Egypt?
What objects were exhibited in Egyptian temples?
Is the mythology of Egypt of much importance to be known!

Did any of the people of Egypt acknowledge but one God; and who were the principal deities of Egypt?

Who were Osiris; Isis; Typhon; Horus; Anubis; Serapis; Harpocrates?

PERSIAN MYTHOLOGY.

The ancient religion of Iran or Persia, according to the most authentic historians, was more rational than that of most other nations of the world. It consisted in the belief of one supreme God, who formed all things by his power, and continually governs them by his providence; in pious reverence, fear, and love of him; in due respect for parents and the aged; in affection for the whole human species, and compassionate tenderness towards even the brute creation.

The ancient Persians regarded the Sun as the peculiar image of the Deity. They represented him by certain fires esteemed holy, and kept in temples to be worshipped. The sacred fire was kindled by concentrated sunbeams.

Priests took charge of the sacred fires in Persia, and they were also instructors of youth. These priests were often wise men, and well-informed. These were the Magi, sometimes called Magicians. They were Magi, mentioned in the New Testament as *wise men from the east*, who visited the infant Jesus.

Besides adoring the sun, the ancient Persians worshipped the moon and the stars. Temples were dedicated to them; images of them were invented, and magnificent festivals and processions instituted to their honour.

The religion of Persia became corrupted, and it was reformed by a philosopher named Zoroaster. He prepared a book of doctrines and of regulations for worship. This book is the Zend-Avesta.

This reformed religion of Persia continued in force till that country was subdued by the Mussulmans, who by violence established Islamism, or Mohammedanism, which is the prevalent system, at present; though numbers still preserve their ancient faith. These are called Parsees, or Guebres.

Orosmades or Oromazes, was the name given to the Supreme Creator, by the Persian Mythology He was adored as the author and principle of good.

It was presumed by the worshippers of Orosmades, that he was at constant war with a wicked being called Arimanius; that Arimanius was always endeavouring to make men wicked and miserable, and that Orosmades willed them to be virtuous and happy. Zoroaster described Orosmades, as residing in the midst of a pure and divine fire which fills the immensity of space.

The ancient Persians regarded it as impious to pretend to form visible images of Orosmades, or to erect temples to his honour, with the idea of him making them his dwelling-place. They venerated fire as his sacred emblem ; the sun as his image ; and their worship of him consisted in bloodless sacrifices and simple rites.

MITHRAS was a deity of the Persians, supposed to signify the sun ; and inferior to Orosmades, but perfectly benevolent. Mithras was represented by Zoroaster as seated next the throne of Orosmades, surrounded by an infinite multitude of genii, of different ranks and various orders, who presided over the divisions of time, the succession of the seasons, and the various operations of the natural world.

It was believed that the good gods, Orosmades and Mithras, would finally defeat Arimanius, that wars and vices would cease, and that all mankind would become good and happy.

This doctrine, and the Persian worship, has been described by an English poet thus :

> ————————————Robed in purest white
> The Magi ranged before the unfolded tent.
> Fire blazed beside them.　Towards the sacred flame
> They turned, and sent their tuneful praise to heaven.
> From Zoroaster was the song derived,
> Who, on the hills of Persia, from his cave,
> By flowers environed and melodious founts,
> Which soothed the solemn mansion, had revealed,
> How Oromazes, radiant source of good,
> Original, immortal, framed the globe
> In fruitfulness and beauty.
> 　　　　　　　　　How with stars,
> By him the heavens were spangled ; how the sun,
> Refulgent Mithras, purest spring of light,
> And genial warmth, whence teeming nature smiles,
> Burst from the east, at his creating voice ;
> When straight beyond the golden verge of day,
> Night showed the horrors of her distant reign,
> Where black and hateful Arimanius frowned,
> The author foul of evil : How, with shades
> From his dire mansion, he deformed the works
> Of Oromazes ; turned to noxious heat
> The solar beam, that foodful earth might parch,
> That streams exhaling might forsake their beds,
> Whence, pestilence and famine.
> 　　　　　　　　　How the power
> Of Oromazes in the human breast
> Benevolence and equity infused,
> Truth, temperance, and wisdom, sprung from heaven ;
> When Arimanius blackened all the soul
> With falsehood and injustice, with desires
> Insatiable ; with violence and rage,
> Malignity and folly.　If the hand
> Of Oromazes, on precarious life
> Shed wealth and pleasure, swift the infernal god,
> With wild excess, or avarice, blasts the joy.
> But yet at last, shall Arimanius fall
> Before his might, and evil be no more. *Glover's Leonidas.*

What is the character of the ancient religion of Persia ?
What among the Persians was the symbol of the deity ?

Who were the ancient Magi?

Did the Persians worship other objects besides the Sun and Moon?

Who reformed the religion in Persia?

Did the Persians believe in more than one governing power in the universe?

Was Mithras a benevolent deity?

How has an English poet described the worship of the Persians?

RELIGION OF THE MEXICANS.

RELIGION is a sentiment which is cherished in the bosom of all men: for it is not an established fact that any people discovered by civilized men have been found entirely destitute of the belief of a superior power which created mankind, to whom men lift up their thoughts, and to whom, in some form or other, worship is offered.

Among the nations of the western hemisphere, previously to the discovery of the continent by Europeans, the Mexicans were the most highly civilized: and it is a truth exhibited in the history of all nations, that the more improved men are in the arts and comforts of life, the more *intelligent* they are. *Intelligence* is the power of thought and reflection. Men must think much before they can do any thing. A house cannot be built, or a garment made without much thought concerning it.

If men are compelled to think much in order to make themselves comfortable, and to employ their hands skilfully, they will meditate upon the objects around them. They will admire the sun, and moon, the earth, and all that grows upon it; and they will inquire who made and takes care of the world they inhabit—who gave them every comfort—who made man, and gave him the power to think and feel, and also what becomes of the soul after death. Thus the most intelligent become the most religious people.

Having heard, from the revelations of God to the first men, some imperfect accounts that God had long ago declared himself to his creatures, savages describe that God as many gods, and fancy that the warm sun. and the mild moon, or the refreshing waters, are themselves gods, or that there are gods who live in the sun, moon, and ocean, to take care of them, and to make them useful to man ; so that ignorant men worship the things which are made, instead of him who made them.

In time they give names to these false gods, add stories of virtuous men, to those that have been related of the gods, and call these virtuous men gods also. To honour the gods properly, it is necessary to have priests to celebrate them, temples to worship them in, and particular days on which people shall leave their labour, and go together to offer prayers and praises to the giver of all they possess.

The Hebrews in Asia were, without doubt, the only nation which, before the birth of Christ, preserved the knowledge of the true God : but it is curious to compare the history of God's people and their worship, with that of the heathens ; and curious also to compare heathen nations with each other. There are many particulars in which the Greek mythology resembled the history related in the Bible, and many others in which the religion of the Asiatics and North American savages resemble the fables of the Greeks and Romans.

The Bible relates the history of the Deluge or flood ; it also gives the history of Samson, and the sacrifice of Jephthah's daughter. The Greeks had a fable that the world had been drowned; that a good man and woman, Deucalion and Pyrrha, survived, and that their descendants peopled the earth. The

MEXICAN ALTAR.

MEXICAN PRIEST.

Greek Hercules was a man of irresistible strength, and performed wonders like the Hebrew Samson. Jephthah, a Hebrew general, offered his daughter tc his god; and Agamemnon, the Greek chief, sacrificed his daughter Iphigenia to Diana. These are only a few of the *analogies* which may be found between true and false religions.

The Romans celebrate the reign of Saturn, and call the time of his government the Golden Age; and they honoured his memory, because he loved peace and detested war, and taught his subjects to be industrious, and to love one another. The ancient Mexicans had a Golden Age, which was commenced under the instructions of a good king, who kept his people in peace and order, and they worshipped him after his death as their benefactor. The Mexicans could never have heard of Saturn: but people honour their benefactors sooner or later everywhere; and this *analogous fact* serves to show how much men of all countries resemble one another.

Are there any people on earth without some religion?

People of what character are the most religious?

What objects first dispose men to religious thought?

What worship do ignorant men first practise?

What are the first religious services?

Does the religion of ancient Greece resemble that of other nations?

Does *fabulous history* afford any facts analogous to those recorded in *sacred history*?

Does the mythology of the Mexicans in any respect resemble that of ancient Rome?

THE Mexicans had no writings, but they represented their religion, as well as their history, by hiero-glyphic paintings. The Spaniards, who discovered them, saw their worship and studied their traditions.
–thus we are informed concerning them. The

Roman gods were less pure in their actions than those of the Mexicans, but the Mexican worship was not so innocent as the Roman, for it was cruel—it required human sacrifices, and they were accounted happy who were thus offered to the gods.

The Mexicans, like the Greeks and Romans, believed in the immortality of the soul. They called Heaven the House of the Sun. They worshipped the sun as a god, by a name which signified the Prince of Glory. Music, dancing, the praises of the gods, and the pleasant society of each other, according to their belief, formed the eternal happiness of the good.

The Mexicans did not confine the blessed to the House of the Sun; they supposed that after a time, they might explore the whole universe—sometimes as birds of beautiful feathers and sweet songs, and sometimes as ethereal spirits borne on light clouds, or that they were permitted to descend once more to earth, to warble heavenly music and inhale the perfume of flowers.

The Mexicans believed also in the *transmigration of souls*, that is, that the souls of dead men animated the bodies of inferior beings; honourable men becoming horses and noble quadrupeds; while mean persons were metamorphosed to bats, beetles, and disgusting reptiles.

The Greeks were taught such a doctrine by one of their philosophers, Pythagoras: they called it the Metempsychosis, and many others professed to believe it. Some of the Hindus believe in the Metempsychosis to this day.

The Mexicans had thirteen principal gods, besides the god Teotl. Teotl was a purely spiritual divinity, supreme, immortal, and invisible. He was infinitely deserving of love and praise, and could be represented by no image.

The god held next in reverence, was TEZ-CAT-LI-PO-CA, or Shining Mirror. He was represented as always young, and was the god of justice; assigning rewards to the good, and punishments to the evil. Sacred stones were placed in the streets of Mexico, for this god to rest upon: and no mortal dared to sit upon them.

The principal image of Shining Mirror was of black marble, richly dressed. The ears were adorned with golden rings, and the breast covered with plates of the same metal. In the left hand, this image held a golden fan, highly polished like a mirror, and set around with gay feathers; and in it, the worshipper of the god fancied that he saw reflected all that happened in the world.

Had the ancient Mexicans letters, and did their worship resemble that of Rome?

How did the Mexicans describe Heaven?

What did they presume was the condition of good and evil men after death?

What is the *transmigration* of souls?

What did the Greeks term this doctrine, who taught it among them, and what people now believe in it?

How many principal divinities were acknowledged by the Mexicans, and who was the chief?

Who was the Mexican god of justice?

How is Tez-cat-li-po-ca described?

How was the image of Tez-cat-li-po-ca described?

———

THE Greeks had a fable, that all the elements which form the universe; that is, fire, earth, air, and water, once lay in a vast mass of confusion, in which there was no light, nor any living thing. This condition of the elements they called Chaos.

The Mexicans held a tradition not unlike this; it was, that the whole world was once involved in night, though men existed in the darkness. In this state, while some of the desolate inhabitants on the

earth, were standing around a fire, one person suddenly declared, that he who should throw himself
into the flames would be transformed to light itself.
Two men, upon this, immediately precipitated
themselves into the fire, and afterwards appeared in
the heavens as the sun and moon.

QUET-ZAL-COT, or Feathered Serpent, was the god
of the air. This god was, like the Saturn of the
Romans, a great improver of rude men. He invented the working of metals, and polishing of
gems; displayed profound wisdom in laws which
he made, and an excellent example in his conduct.
Quet-zal-cot also taught the art of dying cotton, and
of producing corn. Under this wise and beneficent
government, the Mexicans became rich and happy.

In the midst of this prosperity of the Mexicans,
Tez-cat-li-po-ca (Shining Mirror) contrived to banish
Quet-zal-cot, as Jupiter banished Saturn. He appeared to Quet-zal-cot, and offered him immortality,
(for Quet-zal-cot was then mortal,) if he would
drink of a certain beverage which Shining Mirror
presented to him, and then remove himself to
another kingdom, called Tla-pal-la.

Having drunk the beverage, Quet-zal-cot felt inclined to quit Mexico. He accordingly left the
country, but never reached Tlapalla. He was
stopped on his way at the city of Cholula, where
the inhabitants, charmed with his gracious manners,
persuaded him to remain with them; and there,
abhorring all cruelty, and the very name of war, he
taught all the arts of peace, besides many religious
ceremonies, which the Cholulans ever after observed.

The Cholulans could give no account of their
benefactor's death, but that he disappeared from
among them. After his disappearance, temples in
honour of Quet-zal-cot were erected; and he re-

ceived divine honours at Cholula, and at Mexico,—
people of distant provinces repairing thither to offer
their devotions.

What did the Greeks understand by Chaos?

Had the Mexicans a similar fable, and how did they account
for the origin of the sun and moon?

Who was the Mexican god of air, and whom did he resemble?

Who enticed Quet-zal-cot from Mexico?

Whither did Quet-zal-cot go?

How was the memory of Quet-zal-cot honoured?

TLALOC (master of paradise) was the Mexican
god of water. The Mexicans called him fertiliser
of the earth. His abode was on the summit of
high mountains, which are the sources of rivers;
and the people often resorted to mountains, to celebrate his worship.

Tlaloc ruled over some inferior water gods, who,
like the Naiades of the Greeks, presided over rivu-
lets and fountains. Tlaloc was also associated with
a goddess of water, who divided with him the charge
of that useful element, without which animal life
could not be for a moment sustained.

CENTEOT, or she who supports us, was the Ceres
of Mexico, the goddess of fertile fields and of harvest. This goddess had a multitude of priests employed in her worship, and was universally beloved,
because she required no human sacrifices, but was
content with hares and doves.

The Mexicans worshipped a god and goddess of
hell. These were supposed to inhabit a region of
utter darkness; and their rites were performed in
the night.

JO-AL-TI-CIT was the goddess of cradles. To her
protection, they commended their sleeping children.

Three gods of war were worshipped by the different tribes of Mexico; the chief of these, Mex-it-li, was more honoured than any of the gods of Mexico. The Mexicans offered to him the greatest number of human sacrifices.

Three great sacrifices to this god were made every year. These North American savages, besides these gods, had a goddess of hunting, a god of fishing, a goddess of salt, another of drugs, and a god of wine. IX-LIL-TOT, the god of physic, had a temple, to which sick children were carried, in order to be cured of their diseases. The fathers accompanied these children, and taught them how to pray to the god. If the children were able, they were made to dance before the image of the god; and after that ceremony, some consecrated water, which had been blessed by the priest, was given to be drunk as a medicine.

COAT-LI-CUE, the goddess of flowers, had a temple in Mexico. Baskets and bunches of flowers, and beautiful wreaths were brought to the temple by the votaries of this Mexican Flora; who attended the festivals in which she was celebrated.

A god of mirth, one of gold and of merchants, a mother of all the gods, like Cybele, and the *Tep-it-o-tone*, (or little ones;) the same as the Penates, make up the chief objects of the Mexican *polytheism*. The images of the Penates were kept in every house. The kings and great lords kept six of these images, the nobles four, and the lower people two.

The number of these gods, besides those which have been briefly noticed, was very great; and little clay images of them, found by the Spaniards in the woods, houses, temples, and streets of Mexico, were almost infinitely multiplied.

Who was Tlaloc?
Over whom did he preside, and with whom was he associated?

Who was the Mexican Ceres?
Who ruled in the Mexican Hell?
To whom did parents commend children?
Had the Mexicans gods, whom they praised for their pleasures and comfort, and did they worship a god of Physic?
Who was the goddess of flowers?
Had the Mexicans still other gods?
Did the Mexicans possess many images of their gods?

THE Mexicans prayed to their gods either kneeling, or prostrate. Sacrifices, vows, oaths, fasts, and penances were practised by them. All the heathens attached great reverence to the sanctity of an oath. When the gods of Greece swore by the Styx, their word was given, and they dared not depart from it.

When a Mexican *took an oath*, that is, when he made a solemn promise or declared an important truth, he would say, " Does not Mexitli (or any other god) behold me now;" and kissing his hand, he touched the earth with it. His declaration was believed. Who, thought those around him, would dare profane the name of God?

Temples to the gods were erected in all the inhabited country of Mexico. The city of Mexico was commenced, by the building of the temple of Mexitli, at first a miserable hovel. When the city had become populous and rich, this sanctuary was rebuilt with great labour and cost. According to Cortes, the Spanish conqueror of Mexico, it occupied a space sufficient for five hundred houses, and was surrounded by a wall built of stone and lime. The stones of its pavements were wrought to an exquisite polish. It had four gates, fronting east, west, north, and south; contained altars for sacrifices, and was adorned by figures of huge stone serpents.

The temples of the Mexicans were surrounded

by a space for dances and ceremonies, in the open air : near the temples, were houses for the accommodation of strangers who came to worship. There were likewise, reservoirs of water, in which the priests performed their ablutions, and a *consecrated* fountain, from which they drank. Not far from the temples, were buildings, in which the heads of hu man victims offered in the sacrifices were preserved The number of these heads in one collection amounted to one hundred and thirty-six thousand

The Spaniards, at the time of the discovery, supposed that the empire of Mexico contained as many as forty thousand temples ; and besides these, upon the tops of the hills, and in the woods, were erected altars in the open air, for the worship of the mountain gods, and other rural deities.

The priests of Mexico were numerous and rich. Great tracts of land were set apart for their maintenance. The upper classes of the people consecrated their children in infancy, to the more honourable of the temple services ; and the lower orders offered theirs as hewers of wood, and drawers of water : all considering the worship of the gods as the highest honour to which they could aspire.

MEXICAN PRIESTS.
See plate, page 229.

ALL the offices of religion were divided among the Mexican priesthood. Some were diviners, and some were sacrificers ; some composed hymns, and others sung them. Some of the priests kept the temples clean, and to others belonged the care of educating the younger priests, the ordering of the festivals, and the care of the mythological paintings.

Four times a day, the Mexicans offered incense to their idols, and they had censers in all their houses, to use in their domestic devotions. Females were some.imes devoted to the priestly function from their infancy. As soon as the destined girl was born, her parents offered her to some god, and in two months she was carried to the temple, where a small broom, and an equally small censer was placed in her little hands, to denote that at a future time she should sweep the sacred floors and offer incense in the temple. At a suitable age, the Mexican priestess was permitted to marry. The cruelty of the Mexicans in their worship is detestable, and sorry as one may feel for the misfortunes which they have experienced under the dominion of the Spaniards, the abolition of human sacrifices, and the introduction of Christianity into their country, must be accounted a change for the better.

How did the Mexicans exhibit their veneration of the gods ?
Were temples numerous in Mexico ?
What surrounded the Mexican temples ?
Were there temples in the open country of Mexico
Were many persons employed in temple service ?
Were the functions of religious service numerous ?
How were females consecrated to the priestly office ?
Has the Spanish conquest of Mexico produced happy results ?

RELIGION OF THE PERUVIANS.

The Peruvians are said to have worshipped the sun, moon, and the sea, under different names. They did not practise the barbarous rites of the Mexicans, but they devoted young women to the services of the Sun, and these were called the Virgins of the Sun.

RELIGION OF GREECE.

According to the Greek poet Pindar, the twelve principal divinities were introduced into Greece

from Egypt. When the Greeks began to make laws
for the preservation of society, it was enacted at
Athens, that no foreign deity should be worshipped
in that city, without a decree of the Areopagus.
The Areopagus was a court of justice.

Hesiod, one of the ancient Greek authors, says, that
the Greeks worshipped almost innumerable deities.
" There are," says this authority, " thirty thousand
gods inhabiting the earth, who are subjects of Jupiter and guardians of men."

Because Socrates said that his GENIUS inspired
him, his enemies accused him of worshipping an un-
acknowledged deity, and he suffered death upon this
accusation. Those who are familiar with the book
of Acts, will remember that St. Paul saw at Athens
an altar inscribed to an *unknown God*. Upon this,
Paul, addressing himself to those about him, said :
" Whom ye ignorantly worship, him declare I unto
you," &c. When he preached to them concerning
Jesus and the resurrection, the Athenians, jealous
of a new deity, carried Paul to the Areopagus, that
he might give an account of his doctrines ; but from
that day, the old dark superstition vanished slowly
away before the light of the new truth.

About this time, the law against foreign deities
had fallen into neglect at Athens ; for the gods of
Thrace and Phrygia had obtained a place among the
ancient divinities. The philosophers ridiculed the
gods, and at the theatres they were sometimes mentioned with contempt.

The utmost reverence, however, was shown for
the images of the gods. Alcibiades was obliged to
fly for his life, because he was only suspected of ir-
reverence to the images of Mercury. A child suffered death because it accidentally picked up a golden
olive leaf from the wreath of Minerva, and played
ith it.

The Persians, *not thinking the gods to be of human shape, as did the Greeks*, made no images, and worshipped in the open air, conceiving that God's house and temple was the whole world. All the ancient nations held high mountains in reverence. An English poet says :—

"High mountains are a feeling—"

He means, they inspire a feeling of veneration, and make us think of God, who laid their foundation in the beginning ; who lifted their lofty heads to his own heaven, and who has fixed the everlasting hills that they cannot be removed.

The temples of the Greeks were placed in the woods, upon the mountains, or upon the Acropolis, an eminence in a city ; and some stood by a river's or a fountain's side. The temples in the country were usually surrounded by trees, or sacred groves, which were supposed to be honoured by the immediate presence of the tutelar or guardian deity of the place.

Wherever the temple stood, if practicable, it was made to front the rising sun—the image of the god standing in the middle of the temple, and the worshippers facing the west. The temple of Jerusalem faced the *east*. The different apartments of all temples were the *holy* and the *profane*. Into the former the priests only could enter at all times. Besides these, was the *treasury*, or depository of money, of offerings, and of holy vessels used in the temple services.

The objects which are adored by heathens, appeared to be beautiful or unadorned, according to the knowledge and wealth of the people who worship them. The *Mexicans* worshipped before great masses of stone ; and the Achaians, among the Greeks, kept religiously thirty square stones on

which were engraved the names of so many gods
without any *effigy*—any sculptured figure.   When
sculpture was invented, it was used to represent the
gods ; and when the Greeks arrived at perfection in
the arts, they produced such images as the Apollo,
Venus, and Jupiter Capitolinus, which still remain
to be admired in museums and collections.

The Greeks were an intolerant *people*, how did they manifest
it ?

Who suffered death for the charge of *sacrilege*, and how did
the Athenians receive the preaching of St. Paul ?

What at this time was the public opinion in respect to the
ancient religion ?

How did the Athenians regard the images of their gods ?

Did the pagans revere mountains, and why ?

How did the temple stand, and what were the different apartments ?

What were the first images of idolatry ?

PRIESTS are the ministers of religion in all countries and ages of the world.   It is the business of
Christian ministers, to teach wisdom and virtue, as
well as to perform the ceremonies of religious worship.   Our religion teaches us to " add to our virtue,
knowledge ;" and our ministers are bound to teach
both.   Among the Greeks, the philosophers taught
men their duty.

Paganism offered men no instruction ; it consisted
of prayers, sacrifices, and purifications.   Public
prayers were offered for the safety of the state, and
its allies, for the preservation of the fruits of the
earth, for rain, and for deliverance from pestilence
and famine.

The following prayer is found in the writings of
Plato, and was a tradition from some more ancient
author: " O thou, who art the king of Heaven, grant
us what is useful to us ; whether we ask it, or

whether we ask it not! Refuse us what would be hurtful to us. even if we should ask it."

Priests are held in high honour among all nations. In Greece, the priesthood was a numerous order, consisting of both sexes; and the priests were sometimes civil magistrates likewise. The Greek priests were permitted to marry. In Homer, Chryses, the priest of Apollo, appears before Agamemnon, and implores the restoration of his daughter Chryseis.

The Hebrew priests were required to be without any personal blemish; and the high-priest to be richly attired. (Ex. ch. xxix.) The chief priests of the Hebrews were all descended from Aaron. They were solemnly consecrated to their office, and presided at the feasts, sacrifices, and prayers offered up at the public worship.

The priests expounded the civil law, and were assisted in their observances by the Levites. The Levites were appointed to wait on the priests, to keep the temple and the holy vessels in order, and to assist at the sacrifices.

The Greek priests, like those of the true God, were men of a good constitution, and, indeed, preferred for their beauty. Their dress was graceful and imposing, and suitable to the deity they served.

The priestess of Ceres appeared crowned with poppies and ears of corn; that of Minerva, was armed like "the martial maid" herself, in the ægis, the cuirass, and buckler.

Under the Greek priests, was the Neocoros, whose business was to superintend the decoration and cleanliness of the temple, besides sacrificers, soothsayers, and heralds. Soothsayers, or diviners, pretend to foretell future events. Heralds accompanied all processions, and announced to the people the ceremonies that were to be observed.

Who are priests?

What were the prayers of the Pagans?

What ancient prayer has been preserved?

Were the Greek priests numerous?

To what rules were the Hebrew priests subject?

Who assisted them in the discharge of their functions?

What analogies may be perceived between the Greek and Hebrew priesthood?

Who assisted the Athenian priests in their solemn services?

RELIGION OF THE ROMANS.

ETRURIA was the country of Italy, which was the earliest civilized. It is conjectured that a colony of Phœnicians settled there at a period of the same date with the first emigration of the Phœnicians into Greece; and if that be true, the same religion would naturally be cherished in both countries.

Eneas, eleven centuries before Christ, found an Arcadian people in Italy, and they too had carried thither the religion, which supposes that the primitive God of the Greeks, Saturn, took refuge in the Ausonian land, (Italy.)

The religion of the Romans appears to have been that of Greece—a mixture of Syrian and Egyptian fables. The *principal gods* of both people were the same; the demi-gods, or deified men, might have been a little different; because the Romans more readily admitted the *apotheosis* of *heroes*, and were more *tolerant* than the Greeks.

In the latter ages of Rome, after the conquest of Greece, (B. C. 146,) Rome itself and the chief cities of the provinces were adorned with statues and temples, in honour of the gods of Greece. The most celebrated temples of Rome were the Capitol, or temple of Jupiter Capitolinus, and the Pantheon.

The Capitol stood upon the Capitoline hill. This

PANTHEON.

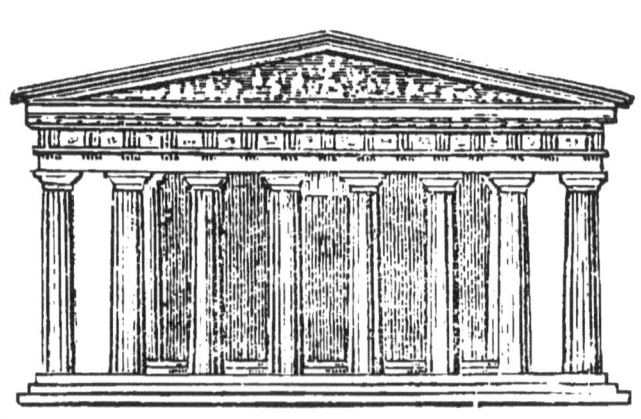

PARTHENON.

celebrated structure was erected by the King Tarquinius Priscus. It occupied four acres of ground, and was approached by an ascent of a hundred steps. During the civil wars, the Capitol was twice destroyed. The last Capitol was raised by the Emperor Domitian; it was afterwards converted into a Christian church; and modern travellers still visit this celebrated monument of antiquity.

PANTHEON.

THE Pantheon is of a later origin than the Capitol. It was built by Marcus Agrippa, son-in-law of Augustus. There are no windows in this edifice. The name Pantheon signifies the temple of *all the gods*. The Pantheon still exists as a catholic church, dedicated to St. Mary and All Saints. It is known at Rome as the Rotonda. It was formerly entered by an ascent of twelve steps; but the surface of modern Rome is so much elevated above that of the ancient city, that this building is below the common level; and those who visit the church, must *descend* a flight of stairs to the entrance.

The consecration of temples was solemnly observed by the Romans. Tacitus describes the ceremony nearly thus: " Upon the 21st of July, being a clear day, the ground upon which the temple was to be raised, was bound by garlands of flowers and fillets. Persons who had *lucky names*, (according to the superstition of the age,) first entered the enclosure with boughs in their hands, taken from those *trees which the gods delighted in.* (Minerva was supposed to prefer the olive, and Apollo the laurel, &c.) Next followed the vestals, attended by boys and girls whose parents were living. These sprinkled pure water on the ground.

"A magistrate, attended by one of the priests,
offered a sacrifice, and humbly besought Jupiter,
Juno, and Minerva, to prosper this holy undertaking; entreating that the divine mercy would ac•
complish what human piety had begun. This prayer
being concluded, a great company, consisting of
priests, senators, knights, and common people, laid
hold of ropes, to which was fastened a large stone,
this, with many lively expressions, was drawn by
their united force to a trench which had been marked
in the soil, for the reception of the foundation stones
in the wall; into this trench, wedges of gold and
silver were first thrown, and the corner-stone was
then deposited, amidst the rejoicings of the people."
A custom like this, of offering prayers, and laying
the first stone of a house of worship with expressions of veneration and joy, is common, at the present time, among Christians.

The memorable fact, that "groves were God's
first temples," is found in the history of all primitive people. "*Trees*, in the old time, served for
the temples of the gods," said a Latin historian.
Dodona's oaks were honoured as the residence of
Jupiter; the ancient Syrians seduced God's people
to their mode of worship; the ancient Germans,
according to Tacitus, worshipped in sacred groves
in the open air; the Druids of Britain observed the
same custom; and the Indians of Asia and America
acknowledged the divinity in the thick shade. The
Romans, after their temples became numerous and
magnificent, still kept up this ancient custom; and
in many parts of the city might be seen Iuci, or
groups of trees, consecrated to some god.

How happened the religion of Italy to be the same as that
of the Greeks?

In what respects might the religion of Greece and Rome
differ; and what were the chief temples of the city of Rome?

Whare, and what was the Capitol?

What was the Pantheon?

How did the Romans remarkably express their veneration for places of worship?

Were religious services performed at the first commencement of edifices for religious uses?

Before the erection of costly temples, what were the places of worship?

THE Romans placed great confidence in *soothsayers* and *auguries*. Soothsayers were persons who pretended to foresee future events; and they discerned these events in certain appearances of things. The soothsayers declared that thunder, lightning, and comets expressed the will of the gods. They also maintained, that motions and chattering of birds intimated what might happen; and these signs, when favourable, were called *auspices;* and when unfavourable, *portents*.

An *auspicious* day is one that promises some happiness. We say a *portentous* cloud, or a *portentous* appearance, we mean a cloud that threatens a destructive storm, or an appearance of some danger.

The flight of birds was divided (by the Romans) into *dexter* and *sinister*, right and left; the former being esteemed *fortunate;* the latter, *unlucky*. If a man, commencing a journey, saw a flock of birds flying in the right hand direction, it was a good *omen*, and foreshowed to him a prosperous adventure; but if the birds took a contrary course, an evil *presage* took hold of his imagination; and he was thrown, by his foolish superstition, into apprehension of some calamity.

Other animals, besides birds, exhibited *good* and *bad* signs; and some inconsiderate circumstances, sneezing, spilling salt, hearing strange voices, were deemed *lucky* and *unlucky*. The art of explaining all these to the credulous and ignorant people, who believed in their mysterious import, was *Augury;* and the *Augurs,* or explainers of mysteries, were respectable men at Rome, and were held in honour by the people.

Divination, or augury, was practised upon chickens kept in a coop for that purpose. Their manner of eating, and of fluttering about their food, was thought to promise happiness or disappointment. Besides the Augurs at Rome, were Haruspices; these persons were commissioned to examine the dead bodies of victims offered in the sacrifices; and to tell by certain marks, what mischance or success was about to happen to the sacrificers, or to the Roman people.

At Rome, were several distinct orders or *colleges* of priests; as the *college* of *Augurs,* of *Pontifices,* &c.

Numa, the second King of Rome, was the principal founder of these orders. They were only few in number, sometimes not more than fifteen persons in an order. The Flamines, Sodales, and Salii, were of them.

The most distinguished of the priests at Rome, were the Pontifices; their duty was to appoint the public worship, to order the sacrifices and festivals, and to punish inferior priests, and the vestal virgins, if they were guilty of any crime. The high-priest of this order was almost as much venerated as the modern Pope of Rome.

So much was religion honoured in the person of priests, that it was said, the liberty of the commonwealth, the virtue of the people, the safety of the citizens, and the honour of the gods were committed to their guardianship.

Cæsar Augustus, and others of the emperors thought proper, in order to exalt the public respect for themselves, to assume the office of Pontifex Maximus, or chief priest.

The Roman history represents the great men of that nation as eminent for wisdom and courage: admirable as warriors, and orators; and distinguished, in their most civilized state, for love of arts, and for magnificent works.   But their superstition, and ignorance of God's character and will, ought to diminish our adoration of them; and make us grateful, that the revelation in which we are instructed in this our day exalts us to the higher excellence of Christian faith and Christian virtue, and relieves us from a burdensome worship, and from fears and error.

What were soothsayers?

What is an *auspicious* day, &c.?

What was the *lucky* or unlucky flight of birds?

Were many unimportant circumstances superstitiously regarded by the Romans?

How did the Romans sometimes regard chickens, and who were the Haruspices?

Were there three distinct orders of priests at Rome?

Who were the Pontifices?

How was the *sacerdotal* or priestly character considered at Rome?

Have we reason to rejoice that we are born in the present age?

SIBYLS.

The Sibyls were virgin prophetesses, held in honour by the Romans.   They were probably fictitious beings; or traditions of some real women. entirely altered from the original fact.   The princi pal were the Delphic, the Erythrean, and Cumeal. Sibyls.

In the Roman history, frequent mention is made of the Sibylline *oracles*.   These were books kept, or pretended to be kept, in the temple of Jupiter Capitolinus, which were committed to the care of certain persons, who, when a difficult enterprise was to be undertaken, affected to consult them, and to find in them directions of what was best to be done

The fabulous origin of the Sibylline books is this In the reign of Tarquin II., a woman came to Rome, and brought nine books to the king, demanding for them certain pieces of gold. Tarquin refused the price; the woman departed from him, burnt three of the books, returned with six, and still demanded the price.

Tarquin refused the Sibyl, for such she was, her demand, and she left him a second time : still she returned again, having but three books, for she had burnt three of the six, and still she demanded the original price. Tarquin, moved by her importunity, applied to the augurs for instruction how to act.

The augurs, after some mysterious consultations, told Tarquin that he had been guilty of impiety in refusing a gift from the gods ; and they commanded him to give whatever the woman required. Upon this, Tarquin purchased the books, and was informed by the augurs, that they contained oracles concerning the future state of Rome. The woman immediately disappeared, and was never seen more.

Who were the Sibyls ?
What were the Sibylline oracles ?
What was the origin of the Sibylline books ?
How did Tarquin treat the Sibyl ?
What instructions did the augurs give Tarquin in respect to the Sibylline books ?

TEMPLES.

TEMPLES were places of worship, constructed of costly materials, of beautiful proportions, and often adorned with exquisite sculpture. The temples contained a statue, or image of the god or goddess, to whose worship it was consecrated. The interior part was entered by the priests only. The apartment at the entrance of the temple was called the *vestibule;* and was open to the worshippers.

The *altar*, somewhat like a table, was an ornamental structure, before which prayers were offered, and upon which sacrifices were laid. An altar, when men worshipped in the open air, was only a pile of turf, or of stones. *Incense* was a fragrant substance burned in the worship of the ancients, in a vessel called a *censer*. To express the deepest humiliation they sometimes knelt, and sometimes prostrated themselves in their prayers. All temples and inferior places of worship were held in reverence. Whenever the Romans passed a temple, they kissed the hand, in token of respect for a sacred place.

Besides the temples and images of the gods, pillars and solitary altars were held in reverence by the nations of antiquity. A pillar would be erected where some extraordinary mercy or deliverance had occurred In the twenty-eighth chapter of Genesis, it is related, that in a dream, Jacob saw a vision of God, which promised him many blessings; and awaking, he felt the presence of his Maker.—"And Jacob rose up early in the morning, and took the stone which he had put for his pillow, and set it up for a pillar, and poured oil upon the top of it." Afterwards, he says, "This stone which I have set for a pillar, shall be *God's house.*" Doubtless, all who came that way knew what had happened there, and stopping, worshipped at the place which Jacob had called "the gate of heaven." In a similar manner, Catholic Christians sometimes erect a cross, or an image of a saint at a fountain, or by a way-side, to remind the passer-by of the sentiments of piety and gratitude.

Temples and altars both were places of refuge for the guilty, and for the unfortunate, who might be innocently persecuted. The altar was often adorned with horns. A man being accused of a crime or having committed one, would seek some altar, and lay his hands upon the horns; or he would enter a temple, and when his pursuers overtook him, 'hey would not tear him from those places. Sometimes the criminal would not be suffered to escape from his asylum, and was thus famished to death.

Besides the protection afforded to the wicked and the outcast by the temple and the altar, private hospitality was sometimes allowed to act against the laws. *Banishment* was a punishment frequently inflicted upon innocent persons, by the Greeks. The exiled person was driven from his house, and was forced to entreat compassion from strangers. Such an unfortunate man would enter a strange house, and without uttering a word, would sit down among the ashes upon the *hearth*, and by his looks express his forlorn condition; and thus appeal to the pity of the family which surrounded him. The *hearth* was sacred to Vesta, and the household gods. The *sacred hearth* is a common expression. The master of a house would not drag from his hearth the unhappy exile who entreated his protection.

What are temples?
What were altars and their uses?
Were other places of worship, besides temples, held in reverence by the ancients: and does any Christian custom resemble this?
Were temples and altars ever made use of, as asylums for the guilty and the unfortunate?
Was private hospitality among the ancients ever permitted to afford protection to criminals?

THE most celebrated temples of the Greeks were those of Apollo, at Delphi; the Parthenon, in honour of Minerva, at Athens; and that of Diana, at Ephesus. The temple of Delphi was chiefly enriched by those who consulted the oracle—the rich. who lived all over the *Greek empire*. The

Greek empire signifies, wherever the Greeks had established colonies. and founded cities, and transmitted their laws and their language, and extended their commerce; this was from Massilia (Marseilles) in Gaul, to the eastern limits of the Euxine sea, all along the European and Asiatic coasts of the Mediterranean, and on the north coast of Asia Minor.

The votaries of Apollo, all who sought knowledge from the Pythia, bestowed tripods, tables, cups, shields, crowns, and statues of gold and silver, upon the temple; and, according to the most authentic computation, the value of these offerings in their largest accumulation, before they were rifled by the conquerers of Greece, amounted to 5,000,000 of dollars. The Roman Emperor Nero carried off at once from Delphi, five hundred statues of brass, partly of gods, and partly of illustrious men.

PARTHENON.

See plate, page 245.

THE PARTHENON is the chief boast of the Greek architecture. It was situated on the Acropolis of Athens; and even in its present state of dilapidation, is accounted the most magnificent ornament of that city. The accomplished Pericles first designed the Parthenon, as a suitable dwelling-place for the "august Athena;" the favourite goddess of all Attica. The architects of the Parthenon were Callicrates and Ictinus.

The Parthenon was about two hundred and eighteen feet in length, and ninety-eight feet, six inches in width. This temple is of white marble, of the Doric order, the columns fluted, and without bases; the number in front, eight. The story of the birth of Minerva was carved on the front pediment, and on the back. was represented the contest with Neptune.

The statue of Minerva, which was placed in the Parthenon, was esteemed among the best works of Phidias, the most renowned of the Greek sculptors. The Parthenon remained entire for many ages. It is said that Christians have worshipped in it as a church, and that Mohammedans have used it for a mosque. In 1687, the Venetians besieged the Acropolis, and threw into it a bomb, which demolished the roof of the Parthenon ; at the same time setting fire to a powder magazine within the Acropolis, which exploded, and did much damage to this temple.

Lord Elgin, a Scotch nobleman, took pains some years since, to pull down and convey to England some of the finest specimens of sculpture from the Parthenon. " Thus," says Dr. Clark, " the form of the temple has sustained a greater injury than it had already experienced from the Venetian artillery." It is to be regretted that a great portion of these specimens of Grecian art were lost, with the vessel on board which they were, in Cerigo bay, near the island of Cythera, in 1802.

The Parthenon was constructed of immense blocks of white marble. " The quarries of Pentelicus, of Hymettus, of the Cyclades, of Lacedæmon, and of the most distant mountains of Greece," contributed the material of which the Parthenon and other edifices of the Acropolis were composed. Modern travellers admire the skill, and mechanic powers, which must have been exerted, in conveying the immense masses of marble up the acclivity of the Acropolis.

" In all that relates to harmony, elegance, execution, beauty, proportion, the Parthenon stands a *chef d'œuvre;** every portion of the sculpture, by which

---

* As this book is written for young persons, it may not be amiss to inform them that the term *chef d'œuvre* is French,

it is so highly decorated, has all the delicacy of a *cameo.*"* The immense quantity of this sculpture serves to show the vast resources of the Athenian state.

——————————Those men are called divine,
Who public structures raise, and who design.

There is something sublime in the character of Pericles, who imagined the appropriation of so much wealth, so much genius and thought, so much labour and perseverance, such concentration of intellectual and physical power; and yet there is something more magnificent in the conception of a people, who consented in such a work; who gave to it money, time, and skill; and the sentiments of patriotism, and of veneration, in which it originated, in such amount as to produce so glorious a result, so lasting a monument.

" Often," says Dr. Clark, " as the Parthenon has been described, the spectator, who for the first time approaches it, finds that nothing he has read can give any idea of the effect produced in beholding it." The most remarkable ornament of the Parthenon is the series of sculpture continued round the whole of the frieze beneath the ceiling. This represents the whole of the Panathenaic Festival, by the best artists of ancient Greece; is one continued sculpture above three feet in height, and originally six hundred feet in length. A very con-

and signifies a perfect or superior work; as we say in English a *master-piece.* The statues of Venus and Apollo in Italy are such.

* Cameo—This is an Italian word : it signifies a sort of medal, composed sometimes of exceedingly fine porcelain, generally white, upon a coloured ground. Cameos represent exquisite heads, and beautiful forms; sometimes groups, and sometimes single figures, wrought with the most perfect delicacy and truth They are often set in gold, and worn as rings, &c.

siderable portion of this remains, and is " alone,"
says Dr. Clark, " worth a journey to Athens."

" The whole population of the ancient city,
animated by the bustle and business of the *Pana-
thenæ*, seems to be exhibited by this admirable
work ; persons of either sex, and of every age,
priests, charioteers, cattle, victors, youths, maidens,
victims, gods, and heroes, all enter into the proces
sion. Every countenance expresses the earnestness
and greatness of the occasion ; and every magnificence of costume, and varied disposition of the
subject, adds to the effect of the representation.

" It is somewhere said of Phidias,* that as a
sculptor, he particularly excelled in his statues of
horses. Perhaps some notion may be conceived of
the magic of his art, when it is related, that of a
hundred horses introduced by him into the Panathenaic *pomp*, there are not two either in the same
attitude, or which are not characterized by a marked
difference of expression."

The figures thus exhibited give a most correct
notion of the fashions of dress peculiar to the Greeks
in the time of Pericles. Among the articles of dress,
may be seen the leathern boot called the *cothornus*,
and resembling that sometimes worn at the present
time. Some of the horsemen of the Parthenon
wore light hats slightly confined by ribands. The
Greeks had two external covers for the head, the
Petasus, and the *Pileus*. Homer mentions no
other covering of the head, but the *helmet* of the
military. The Romans usually, when there was
occasion, wrapped their heads in their robes or

---

* Phidias, the celebrated sculptor at Athens, died B. C. 432
Phidias was banished by the Athenians, because they accused
him of carving his own image upon the shield of Minerva.
Phidias retired to Elis, where he produced a statue of Jupiter,
which was the most admired of his performances.

mantles. This Greek cap was only an ornament sometimes worn by men of fashion.

"'The Parthenon, in its entire state, either as a hea then temple, or as a Christian sanctuary, was lighted only by means of lamps ; it had no windows.''

" The remains of many ancient buildings in Egypt, and in Greece, seem to prove that the earliest places of idolatrous worship were all calculated to obstruct, rather than to admit light. Even in its present state, the Parthenon still retains something of its original gloomy character.''

Dr. Clark observes, that the prospect from the western entrance of the Parthenon is truly affecting " Every portion of territory comprehended in the survey has been rendered memorable, as the scene of some conspicuous event in Grecian story ; either as the land of genius, or the field of heroism ; as honoured by the poet's cradle, or the patriot's grave ; as exciting the remembrance of all by which human nature has been adorned and dignified ; or as proclaiming the awful mandate, which ordains that not only talents and virtue. but also states and empires, and even the earth itself shall pass away.''

The temple of Diana, at Ephesus, was of immense extent and magnificence ; but as no remains, nor any correct representation of it exists, it needs no description. In Italy, all over Greece, and the islands, wherever the gods of Greece and Rome, of Syria, and of Persia, were worshipped, in all those countries, the ruins of temples may be found, and all serve to show that the sentiment of religion, however perverted, is expressed everywhere, by the finest works of human art, and the universal concurrence of mankind.

What were the principal temples of Greece, and by whom was that of Delphi enriched ?

What were the offerings at Delphi, and what became of them

What was the Parthenon, and who projected it?

What were the dimensions of the Parthenon, and what was sculptured upon it?

What statue adorned the Parthenon, and how has that fabric been impaired?

What further injury has the Parthenon sustained?

From what places was the marble of the Greek temples taken?

Is the Parthenon one of the most beautiful specimens of the ancient architecture?

In what manner does the Parthenon exhibit the Grecian character?

What is the most remarkable feature of the Parthenon?

What is exhibited by the frieze of the Parthenon?

What is remarked of the genius of Phidias?

What particulars in the article of dress are exhibited in the sculpture of the Parthenon?

Was light freely admitted to the heathen temples?

What thoughts are suggested by the prospect from the Parthenon?

Are there any remains of the temple of Diana, at Ephesus?

THE Hebrew Scriptures give us accounts of prophets; men who were endowed by God with superior wisdom, and who were enabled by divine assistance to foretell events, which afterwards were accomplished; and, moreover, to direct others wisely what they ought to do. When Herod inquired of the Jews were Christ should be born, they answered, in Bethlehem of Judea, for thus it was written by the *prophet*.

It appears from all antiquity, that though the Hebrews alone had true prophets, all nations believed that the gods communicated their will to some men, that those favoured persons might convey that will to the rest of mankind. The word *oracle* signifies the words which express the will of God. The ancients believed that some persons were instructed to express and explain God's will; and these persons uttered oracles.

Among the ancients, certain places were fixed upon, where priests, when they were consulted, gave information of the god's purposes. Thus, Lycurgus, the Spartan lawgiver, went to the oracle of Apollo at Delphi, and inquired if it were the will of the gods, that the Spartans should adopt his laws. The oracle replied that it was the divine will: and the Spartans obeyed. Those who consulted oracles were forced to pay for the information they sought; so that rich people only could be benefited by them.

One of the most celebrated oracles of Greece was that of Jove, at Dodona, in Epirus. Here black pigeons congregated in oak trees, and made the usual noise of pigeons; but some persons fancying their noise to have some meaning; and pretending to explain that meaning as the will of Jupiter, other credulous persons repaired to that place, to learn what they should do, or what they might.

The most famous oracle of Greece was that of Apollo at Delphi, a city of Phocis. So many persons resorted to the Delphic oracle, and such large presents were made to it, that the institution became immensely rich; but the oracle was uttered by a poor old woman called the Pythia: who was made to sit upon a stool, called, from its three feet, a tripod; and to inhale some deleterious gas, which convulsed her body, and made her utter strange words; which artful priests explained just as they chose, to those who consulted them. In Greece, besides these, were many other oracles; but those of Dodona and Delphi were the chief.

Does it appear from sacred history that true prophets have existed?

Who uttered oracles among the ancients?

Had the people of Greece confidence in oracles?

How is the oracle of Dodona described?

What was the most famous oracle of the Greeks?

THE victims offered in sacrifice were often highly ornamented, and the priests on those occasions were richly dressed ; the worshippers wore white, and brought wreaths and baskets of flowers to the sacrifices. *Lustration* or purification was a ceremony necessary to be observed by devout persons attending a sacrifice. When a very wicked person came, he was said to be *polluted*, unfit for a religious service, till he should be put into a proper state by a suitable ceremony.

A large vessel of water stood near the entrance of the temple, and the priest having plucked a burning brand from the altar of the god, extinguished it in water designed for the purification ; this act was supposed to *consecrate the water:* and this water being sprinkled upon the worshippers, was supposed to make them *pure*, or fit to address the divine being. Catholic Christians have a vessel of holy water in their churches.

Washing the hands upon any solemn occasion was accounted a purification. Hector says,

> I dread with *unwashed hands* to bring
> My *incensed* wine to Jove an offering.

Washing the whole person was an expression of innocency. In the xxxvi. chapter of Ezekiel, in which the prophet tells the Israelites that God will turn them from their sins, he says, in the name of God, "Then will I sprinkle clean water upon you, and ye shall be clean ; from all your filthiness, and from all your idols will I cleanse you." When Pilate, the Roman governor of Judea, against his conviction of his innocence, was about to give up the blameless Jesus to his enemies, " he took water, and washed his hands before the multitude, saying, *I am innocent* of the blood of this just person, see ye to it "

It was customary, during the performance of religious services, on some occasions for a part of the worshippers to dance round the altar while they sung their sacred hymns. These hymns consisted of three stanzas or parts; while the singers sung the first, they moved from east to west, this stanza was called the *Strophe;* the second stanza, the *Antistrophe,* was sung while the singers returned from west to east; they then stood still around the altar and sung the *epode,* or last part of the song. The hymns were composed in honour of the gods, and celebrated their actions, and their beneficence to mankind. They usually concluded with a petition that the god who was addressed would continue his favour to the supplicants.

Various offerings besides sacrifices were brought to the temples; these were either designed to pacify the deity, if he had been offended, or to procure some favour, or to express the gratitude of the giver. Crowns, garlands of flowers, cups of gold, or any thing which might adorn the temples, were presented to the gods, and hung upon the walls, pillars, and roof, as was convenient. Poor people made such humble offerings as they could afford.

One mode of supporting the public worship was by *tithes*—a tenth part of any thing, as the tenth of the metal from a mine, or the tenth of the wheat, &c. The collecting of the *tithes* or taxes was called the *gathering of tribute.* In the xiv. chapter of Genesis, Abraham is represented as giving tithes of all to Melchisedek, King of Salem, and priest of the Most High God.

How were animals to be sacrificed prepared, and what was required of devout persons?

What was the mode of *purification?*

What is expressed by the washing of hands, and what examples may be given of that meaning!

Did the worshippers among the ancients dance and sing, and what were their hymns ?

What other offerings besides sacrifices were presented to the gods ?

What are *tithes ?*

THOUGH the Greeks and Romans did not worship one God as we do, nor were those they worshipped holy beings, they always confessed that Jove was supreme. Those who acknowledged one, " high throned above all," called him *Theon,** or the God. *Piety* is a disposition to bear God in mind, to thank him always for his manifold goodness. This disposition was always cherished by the most virtuous of the ancients.

" 'The piety of the ancient Grecians," says a writer eminent in the knowledge of their antiquities, " was in nothing more manifest than in their continued prayers and supplications to the gods ; for no man among them who was endued with the smallest prudence, said the philosopher Plato, would undertake any thing without having first asked the direction and the assistance of the gods ; for this they thought the surest means to have all their enterprises crowned with success." This was practised by *all the people* as well as by the philosophers, says the same authority.

Every morning and evening supplications were offered. " Both at the rising of the sun and moon, one might every where behold the Greeks and barbarians, those in prosperity, as well as those under calamities and afflictions, prostrating themselves, and hear their supplications." One of the Roman poets says, " *we pray* for the prosperity of Italy, both in the morning and in the evening." The Spartans only prayed that the gods would grant

* See note to Francklin's Sophocles, Œdipus Tyrannus.

what was honourable and good for them ; and they added one petition more, viz. that they might be enabled to suffer injuries with patience.   Petitioners, both to gods and men, used to supplicate with green boughs in their hands, and sometimes with garlands on their heads.

Imprecation or cursing, was practised by the ancients : this is sometimes called MALEDICTION.   A *curse* is a supplication to some god, that he would inflict shame and misery upon the *accursed* person ; that is, the person hated by him who entreats the curse.   The misfortunes which happen in consequence of our own or other person's faults, are sometimes called *curses*.   The Greeks had a most superstitious fear of curses.   Kings, parents, priests, and prophets, uttered imprecations upon detested persons ; and those who heard the *malediction* believed that all the evils which it threatened would actually overtake the accursed person, and sometimes all his posterity.   " All men are afraid of imprecations," said one of the Roman writers.

Blessing, or *benediction*, was the reverse of cursing.   It was a supplication that God would make those blessed, prosperous and happy.   A memorable example of *blessing* and *cursing* is given in the forty-fourth chapter of Genesis.   The patriarch Jacob assembles his children around his death-bed, and upon some, he pronounces blessings, on others curses.   The blessing was supposed sometimes to express the will of God, and could not be recalled. When Isaac had blessed Jacob, and given him the inheritance of Esau, he could not withdraw the blessing, and give his property to the first-born, because he had, as it were, promised them in a solemn manner to Jacob who had deceived him.

An oath is a solemn promise made in the name of God   If a man says, *I declare in the name of God,* (that is, I declare that I believe God hears me, and that he will punish me if I speak falsely : I declare that I speak the truth at this moment;) such a declaration is an *oath*. When a man declares he will surely do a certain act, he makes a *vow*. The Hebrews were permitted to take oaths upon solemn occasions. " Thou shalt fear the Lord thy God, and serve him, and shalt *swear* by his name."—*Deuteronomy*.

There was another mode of swearing besides using the name of God, as by the elements, the sun, moon, or stars ; or, a king would swear by his sceptre, a soldier by his spear, a fisherman by his nets, &c. Thus Achilles, in the Iliad, addressing himself to Agamemnon, exclaims,

> Now by this sacred sceptre hear me swear
> Which never more shall leaves or blossoms bear,
> Which severed from the trunk as I from thee,
> On the bare mountain left its native tree.
>
> * * * *
>
> *By this I swear,* when bleeding Greece again
> Shall call Achilles, she shall call in vain.

This swearing by certain objects signifies, as surely as this thing, the *sun*, or *moon*, for example, exists, and as God hears me, I speak truly. Achilles means, truly as I hold this *sacred sceptre*, I swear, that let the Greeks need my services ever so much, I will never again unite myself to you, Agamemnon, in their defence.

After this explanation, it is easy to understand our Saviour's prohibition,—" Swear not at all ; neither by heaven, for it is God's throne ; nor by the earth, for it is his footstool," &c. This injunction was given because the oaths were sometimes taken falsely, and sometimes needlessly by the people of that time ; and they did not hold God in suitable reverence when they thus used dishonestly and lightly to call upon him.

All important agreements, or *covenants*, among the ancients, were made with mutual oaths. False swearers are abhorred everywhere, and never after they are detected believed. False swearing is *perjury*. A person hired to swear to a falsehood is *suborned*. Perjury, among the Greeks, was punished with death ; among us, as it ought to do, it makes the perjured person liable to imprisonment and disgrace.

Did any of the Greeks worship one God, and what is signi fied by *piety ?*

Were the Greeks a religious people, and how did they manifest their piety ?

When did the Greeks offer their devotions, and what did the Spartans pray for ?

What is meant by a curse, and who stood in fear of curses ?

What is a blessing or benediction, and what is a memorable example ?

What is an *oath* and a *vow*, and who were permitted to take oaths ?

Was there any other mode of swearing except in the name of some god, and what is an example of it ?

What is meant to be understood when a person swears by the sun or moon, &c., and what is the reason of our Saviour's prohibition of swearing ?

What is perjury, and how are perjured persons regarded everywhere ?

Whenever the Greeks were about to embark on a voyage, previously to their departure, they made a sacrifice, and put up prayers for safety and success ; and the sea-faring men were joined in their devotions by their friends and neighbours. Being arrived in port, the first act of mariners was to thank the gods for their preservation ; and if they had been safely landed after tempests, their custom was, to consecrate the garment in which they had escaped, out of gratitude to their deliverers, and to engrave upon a tablet a short account of their deliverance.

Those who undertook a journey, first implored the divine protection. When they departed for a foreign land, it was customary to take leave of the gods by kissing the earth; and when they returned, they repeated the same act as a salutation to the guardians of the country. In a strange place, the Greeks worshipped the local deities as the protectors and patrons of those who sojourned in their land; and when they were restored to their homes, offered thanks for a safe return to their peculiar divinities.

THE MOSAIC DISPENSATION.

LIVING, as we do, in the knowledge of the gospel, when we read of the false and foolish religions of antiquity; of those nations who worshipped they knew not whom, we have reason to thank God always that he has given us a true religion, while it has pleased him to leave millions of mankind for so many ages in ignorance of himself; though men of all times had *some* true notions of the divine character and government.

Nineteen centuries before Christ, God instructed Abraham, who had then no child, that from him should descend a race who should preserve the knowledge of one true God; and that from him, in due time, should also descend, one in whom all the families of the earth should be blessed, namely, our Lord Jesus Christ.

Four hundred and thirty years after God had given this promise to Abraham, his posterity was increased to six hundred thousand persons, and then God appointed one of this nation to be instructer of his people, Israel. This person was Moses. God, about fourteen centuries before Christ. gave to Moses a law for his people to observe. This law is con tained in the Pentateuch, or the first five books of the Bible.

The law of Moses, or more properly, the dispensation of the true God. was received by the Hebrew people, and observed by them in their belief, and in their worship, very near the time that Athens was founded, (B. C. 1556,) and at the time in which these polished nations of Greece, of Egypt, and those of Italy, and of Syria, were bowing down before idols

There is no doubt that the Phœnicians were informed of many facts which are contained in the Old Testament. The Flood, the Tower of Babel, and the exploits of Samson, appear to have been celebrated by the heathens under the deluge of Deucalion, the wars of the giants with Jupiter, and the labours of Hercules. They introduced these facts into the fables of their religion.

The worship which God appointed for his people the Hebrews, is described in the book of Leviticus. This worship or ceremonial, was not unlike that of the heathens, only it was paid to a true God, and not to false divinities, and it was offered to an invisible Spirit, and not to gold and silver, or things of man's device.

The differences between the Hebrews and heathens were these. The Hebrews were instructed by God himself; the heathens were left to seek out God, if haply they might feel after him and find him. The Hebrews worshipped *one God*, who is above all, who created all, and who is in all ; the heathens worshipped gods many, and lords many.

The Hebrews had a moral law that taught them their duty to God and their neighbours ; the heathens were a law to themselves ; they had not the ten commandments which God gave to Moses.

The Hebrews had a holy Sabbath ; the heathens

had no day of rest, and of instruction. The Hebrews had true prophets, whose predictions were
accomplished ; the heathens, false oracles and diviners, whose lies were only delusions. The heathens
had a religion which lasted for a few centuries, and
then gave place to another and a better ; the Hebrews had a religion which was the first lesson of
eternal truth, and which was not destroyed, but im
proved, advanced, and perfected by the Messiah ;
who only laid aside the ceremonies of his country,
but has preserved through all time, the piety and virtue, which were the weightier matters of the law.

Having been shown some of the most remarkable
differences between Judaism, and Polytheism, it
may be well to learn a few particulars of the worship of the Jews, which bear some resemblance to
those of the Pagan nations : these were considerable
in number.

How should we feel in respect to our own privileges and
advantages ?

Who was the person appointed to preserve true religion in
the world ?

At what period of the world did God impart the Mosaic dispensation ?

What was the condition of the most polished nations in respect to religion, for fifteen centuries before Christ ?

Were the Phœnicians informed of any of the facts which
are recorded in the Old Testament ?

In what book are the religious services of the Hebrews described ?

What differences existed between the Hebrews and heathens,
in their knowledge of the character of God ?

What moral advantage had the Hebrews over heathens ?

What superior religious institutions had the Hebrews ?

Did the *ceremonies* of Judaism at all resemble those of poly
theism ?

JEWISH HIGH-PRIEST.

THE Hebrew religion, like the Pagan, had its holy *persons*, holy *times*, holy *places*, holy *actions*, and holy *things*. Those *things* are termed *holy*, which belong to God ; or such objects, services, and thought, as belong to the Deity only.

The Priests, the Nazarites, and the Levites, were the *holy persons* among the Israelites or Hebrews. Aaron, the brother, companion, and counsellor of Moses, was appointed the first high-priest.

The *office* of *supreme pontiff*, or a priest, distinguished above all the rest, is a dignity which all the ancient nations conferred upon their priesthood. The Egyptians, and all the distinct orders of Greek priests, had their hierarch.

Christian churches have followed this example even to the present time. The pope of Rome, and the primate of all England, who is the archbishop of Canterbury, are instances.

The Hebrew high-priests were the descendants

of Aaron's eldest son, whose eldest sons were hereditary high-priests ever after, provided they had no bodily imperfection. The rest of Aaron's descendants were inferior priests. The priests entered upon their office at the age of thirty years, and were solemnly introduced to their public duty, by prayers and purifications.

The office of the Hebrew priests was to offer sacrifices, to burn incense in the holy place, to kindle the lamps, to do the higher services of the temple, and to instruct the people. They also pronounced solemn blessings upon the people in the name of the Lord.

The Hebrew high-priest was appointed to enter that apartment of the temple which was called the *most holy place*, into which no other person could enter, and to oversee all the public worship. He was a judge in civil, as well as religious affairs.

Among the *holy persons* of the Hebrews, was a religious order, called the *Nazarites*. These were persons who made a vow to devote themselves to the service of God, instead of attending to the common business of life. This vow was only made for a time. The Nazarite permitted his hair to grow during the time for which the vow was made.

The other holy persons were the whole tribe of Levi, called the Levites. It was their business to wait on the priests, and to keep in order the temple and the sacred vessels, and to attend in public services of religion.

What resemblances may be found between Paganism and Judaism?

Who were the holy persons among the Hebrews?

Had all the nations of antiquity high-priests?

Have Christian churches chief high-priests?

Who were the Hebrew priests?

Who were the Nazarites?

What was the office of the Levites?

AFTER holy persons, *holy places* demand some attention From the days of Moses, to those of Solomon, about four hundred years, the *Tabernacle* was the chief place of worship. After Solomon, B. C. 1070, the Temple which Solomon built was the *Lord's house.* Both the *Tabernacle* and the *Temple* were called the *Sanctuary.*

The Tabernacle was a movable tent, a building made of pillars, boards, and curtains, kept together by fastenings of gold and silver, and which could be taken to pieces, and removed from one place to another. *See* Exodus, ch. xxvi.

The Tabernacle was divided into two apartments, the outermost called the *holy place*, and the innermost, called the *holy of holies.* The high-priest only entered this apartment, and that but once a year. The *most holy place* was divided from the *holy place*, by a veil or curtain adorned with gold and embroidery.

The Tabernacle was enclosed by a row of pillars, with curtains between; and the space within this fence, and around the Tabernacle, was called the *Court of the Tabernacle.* The Tabernacle was carried by the Jews wherever they went, during their sojourn in the wilderness, and when they were established in Canaan, it was set up in Shiloh, and is thence called the *Lord's* House in Shiloh.

The Temple was built by King Solomon. It was a magnificent building in the city of Jerusalem. The first temple was destroyed when Jerusalem was taken by the Babylonians. It was rebuilt after the restoration, adorned and beautified by Herod, and finally laid in the dust by the Roman army, when Jerusalem was taken under Titus, A. D. 70.

We read in the New Testament, that at the crucifixion of Christ, the *veil of the temple was rent.* The Temple, like the Tabernacle, contained the

apartment called the *most holy*, and it was concealed
from common eyes, by the sacred curtain.   When
nature was convulsed on the occasion of our Lord's
violent death, this curtain, or veil, was torn by the
shock of an earthquake.

Jerusalem was called by the Jews, he *Holy City*,
because the Tabernacle was removed tnither by King
David, and set up on the *holy hill*, Mount Zion; and
there, on Mount Moriah, afterwards stood the Temple of Solomon.   During the reign of David, Jerusalem became the metropolis of the Jewish state;
and thither the whole people, or as many as were
able, annually repaired to celebrate certain religious
festivals.

What is signified by holy places in the Hebrew worship?
What was the Tabernacle?
How was the Tabernacle divided?
How was the Tabernacle enclosed?
Who built the first Temple, and who destroyed the last?
What was the veil of the Temple?
What was Jerusalem?

———

THE *holy things* were altars, garments, and vessels, besides incense, and other substances used in
the Hebrew worship.   The ark of the covenant, the
mercy-seat, the altar of incense, the table, and candlestick, the altar of burnt-offerings, the laver, the
priest's robes, purifying water, holy oil, and holy
perfumes, together with instruments used in the
sacrifices, were *holy things*.

ARK.

THE Ark was a box or coffer of wood, overlaid with gold. In the ark were kept the *Tables of the Law*, these were stones on which the ten commandments were engraved. The book of the Law was that commonly called Leviticus.

The *Mercy-Seat* was of pure gold, and formed the covering of the ark. A *cherub* was placed at each end of it. A cherub was the image of a human face attached to a form with wings. It was an emblematical figure, denoting God's presence.

It is said, that between the cherubs, on the mercy seat, a perpetual and vivid light was apparent. This light was called by the Jews, the *Shechina*, or the habitation of God, and sometimes, the *glory*. The ark was kept in the *Holy of Holies*, within the veil.

The *Altar of Incense* was made of wood covered with gold, and upon it a perfume of sweet spices was offered morning and evening. Incense was a perfumed substance burnt in a censer. The *table* used in the religious services of the Hebrews was furnished with golden dishes and spoons. Upon this table were set every Sabbath, twelve cakes of fresh bread called the *show-bread*. This conso crated bread, according to the law, could only be eaten by the priests.

The *Candlestick* was a pillar of pure gold, from which several branches were extended which supported lamps. The lamps were daily supplied with fresh oil, and kept always burning. The *Altar of Incense*, the *Table*, and the *Candlestick* were kept in the *Holy Place*.

The *Altar of Burnt-Offering* was overlaid with brass, and was that on which sacrifices were offered. The fire used to enkindle the fuel used in the sacrifices was fire from heaven

The *Laver* was a vessel of brass, which would contain a large quantity of water. It was designed for the priests to wash their hands and feet in, when they went to do service in the sanctuary ; thus to intimate, by outward purity, that " clean heart" which is proper to the ministers of religion. The *Altar of Burnt-Offering* and the *Laver* stood under the open sky

The sacred vestments of the High-Priest were principally the *Ephod*, the *Robe*, and the *Mitre* The Ephod was a short vest, without sleeves, worn over the Robe. The Robe was a flowing garment which covered the whole person. The *Mitre* was a pointed cap worn by the High-Priests only. On the front of the Mitre was a plate of gold, upon which was engraved the inscription, Holiness to the Lord. The Mitre is still worn by Catholic and Protestant Bishops.

The Breast-plate of the High-Priest was an ornament of a square form, consisting of twelve jewels set in gold, representing the twelve tribes of Israel. The Robe was of blue cloth with a wrought border of pomegranates and little bells suspended from the hem. This was emblematic—*fruit and sound*—intimating that the *fruits of righteousness*, that is a virtuous conduct, should always attend the *sound*, the fame or reputation of the priest's sanctity.

The corn, wine, and oil, and the birds and beasts offered in the Hebrew sacrifices, and in those of all the nations of antiquity, were required to be of the best quality that could be procured. Things of the greatest value being the most suitable to express the highest sense of gratitude and homage which human beings can feel. These sacrifices were offered daily, weekly, monthly, and yearly.

What were the holy things used in the Hebrew worship?
What was the Ark?
What was the Mercy-Seat?
What was the Shechinah?
What was the Altar of Incense?
What was the Table?
What was the Candlestick?
What was the Altar of Burnt-Offering?
What was the Laver?
What were the High-Priest's garments?
What were the substances offered in sacrifices?

The *holy times* chiefly observed by the Hebrews, were the morning and evening sacrifice, the Sabbath, the new moons, and the feasts of the Passover, the Pentecost, and the feast of Tabernacles.

JEWISH SACRIFICE.

The Passover was celebrated during seven days of Abib, the first month of the Hebrew year. The Passover commemorated God's *passing over* the dwellings of the Hebrews in Egypt, while an angel smote with death the first-born of every Egyptian family. The lamb sacrificed and eaten by the Hebrews on this occasion was called the paschal lamb. Ripe corn (barley) was also offered at the Passover. On the last day of the Passover was held a solemn assembly of the people, called a holy convocation.

The Pentecost was observed fifty days after the passover. It celebrated the beginning of the wheat harvest, and was a thanksgiving for the divine mercy in bestowing the fruits of the earth.

The Pentecost also celebrated the revelation of the law to Moses on Mount Sinai.

The *Feast of Tabernacles* was kept to preserve the remembrance of the time when the Hebrews wandered in the desert, and rested in booths and tents without any fixed habitations. To these solemn feasts the Hebrews were commanded to bring a tithe or tenth part of their corn, wine, oil, and the first-born of their cattle.

The *holy actions* of different religions are different, but the sentiments are the same, except in those where human sacrifices are permitted; they are the natural worship of frail and weak creatures to a powerful and gracious benefactor, and consist chiefly of praise, and prayer, and confession; and in acknowledgments of gratitude, weakness, penitence, hope, and trust.

What were the holy times observed by the Hebrews?
What was the Passover?
What was the Pentecost?
What was the feast of Tabernacles?
Are the actions and sentiments of different religions alike?

THE END.